Heavenly Detour

HEAVENLY DETOUR

JOANNE MEYER

KENSINGTON BOOKS
http://www.kensingtonbooks.com

KENSINGTON BOOKS are published by

Kensington Publishing Corp.
850 Third Avenue
New York, NY 10022

All Kensington titles, imprints and distributed lines are available at special quantity discounts for bulk purchases for sales promotion, premiums, fund-raising, educational or institutional use.

Special book excerpts or customized printings can also be created to fit specific needs. For details, write or phone the office of the Kensington Special Sales Manager: Kensington Publishing Corp., 850 Third Avenue, New York, NY 10022, Attn. Special Sales Department. Phone: 1-800-221-2647.

Library of Congress Card Catalogue Number: 2002106112
ISBN 0-7582-0260-1

First Printing: February 2003
10 9 8 7 6 5 4 3 2 1

Printed in the United States of America

For my husband, John

ACKNOWLEDGMENTS

The old cliché that writing is a lonely business is an understatement. It can be lethal. Without the support of family, friends and fellow writers, my first novel might never have been born, and I might never have survived. Therefore, it's only fair to thank those who stood by, cheering from the sidelines, as I negotiated the hazardous trail.

My husband, John, deserves the croix de guerre for his assignment as first reader (he had no choice) and for putting up with our newly wacky lifestyle. A higher power gave me three children whose combined education and experience amounts to an in-house library for all sorts of research plus free legal services: Thanks to Ellen for the technical legal data, advice and encouragement; to Howard for his NYC real estate background, which not only provided choice locations but also included better restaurants; to Ken, who must have had a sixth sense when he decided to focus on entertainment law. I'm grateful to Emerald Coast Writers and West Coast Writers for keeping me firmly on the path, and also to Jan Wheeler of New College. A special thanks to Dr. Carlos Caballero for sharing his medical know-how.

Lastly, this book would never have reached the bookshelves if it were not for two special people: Alice Martell, my wonderful agent who believed in it (and me), and John Scognamiglio, editor extraordinaire.

HEAVENLY DETOUR

One

No one was more surprised by my drowning than I, an event that occurred two weeks ago after a splendid summer's day at Sands Point, Long Island. The shock was followed by something even more unsettling: The revelation that death, after all, is not the end. Since the event, I've discovered a whole new dimension, but it's neither milk nor meat, as my mother would say, meaning a thing has no real definition. Using my mother's logic, therefore, a person should be either living or dead. In spite of that I am still here.

My name is or, rather, was Annie Dowd (née Edelstein). I kept the name after Frank and I divorced more than eighteen years ago—first, because I really loved the name and, second, because I still loved the guy. I also had a great job, good friends and a perfectly wonderful life—while it lasted. Now I find myself in a confused state of unreasonable limbo. If I were alive, I'd probably go out and get really drunk. In my case, that's not a viable option. Between a rock and a hard place is nothing compared to the fact that I'm caught literally between two worlds. It's like a bad case of constipation. To put it bluntly, I need to move on.

I suppose I ought to start with the drowning and work my way back through the events. The part about the drowning is not something I like to think about, but the rest of it was, well, heavenly.

We were just finishing a whole day and evening at the estate of our company's titular head, the ever-intimidating Agnes

Spurgeon. Agnes is the mother of Harold Spurgeon who now runs the company, a real estate brokerage firm dealing in astronomically priced Manhattan rentals and subleases. Now in her late-seventies, and with fading health, Agnes still carries an air of well-bred hostility. She looks at the world through a curtain of faded green eyes—two uniformed guards, weary but still dangerous. The effect is hypnotic, and one soon gets the impression that to hide behind words is an exercise in futility. No one lies to Agnes Spurgeon, at least not to her face.

We'd driven out from the City, a group of us, in a rented car and melded into the exodus of other holiday-minded apartment dwellers headed toward the beautiful beaches of Long Island. Where better to celebrate the Fourth of July? It was Friday, a perfect morning. The sun had risen in a cloudless sky of bright cerulean blue, and the predicted combination of seventy-eight degrees and low humidity made us all feel as though New York had been kissed by angels. I remember feeling really happy—anticipating the day, whatever it would bring. Certainly, Death was the last thought on my mind.

The Long Island Expressway groaned under the weight of its heavy load. Not recommended for the faint-hearted, the L.I.E., as it is affectionately known, is an obstacle course composed of potholes and unhappy drivers intent on getting to their destinations ahead of everyone else. As we moved eastward toward the more affluent establishment, the road became smoother. We crawled along with the rest of the traffic, determined to get to Sands Point in one piece. By default, Roger Franklin drove. He had the only valid driver's licence.

Roger had been with the company, Royal Roosts, Inc., more than eight years. An easygoing personality, he was the likely choice to safely navigate the holiday traffic. A bachelor in his late forties, Roger's prematurely graying hair and soft voice lent an air of stability that gave clients confidence and women, in particular, hope. There had never been any chemistry between Roger and me, so it was easy to say we were friends. I sat next to him with the map; Matt Sterling and Marian Hingis shared the back. Claudia Harmon, we knew, had gone out the day before. Claudia had in mind to become the next Mrs. Spurgeon, but we were betting on Agnes to blow that deal—

two immovable forces, as it were. It would be interesting to see how the campaign was shaping up.

The car swerved suddenly when a white Ford Escort, loaded with raucous young things, cut in front of us. My stomach lurched with the unexpected move, making me glad I hadn't eaten the other half of my bagel. At the same time, it occurred to me how easily life could disappear when one least expects it. Roger raised his fist in anger but was greeted with derisive laughter and an arm that extended out the window on the driver's side, punctuating the moment with a vertical finger for emphasis. "Nice job," Matt yelled from the rear, but the Ford was already two car lengths ahead.

While the others chewed over the behavior of the unrepentant miscreants, I began to focus on being pleasant to Agnes. Although she was no longer an active participant in the firm's daily operation, she remained, nevertheless, the wielder of whips when it came to deciding factors. I'd managed to stay out of Agnes's way for ten years and intended her dossier on me should contain nothing but the bare facts: Dowd, Annie; Licensed Real Estate Broker; height: 5 feet, 4 ½ inches; weight: 118 pounds; hair: red; eyes: gray; age—well, never mind—privacy in some areas is allowed. Suffice it to say, I'd been loyal to the Spurgeons. Only an unforgivable error on my part or the overt action of a living virus could rock my boat.

When I say virus, Claudia Harmon is a name that immediately comes to mind. Her methods may not be original, but the results are guaranteed. When she first joined the firm, Claudia began exploring the best and shortest way to success. Harold Spurgeon was her ticket. A mama's boy in every sense, Harold had taken over Royal Roosts only after Agnes, the matriarch from hell, had suffered her second heart attack. Handwriting on the wall and all that, the doctor assured Agnes she'd be dead within six months if she didn't retire. She conceded, only because she thought she could run the company from Sands Point. Agnes, however, never counted on Claudia.

Claudia is a tall, attractive brunette in her late thirties with a body that cries for designer clothes and a Ph.D. in how to enter a room. I've seen grown men of high station sigh without shame. Claudia will do whatever it takes to sign, seal or deliver an account: Lie?—without a second thought. Step on toes?—an everyday occurrence. Murder?—well, that remains to be seen. She already has her long, perfectly manicured fingernails into any client worth having. And let's not forget Harold, with whom she formed an immediate, unbreakable attachment. Not even Agnes could persuade her son to keep a perspective once his ling-ling became the ruling organ of note. And who had control over that? Never mind that the guy is not much to look at, or even that he is downright dull. He has money, lots of it. And power. The combination is like a bowl of cream to the feline Claudia.

My other co-workers, most of whom had been with the firm for years, were people I could count on. Some were just starting out. Matt Sterling, for instance. He's young, twenty-something, and new on the payroll, though not new to the office. Matt had been putting in his time during the last two summers and managed to make the leap to full-time after graduation from New York University in June. Having caught Claudia's eye might have something to do with it. What Harold isn't, Matt is: tall, boyishly handsome with sun-streaked blond hair that has recently discovered gel and incredibly sexy eyes. He also works out three to four times a week at Gold's Gym, which doesn't hurt. Claudia is attracted to his, uh, charms, and some of us are taking bets to see how long before she gets him on the casting couch. He blushes easily, so it won't take a rocket scientist to figure out when the denouement takes place. How will she get away with it in front of Harold? Puh-leeze! The wool she pulls over his eyes is two feet thick.

Marian Hingis, who has operated the switchboard for twelve years, is our firm's version of CNN: all the news every half hour. Marian's okay really, maybe just a little lonely. Fiftyish, overly thin and possessed with a penchant for changing her hair color often, she never married and lives with her mother. There's never been a helluva lot of excitement in her life, and I knew she was looking forward to our outing today.

The trip did not take as long as expected, and we were much relieved when our car left the highway and made its way along Searington Road and past the town of Manhasset. Fifteen minutes later, we turned off Old Sands Point Road and drove through the outer gates of our destination along a private stretch that led toward the sprawling Victorian home on the edge of a low cliff. The graveled, circular driveway, and its connecting road leading to the garages, were already dotted with prestigious automobiles. I spotted two Mercedes—a sedan and a 450-SL convertible—one Jaguar XJ12, and a vintage Rolls. Roger parked our humble Honda Civic behind the Rolls, and we exited the car, dragging an assortment of satchels and garment bags. Our long day would include a variety of lawn games, swimming, buffet lunch at the pool and dinner in the formal dining room. Each activity required a different costume and, in deference to Agnes and her *noblesse oblige,* the least we could do was comply. As it turned out, the effort was worth it. What made it even more interesting this year, though, was Michael Rheims.

I found myself standing next to him later while choosing up sides for volleyball. "Hello!" His warm voice blew past my ear like a lover's kiss. He had a wonderful smile with white, even teeth. "Hello back," I breezed, but staring up into his incredibly blue eyes, I was suddenly transported across a vast chasm of charm.

Michael was Agnes's cousin from the British side of the family. An executive with Marks and Spencer, he planned to be in the States for about a year. Already, I could hear my mother yelling, "Another *shaigetz?*" But religion was not my primary focus. Michael was six-plus feet of appealing hunk.

He took my hand and led me away soon after the game ended. "Are you one of Spurgeon's girls?" he asked.

"Whoa," I countered, "if you're planning to 'get past Jail' and 'collect two-hundred dollars,' we'd better lay a better foundation."

His perplexed look told me he didn't have a clue. "Listen," I began. "In this country, women are called women. A two-year-old might be a girl, but a twenty-two-year-old female is a woman." I had used the last number arbitrarily, which must have been obvious. A team of wild horses couldn't make me confess to forty-six.

He grinned down at me. "Yes, ma'am, and can we go on from here?"

And go on we did, my stomach riding the wheels of a roller coaster with his every gesture. There was his open smile, the little furrow between his dark brows that awaited patiently the translation of an American slang or Yiddish phrase, his frank expression of tender feelings. No game player, this. He liked what he saw and made no effort to deny it. The effect for me was spontaneous and deep. I was falling.

"What is it about you—?" he began, taking hold of my hand and running with me into the house, where I saw more of Agnes's grand home than ever before.

Never knew, for instance, that her library held so many first editions, or that the thick piled rugs were imported directly from the Orient, or that the heavy velvet curtains there allowed one wildly horny couple their first kiss. Already, we were making plans for the next day.

"You are the most adorable creature," he whispered huskily.

"And you're the closest thing to a double-oh-seven I've ever met," I countered. "Uh, that's Bond, James Bond."

When we stood close together like this, my eyes were level with his collar bone, and I could see the pulse in his neck beating like the wings of a wild bird. Hands slid around my waist, gliding up and forward and stopping just short of each breast. A moan escaped from deep inside me. My body was an orchestra, Michael the conductor. I nestled closer, encouraging the intimacy.

He liked my untamable mane of curly red hair. I was crazy about the cleft in his chin. We wondered aloud about the parts of our bodies we'd explore at our next meeting. Neither of us cared if anyone else had noticed nor what they thought. "Tomorrow," he whispered, "we'll be together tomorrow." It all seemed so infinitely possible. . . .

Nearing ten o'clock there was a ruckus at the front gate. A gang of happy celebrants from the nearby country club apparently mistook the Spurgeon estate for a friend's house. Their loud voices created a terrific din as they surged onto the grounds. Servants were dispatched to rectify the situation, but by that time the interruption had served as a reminder that it was time to return to reality. Belongings were collected, farewells and thank-yous expressed, all in preparation for the trek back to the

City. It was then someone finally noticed I was not there. An ensuing search also revealed I was no longer among them in any sense of the word!

"What's that in the pool?" someone yelled in horror. And that was the beginning of it.

In a strange way, I was as much an observer in the chaos that followed as I was the object. It took me a while to get my bearings, but I must emphasize that I was as profoundly shocked as everyone else to discover my demise. *Me?* I kept thinking. *Dead? Are they talking about me?*

Oh, there was an attempt at resuscitation while someone called 911, but of course, it didn't work. Dead is dead. Still, it was nice to feel Michael's firm lips on mine while we waited (even though it was just mouth-to-mouth resuscitation) and his strong hands desperately pumping at my chest. Claudia looked away. Marian Hingis's eyes grew to proportions I didn't think possible. Most of the others hung back.

I kept thinking I would wake up. Surely this was a dream. I mean, dying. . . . Wouldn't you think one could remember how it happened? Not necessarily, at least not in my case. It's difficult to describe the process because that segment of time is completely blocked out. Yes, it's the part where one's ticket gets punched for "the big ride"—when one makes the transition from a living state to . . . to the other. Well, you know what I mean. Suffice it say, the big mystery we wait all our lives to find out about is still unknown to me, but only temporarily. Eventually, I'm sure I'll come to know it all, after the facts come to light.

In the meantime, the police arrived and interviewed everyone, including the servants. The lights in Agnes's mansion stayed lit throughout the night, even after the police took me away. Just like that, they took me. . . . I couldn't get over it.

Wait until my mother finds out, I thought. *First, she'll plats, and then she'll have a thing or two to say about this!*

Two

The first thing that hits me as I approach my mother's apartment at two o'clock in the morning is the noise. AHIEEEE! . . . I hear the wailing, and I am reassured. Ma is not alone. My mother has two different ways of expressing grief: The first, when she's alone, is the scariest. Her sorrow swells like an expanding balloon that threatens to explode. Without an outlet, she will beat her fists into a pillow and gulp for air. Shoulders shake, eyes redden and overflow with tears, but not a sound is heard. The second, infinitely more healthy, involves the full menu of expression, and that is what I hear now from outside in the hallway.

My mother was not taking the news about my drowning gracefully. She gave a huge *g'shrei* when she was notified. Two policemen, each holding an arm, helped her to the couch. The tears, the screams, I saw and heard it all, but was helpless to do anything for her.

Ma, Ma, calm down, I yelled, but she couldn't hear me. I'd always heard that losing a child is the worst thing for a parent, and now, in a convoluted way, I witness the sadness. My mother would not be comforted. She retreated into herself, unable to cope.

The policemen exchanged looks. "Do you have any family in the vicinity, Mrs. Edelstein?" one of them ventured.

Her small, plump body was eclipsed by the two uniforms from the Forest Hills Precinct. Because of the hour, the Nassau

County authorities had prevailed upon their comrades in the Queens area that served the neighborhood where Ma lived.

"Family?" she repeated, too stunned to focus. Well meaning though they were, the good officers were having a problem getting through.

It was true what my father had said before he died. Ma was wonderful in the kitchen; she could nurse a sick child back to health with her chicken soup and *bobbeh meisehs*; she could bandage a scrape, bargain with the butcher, argue with Aunt Sarah (and win!)—but accept death and deal with it? No. My mother needed a strong arm to lean on. When Pop was here, it was his. After he died, it was mine. Whose would she lean on now?

When my father took ill, I had just completed my first year at the University of Stony Brook and was trying to get used to living within the confines of parental supervision again. The rapidity with which his health deteriorated from a severe cold to pneumonia astounded us all. Poppy was rarely ill, and we were later to take ourselves to task for what we thought might have been our fault. The doctors assured us that nothing we could have done would have changed the course of history. Ma and I never quite accepted that. My father died within three weeks of the onset of his illness. I was nineteen. Now my mother stood alone, supported by two well-meaning police officers.

I thought of my sister in Ohio and hoped the police had the good sense to look in Ma's personal telephone book for someone else, perhaps closer. They did better; they called in Myrna Brandt, Ma's neighbor, and through the ensuing wailing and distress, they made their exit.

As things went, my mother was in pretty good hands. Mrs. Brandt and her husband had lived next door to my mother for ten years. They were good neighbors: There for each other, but not in each other's plate, if you know what I mean. But this situation was different. I knew Mrs. Brandt would contact my sister Miriam and that she would not leave my mother alone until the family arrived. My next priority was to find Frank. The problem was where in the heck was he? I could sense a searching expedition on my part was imminent and concluded that the only good thing about this job was that I didn't have to worry about transportation. Naturally, I still preferred the alternative.

Saudi Arabia—somewhere in the frigging desert: Gimme a break! What does Frank get out of this besides earning a darned good living? My former husband Frank is still my best friend. The only competition I ever had was his chosen profession. An investigative reporter who travels the globe cannot help with supermarket shopping on the weekend because somewhere something big is happening, and wherever that is, Frank will be there. An assassination? Look for Frank. A war? A coup? He's Johnny-on-the-spot. And I have to suppose he's at this dreadful spot because there's a major story lurking. I observe him and two other men in Western attire sitting cross-legged on a blanket inside the tent of an Arab chieftain discussing the finer points of why Saudi Arabia chooses to remain outside the lines of progress. And, I notice, the good ole boy network is still in business. Women demurely draped in black abayas are serving their chief and his guests tea. They move like shadows across the earthen floor and are just as dispensable. The chief dismisses them with a wave of his hand. Wouldn't you know I'd run into this sort of stuff on my first visit to this part of the world?

Frank, I whisper, *can you hear me? Listen, I've got to talk to you privately.*

Instead, one of the other men begins to speak. "I say," his British rolls out toward his host, "one suspects you might know a little something about what Saddam Hussein is really up to—under the skirts, so to speak."

The chieftain smiles haughtily and takes a long sip from his tea. Looking up from under a brush of dark eyebrows, he stares at the foreigner a full minute before responding. "The camel does not look for water in just any part of the desert."

There is general assent among his guests, but I'll be damned if I know what he means. Anyhow, I'm not here to learn about the habits of exotic, smelly animals.

Psst, Frank, something terrible has happened. I need to talk with you now! He doesn't look up, but I notice he's adjusting his position. Ah, maybe this is a sign. I persevere. *I hate to break this to you like this, hon, but I've suffered an awful mishap*—now I'm rudely cut off by the other member of the group, a soft-spoken Italian.

"Leeson, please. We all-a-know that-a Saddam has the abeel-ity for nuclear warheads. Why we play these games? Hah? The man, he ez a dog, a crazy animal—" At this point, the Italian is interrupted by an armed guard who has entered the tent and begins whispering in the chief's ear.

I take this opportunity to try again. *Frank, please try to hear me. I need you, for God's sake. This is bigger than even Saddam Hussein!* But all I get for my efforts is the sight of his hand reaching behind his head to slap an annoying sand flea from the back of his neck. I'm sure there's a way to establish contact, but my present condition did not come with a how-to manual. Then I get a brilliant idea. I bend over him and begin to blow in his ear, or try to. That always used to work. He slaps at the side of his head. I can't tell if it's me making progress or if the sand fleas are getting turned on. *Frank, if you ever loved me, pay attention! Nada.* Zilch. Nothing. I'll have to rely on someone else in the family to get the message across. Someone else means my sister Miriam. Well, beggars can't be choosers. So now, I head back to Ma's.

AHIEEEE! Either the concert is still in progress or else there was an intermission in my absence and the second act has begun. That can mean only one thing . . . my sister has arrived.

From the very beginning, Miriam's arrivals have elicited such reactions. She was the unexpected consequence of an amorous encounter between my parents when I was almost seven. Their previous attempts to create a sibling for me had ended in failure, and they finally accepted what appeared to be God's will. But the Lord does have a sense of humor—ergo Miriam.

From the start, my sister seemed to have bypassed the modern era, riding into our lives on some obsolete cloud of Edwardian piety. She obeyed her parents, never lied and was potty-trained at one and a half. And as the years progressed, Miriam attended religious services on a regular basis. Conservative, devoted to rules, she fit the profile of an old woman from the age of five on.

As I study her now, one glance tells me she's been frequenting the wrong beauty parlor again. Her "honest" brown hair has been streaked with something resembling mustard. Maybe this is my sister's version of "a walk on the wild side," or maybe this is just what living with her husband Herbie has driven her to. Whatever. Everyone needs a change, I suppose. Unfortunately, this one does not enhance. I observe that my sister becomes more matronly every time I see her. Then I am jolted with the reality that she will be forty this year and forgive her the few extra pounds and double chin. I dwell ungenerously on the question of how happy could anyone be with the unexciting Herbie? That plus the fact that she's just been hit with the news of my death softens my stance.

After she married, Miriam glided easily into her role of "Stepford" wife. Whatever discrimination I hoped my intelligent, college-educated, properly reared sister possessed became diluted in the everyday, humdrum routine of a suburban wife and mother. And the strange thing was, she thought she was lucky! Furthermore, whatever Herbie wanted, Herbie got. It was enough to make a normal person gag. Now here she was, with husband in tow, newly arrived from Cleveland, *his* place of origin, the two of them taking over Ma and *the arrangements*.

"I called Rabbi Friedman," my brother-in-law announced, fully in charge, "and he will be here this afternoon." My sister stood there nodding like a metronome. Herbert Rosen, vice president of Rosen Plumbing Supplies (his father is president), made the announcement like the true heir of the plumbing dynasty he was, expecting nothing more than applause from those around him. Stretching himself to his full five feet, eight inches, he rocked back and forth in place. There being no response from his audience, he went on. "My parents are arriving tonight. I reserved a room for them at the Holiday Inn, which is good because they can help keep an eye on the kids."

Responding to the magic words, my mother looked up. "The children? They're here?" Her eyes were red and swollen, but there was hope in her voice.

"Of course, we brought them," said Miriam. "They're in the living room watching television."

Television, the nanny of the millennium.

The first ray of sunshine crossed my mother's face as she rose from her bed. Miriam put out her hand. "Where are you going?"

"I'm going to see my grandchildren!"

"You don't have to get up, Ma, I'll bring them in here." Mrs. Stepford on the job.

"I'm not a cripple!"

Good, Ma. You tell her.

Miriam turned to Herbie, who shrugged his shoulders, and Ma brushed past them both and went into the living room. There she held out her arms to her two darlings, aged nine and eleven. My niece, Cheryl, was the first to respond. She was the mirror image of her mother in every way except she was too young to experiment with hair color. Hers was still the original graham-cracker brown, a shade lighter than her eyes. She was a pretty child, though a bit on the chubby side. Yes, Mother Miriam knew how to overindulge, but was she doing her daughter any favors? My guess is the child will swing the other way when boys become more important than strudel. And how will her mother, the control freak, manage anorexia?

Given to drama for most of her eleven years, Cheryl fell against her grandmother's breast, eyes closed tightly. "Poor Grandma," she whispered, in excellent Actors' Studio diction.

"Oy," Ma declared. "Your Aunt Annie loved you." And it's true, I did. She was a bright child with whom I'd shared my love of literature.

"I know," the actress emoted, "and she loved you too, Grandma."

A few soft tears rolled down Ma's cheeks, but before she would let grief take over, she held out her arms to her grandson. David, however, was preoccupied with a rerun of *NYPD Blue* and didn't readily pick up his cue.

"Go to Grandma!" ordered Cheryl, sounding more like she was commanding a golden retriever than her kid brother. I didn't have to wonder where she got that from.

My nephew eased toward Ma, stretching his neck sideways

in what looked like an awkward imitation of a Siamese dancer. He managed to keep his eyes trained on the screen and never lost a word of dialogue. Coldhearted little bastard. I don't care what the new rules are today. One good kick in the rear would go a long way toward his education.

Ma didn't seem to notice; she was *kvelling*. Family, especially children, made her complete. Never mind the altitudes women have soared to in modern times, Ma was the best of her era: the maven, the Ph.D., the elder stateswoman of family love. Ma's blissful reunion with her family was short-lived, however. The rabbi arrived within a few minutes, and Ma reverted to her operatic best.

Rabbi Abel Friedman, with his smooth-shaven cherubic face and serious, metal-rimmed eyeglasses, was a good man from the Conservative sector of Judaism, the middle ground between Orthodox (strict, industrial-strength religion) and Reformed (also known as the *other* white meat), where almost anything goes. My parents were reared in the old ways, but after my sister was born, they moved toward the Conservative, midway between the two extremes. Figuring that he would never be blessed with sons, Pop decided there was no sense in schlepping halfway across town to give us the industrial-strength education when the Conservative Temple was only a half a block away. Of course, my parents still retained two sets of dishes, observed the *Shabbes* and other Orthodox rules, but fanaticism took a backseat to the easier life. Enter, Rabbi Friedman, a youngish, more contemporary version of the Old Testament.

Friedman fit in everywhere. Intelligent and well educated, the man was sharp enough to attract the younger generation and at the same time knowledgeable enough to command the respect of the established congregation. He did weddings, bar mitzvahs, funerals and acquitted himself reasonably well when called on to counsel members in distress. Grieving widows were his forte, and he arrived ready for business.

"Mrs. Edelstein, I'm so very sorry for your sad news."

AHIEEEE!

Ma was off and running again.

Friedman's flushed face resembled a bowl of borscht.

Miriam ran for the tissues."Ma, Ma," she clucked, "this is not doing you any good!"

Real smart, huh? And you wonder why you failed Psych 101?

"I understand," the rabbi interjected, "it must have been quite a shock."

"Shock?" my mother countered. "Shock? You don't know the half of it! Oy! My Annie, my darling, my baby! How?"—and here she raised her eyes to the ceiling—"How could such a thing happen?"

As expected, no answer was forthcoming.

The rabbi turned toward Herbie and raised his eyebrows wisely. Cue: Herbie.

"Ma," the *man* of our family began, "the police do not have all their facts yet. We're going to have to wait and see . . . We need to be patient. Give them some time to, ah, iron things out—"

AHIEEEE! "My baby, my—Where is my darling now? I want to see her!"

Herbie flicked his eyes at the rabbi while draping an arm around his mother-in-law. With an expression that translated as *get this!* he said, "Well, Ma, you'll need to get hold of yourself while I explain. . . . Ah, since the circumstances were, um . . . unusual, the police need to keep Annie's body a little longer in order to, ah, to try to figure out what happened. . . . Well, we want to know who did this, don't we?"

"So?"

"Look, there's no nice way to put this. The police want to perform an autopsy."

"Oh, my God! My God! That's *sacrilege!* Rabbi! What should I do?"

My mother's voice had risen to a level that penetrated even television's distraction, and within seconds, two young heads appeared around the doorframe. Mother Miriam sprang into action: "What are you doing in here?"

Duh. They're not deaf!

"Now let's get right back to the living room!"

Another half-hour passed with the good rabbi offering spiritual consolation as well as practical suggestions regarding procedures. But he stayed away from the subject that troubled my mother the most. "Under, ah, normal circumstances, you know we would have arranged burial immediately. This being the Sabbath, the funeral would have taken place tomorrow—Sunday . . ."

"But, Rabbi," she pleaded, "what should I do?"

Herbie to the rescue. "Maybe the police will find enough evidence and the autopsy won't be necessary." Soft, plump tears rolled down Ma's cheeks; she hung her head, accepting something awful over which she had no control.

I, too, was shocked. In the Jewish religion, burial takes place soonest. There's no waiting around. You live; you die; they stick you in the ground. Period. Within two days, wherever possible, except if death occurs on a Sabbath. Jews do not bury on Sabbath. They also don't marry on Sabbath. They don't even work on Sabbath. They're not even supposed to—but that wasn't even the question. The parade couldn't start without the body. Ahem, that's me, or at least the part of me that was before all this began, which brings me to the next question: Where the hell were they keeping me anyway? Along with this thought I felt a sudden inspiration: If he were here, Frank would know!

As if by magic, my mother suddenly cried out, "Somebody has to tell Frank!"

Good for you, Ma! At last, somebody's paying attention to details.

At the same time, I sensed a new energy. Maybe I wasn't so impotent after all.

Three

The first of Ma's "almost" heart attacks had occurred years before when she discovered that the man she thought I was just dating (but was actually living with) wasn't Jewish. "What is your young man's last name?" she asked, pointedly, and after several months of uncharacteristic patience. "Dowd," I replied clearly, "Frank Dowd," and stared her down. Only one word escaped her thin, compressed lips: "Oy." And then, in a low whisper (the neighbors shouldn't hear): "He's not Jewish?" Her eyes were wide, frightened and disbelieving. "Ma," I began, but she held up one hand, palm outward as if to ward off the evil she assumed had overtaken me, and clutched her chest with her other hand. "A *shaigetz!*" She pronounced the word and looked toward the ceiling moving her lips, but no sound was heard. Pop had been dead for six years at that point, and I figured she was making an effort at contact so as to inform him of my shocking behavior. That didn't work either.

"He's a wonderful man, Ma," I reassured her, "and I know you're going to love him in spite of everything."

She looked at me as though I was speaking in a foreign tongue and clasped her hands in prayer: "You're a beautiful girl, Annie, a smart girl. You could have your pick. Why? Why? I don't understand." She set her mouth in a thin line (not a good sign).

"You will when you meet him." I put my arms around her soft shoulders and kissed the top of her silky white hair, easily accomplished for, at five feet, one inch, my mother was three inches shorter than I. She loved me, dammit; we both knew that, and the familiar gesture settled the two of us.

Her eyes were warm when she reached for my hand, and her voice had softened. "Annie, Annie . . ."

Much against all she had ever lived by, my mother consented to meet the stranger who had stolen her daughter's heart. Frank appeared the following Friday in response to her dinner invitation. I'd left the apartment we shared an hour before, in order for him to arrive as a bachelor, so to speak. He was wearing the gray suit I had picked up at the cleaners, the red paisley tie I'd given him last Christmas, a freshly laundered white shirt and polished shoes, all of which I had carefully selected and prepared. There was a tiny mark on one side of his chin, that probably only I would notice, but a part of me applauded the reality that even the great Frank Dowd could be nervous enough to cut himself while shaving at the prospect of meeting his future mother-in-law for the first time.

My mother would appraise the whole of the man: his height, upwards of five eleven, was a mountain for her eyes to climb. She would take in the neatly brushed hair with its reddish brown tints that shone like autumn leaves, the Irish blue eyes softly framed in a gentle whirlpool of creases and his wide, direct smile. And in her own good time, Ma would decide what the man was made of.

I had already prepared him for my mother's *Shabbes* menus, warning him to eat heartily; to do otherwise would automatically disqualify him from further consideration. With my mother watching carefully, Frank scarfed the stuff down like he hadn't eaten in a week. A shnapps—whiskey—to begin? Of course. Chopped liver on rye? Down the hatch. And a new one for the brave stranger: *gefilte* fish. I must say I admired his tenacity on this one. Chicken soup with *k'naidlech,* boiled chicken, beef brisket with horseradish sauce, boiled potatoes and string beans followed. Frank was in the war zone, and he knew it. My mother graded every bite, every expression. Detente was established sometime between the soup and the brisket. By the time Ma brought the honey cake and tea to the table, the two of them were laughing together like old friends. As unlikely a match as ever there was, the ingredients were all there: the wanting, the loneliness, the need. Frank is a warm and hearty Irishman who loves to eat, and Ma loves to cook and afterward to protest that her dishes really didn't turn out all that well. And just like the poker player who bluffs, feints and wins the big one, she sits back and rakes in the chips—in this case, the compliments.

"So, Ma," began Frank, as he settled back in the big easy chair to smoke an after-dinner cigarette (yes, they were already on a Ma/Frank basis), "where did you learn to cook like that?" What an opening! I knew it was safe to leave them alone and went down the hall to the kitchen to start the cleanup. One glance around told me my mother had not stinted on her efforts. Every pot, pan and utensil had been called to the front for action. I organized the mess and a half an hour later joined the other two inside. "So, no World War Three?" I chirped.

They looked up, grinning.

"Come," said my mother, patting the couch beside her. She seemed very happy and at peace as she stroked my hand. "Your young man—he's all right. Why didn't you tell me he *farshtaist Yiddish?"*

"I didn't know."

Frank and I exchanged looks, and he was grinning. I should have known. The man had traveled around the world and, by this time, could certainly say "hello" and "how are you" in a dozen or more languages including Arabic, Swahili and Russian. Why wouldn't he understand my mother's intermingling of Yiddish with English? Frank had found the door. It was a combination of a number of things, though, not just compassion for her style or appreciation for her cooking. He missed his own mother, who had died when he was twelve. The evening had developed like a successful help-wanted ad, "Mother Wanted." Ma managed to pull this out of him during their tête-à-tête. And in no time at all, he had crept into her heart.

I stayed over with Ma that night after Frank left, and she admitted how pleased she was to meet him. "I really like your young man," she confided. "He's a real *mentsh*." The literal translation for this word is "man," but *mentsh* means much more than that. It refers to an ethical person, a man of strong moral fiber, a human being whose worth cannot be calculated. That was Frank, all right. It was the highest compliment Ma could offer. And for the two years we were married, she couldn't get enough of him.

Frank and I had met at a party in Greenwich Village. Always intrigued by forbidden fruit, I was drawn to the Irishman like a hot fudge sundae. Particularly delicious were his quick-action retorts; he matched me wisecrack for wisecrack. I thought I was hot stuff, but Frank suspected that I was not as wild or experienced as I pretended. We retreated after an hour to a nearby coffee house for uninterrupted conversation. An hour later, we were in bed together in his apartment. Looking back now, I realize that my education was just beginning. I moved in with Frank a month later but told my mother I was taking my own place.

"It's close to work, so I don't have to worry about subway breakdowns, and I have a roommate, so we're sharing expenses." I felt like a shit, lying to Ma, but the truth would have been more destructive. It all sounded perfectly logical, except for the fact that my "roommate" seemed always to be visiting her parents out of town when Ma came to the City on one of her rare visits. Even though it was the seventies, I could never explain that I was (God forbid!) living in sin.

Five years later, Frank's and my parting was painful for us both. But his work as a journalist took him away so much of the time that marriage became a commitment he couldn't keep. It was because we really cared for each other that we could let go. By that time, of course, Ma had grown so fond of Frank, she cried more than I did, expressing her displeasure at our separation by a dramatic repetition of her first "almost" heart attack. In this, her second episode, she included breast-beating. Award-winning performance that it was, it didn't change the course of history. Frank left on one of his exotic assignments shortly after, and I tried to find a new way to live. Now, I found myself once again trying to make sense out of disaster.

Looking back now at their first meeting, I realize that Frank became one of Ma's kids that day, as surely as if she'd carried him the required nine months. He would always be an integral part of the equation, and that was why it was essential that he be here now.

Monday, Persian Gulf time, Bahrain: It's amazing how easy it is to travel when one doesn't have to worry about clothes or makeup. Guess that's why Frank and his ilk never want to settle down. They can wear what they damned please, go where they want, when they want, and never have to get bogged down in explanations, except with their supervisors.

The Bahrain Hilton cocktail lounge was filled with an assortment of ragged, unwashed folks who were congregating for what appeared to be Happy Hour. The bartender was gesturing toward the noisy group at the end of the bar. "Hey, Frank," he yelled. "Pick up the phone. It's your Bureau Dispatcher."

My beloved Frank pulled the beer away from his mouth for just an instant, nodded, then took a generous gulp. "Coming."

Be brave, my darling, I whispered. *This will be a terrible blow.* I inched closer, so I could hear his office breaking the awful news.

"Yeah, Frank here."

"Hey, pal, it's Maggio. How're doing? "

"Yeah, Maggio. What's up?"

"Brace yourself. This is reeeely big!"

Oh, poor Frankie, how I wish I could have told you myself!

"Remember that story you filed on the Kurdish refugees?"

Kurdish refugees? What kind of crap is that? Give him the REAL *news, for God's sake!*

"So?"

"CNN picked it up. They want to expand the piece and update their bio on you, maybe fly you back for a little fill-in. Huh! Whaddya say to that?"

"That ain't bad, but I'm in the middle of some other good stuff and can't leave now."

"Okeydoke—your decision. Got some other news for you."

Uh-oh, here it comes. Be brave, honey.

"Marcia called."

Marcia? Who the hell is Marcia?

"She wants you to consider covering the Bush conference in China next week."

"I'll think about it. Anything else?"

"Yeah. Herb Rosen called."

Herbie! At last. I never thought you had it in you!

"Herb? . . . Uh, what did he say?"

"Sorry, pal. This is gonna be bad news. . . ."

"Wh-what is it?"

"It's Annie . . . uh—there's been an accident. Look, there's no nice way to tell you this. Annie's dead."

"Dead?" Frank croaked, struggling to find his voice. "Annie? Wh—how? What happened?" His blue eyes filled, and the deep crags in his face hardened as he gripped the phone. "Tell me what happened!"

Maggio related the brief message from Herbie. "There was a drowning. The police suspect foul play. They've been questioning everyone who was at the house: the Spurgeon place in Sands Point. The main thing Herb wanted to get across is that Annie's mother would like you to come. She's upset about everything, especially that the funeral has to be delayed until the police are done investigating. I told him I would try to get to you, but nothing was certain."

"I'm taking the next plane out."

"But—"

"I said I'm headed back! Call you when I know the flight info." Frank clicked off but sat looking at the phone for a few more seconds.

Psst, Frankie, can you hear me? I'm here, hon. I'm here!

He picked up his head and looked around. For one wild moment, I thought I'd actually made contact, but then I realized he wasn't aware of anything in this world or the next. Pain and disbelief crawled over his face like maggots on a corpse. I'd never seen him so vulnerable.

Frank, listen, I'm sorry. I want to help. Won't you please try to hear me? Nothing. Dammit! I'm entitled to connect with my own husband, er, ex-husband, whatever. I'm getting really mad now and will have to speak to a supervisor if this continues!

I watched Frank move slowly back to his group, exchange a few words and head toward the elevators. I slipped into the room with him. Hell, I would have been glad to help him pack if I could, anything to get him back to the States. After calls to the airline and his office, he showered and threw his clothes into bags, all the time muttering my name and shaking his head in continued disbelief.

Ah, he still loved me. . . .

Four

The time variance being seven hours, I figured I could get more accomplished back in New York than spending half a day on a plane, so I blew a few well-placed kisses Frankie's way, wished him *bon voyage* and departed, in my newly acquired method. It was Monday morning in New York, and I was curious about the disposition of my accounts. Would Claudia get them all? At nine sharp I sat in the reception area watching Marian Hingis dabbing her eyes. Bless her soul, she was having the time of her life breaking the news to all and sundry. Even the Fed-Ex deliverer couldn't get away from her lurid account of THE DROWNING.

Wriggling in her chair, Marian said, "It just gives one the goose bumps, if you know what I mean . . ."

"Can't say that I blame ya. And the police?"

"So far, they haven't named a suspect. But one wonders—I mean, who would do such a thing? Annie Dowd? She was a fun person." Lowering her voice, she whispered, "Divorced, you know."

"Oh?"

"Yes, she was married to a famous correspondent."

The Fed-Ex guy cut her off. "Is that right?"

"Oh, yes. He writes for the *Washington Post* or The *Inquirer* or some such—very important."

I winced. Frank would have a hissy fit if he heard this. But the Fed-Ex deliverer seemed unimpressed. In fact, he looked like he was anxious to get away.

He tapped his pile. "Better be on my way. Gotta lotta stops to cover. Uh, sorry for your loss."

Marian dabbed at her eyes, sniffled and waved him out the door, through which a well-dressed, middle-aged couple were just about to enter. They barely got past announcing their appointment with me when Marian's early-morning glow took on new luster.

"Annie Dowd? Oh my. Well, Ms. Dowd's been . . ." Marian began to shake her head. "No, you can't see her. Annie Dowd *died* yesterday!"

Her audience responded as promised, and the Broadcast Queen took the opportunity to provide all the (by now) embellished details. She was riding the crest and Mr. and Mrs. Almost Clients responded as programmed. They turned green and backed out of the office. If only Agnes could have been there.

Safe in the knowledge that Marian was keeping the home fires burning brightly, I slipped down the hall to see how the rest of the team was faring.

Roger and Matt had arrived fifteen minutes before, but Claudia (a.k.a. Dragon Lady) was late. Well, of course, Harold hadn't arrived yet either. I'm thinking they had a strategy session that took all night. Right. When they finally walked through the front door, Harold looked—well, a little worn but quite satisfied. Claudia's eyes were glistening, and the sweet smell of success moved along with her. In other words, the bitch got my accounts.

Well, she was welcome to them and all the *tsores* that went with them—trouble like Fannie Shine, for one. Signs on with my firm to sublease her duplex on East Sixty-fifth so she can join her producer husband out on the West Coast for a year. At least that was my understanding. Simple fool that I was, I entered her apartment with two clients, thinking it was uninhabited, and was halfway down the hall before the sounds from the master bedroom reached me. You know the kind: throes of sexual ecstacy, rhythmic groans interspersed with little doggie yelps, the latter coming not from any puppy I ever knew.

"Wait just a second," I whispered, sotto voce to the clients, a sedate Belgian couple with royal bearing. Another step or two in the direction of the bedroom, the door of which was ajar, and I was staring into the wild, very displeased face of Johnny Romano, otherwise known as the hatchet man for Luke Snyder, the underworld mob boss. Romano zoomed in on my face. Backing away was already too little and too late. We left, the Belgian couple and I, with me shouting loudly enough for the devil to hear: "HOW STUPID OF ME! DEFINITELY THE WRONG APARTMENT." Who was I kidding?

So, Claudia, lottsa luck. Gangland's Casanova is all yours now.

Now I observed my nemesis, stunningly dressed in her two-piece beige and cocoa Donna Karan ensemble (with coordinating Joan and David shoes) picking up her messages—and MINE too! Guess I'd have to get used to it, though it wasn't fair.

Life's not fair, Frank tried to teach me long ago. How right he was. Frank was right about most things, especially the fact that staying together would stunt us both. But he'd always be my best friend, and I couldn't wait for him to get here and help me unravel this mess. In the meantime, I'd start with the usual suspects. Who could I rule out? I went over the list of my co-workers and, outside of my inglorious feelings toward Claudia, I couldn't think of anyone who would want me dead. I had to admit that even Claudia had nothing much to fear from me.

Yep, there was a lot of work to do. Just because I was dead, didn't mean I could lie back and relax. Ma, for instance, and the explanation behind my untimely demise. And, oh! now there was the funeral to contend with. How could I not attend that?

Okay, but first things first. I had to get organized. In terms of priorities, the office was interesting, in a voyeuristic way, but not number one. I needed to find out *who* did this to me and *why*. The police—ah, yes. What was the guy's name? Martola. Yes, Detective Louis Martola, a bit hard-nosed but a lot of street smarts. Gets the job done, I'll bet. I think I can work with him.

From what I could ascertain, Detectives Louis Martola and Charlene Williams had been partners at the Nassau County Police Headquarters in Mineola for more than two years and had covered crimes ranging from jewelry theft to murder. I helped myself to a quick scan of their files. Evidently, Martola was a tough cop who came through the system in Brooklyn's Flatbush area before moving his family out to Levittown. He was well versed in city scum, their underhanded deals and shortcuts to better living. His younger partner had been with the force for eight years. Charlene Williams grew up knowing exactly what she wanted to do. Her dad had attained the rank of captain in the Glen Cove Precinct and two older brothers still worked there. But there was more.

Charlene had suffered an unusual accident early in her career. That she was still alive to talk about it was part of the miracle. According to the incident report in her file, Charlene's weapon misfired one day on the practice range. In the ensuing explosion, a tiny fragment of metal lodged just inside the temporal lobe. A millimeter in any direction could have ended the chapter right there. But the only price the rookie paid was a tiny sliver of metal in her skull and a small scar next to the hairline, easily disguised. The Academy was lucky; it almost lost a terrific cop.

Satisfied their backgrounds equipped them to handle my case, I perused some of their superiors' comments contained therein: "work well together," "seem to read each other's minds," and my personal favorite—"like professional ballroom dancers, they rarely miss a step." Their captain referred to them as "the yin and yang of crime solutions." When my case fell on their desks, it didn't take them long to get organized. Out came the legal pads, known facts were sifted, relevant characters noted and a list of questions compiled. At least until Frank arrived, I was in good hands.

"Who do you like for this job?" asked Charlene Williams, a brunette of medium height who was currently bent over a pile of notes on her desk.

When she lifted her head after a few seconds, intelligent brown eyes dominated a pretty face, devoid of makeup or prejudgment. I liked her immediately. I was to learn that Charlene's talent in maintaining an innocent, deadpan face stood her in good stead as a detective. Criminals mistook her pleasant expression as ignorance, their lawyers as inexperience. Both groups underestimated her tenacity. Charlene was no easy mark.

She had been Phi Beta Kappa at Columbia University and possessed enough brains to meet any challenge. At this moment, the overhead lights caught the glint of interest in her sparkling eyes as she focused on her partner.

Louis Martola, an athletic-looking specimen in his early forties reached for his coffee mug and pushed back his chair, the back of which was draped with a well-worn tweed sport jacket. When he stood, Martola's knit shirt rode the muscles of his upper arms and torso, leaving no doubt of his original training as a fighter. I gazed longingly, regretting the loss of some of Earth's pleasures. I could guess he still worked out in the gym two or three times a week, leaving nothing to chance.

Martola indicated he was going for a refill and pointed a finger at Charlene's cup, raising his eyebrows. They spoke in silent shorthand. She shook her head. He strode over to a table in the middle of the squad room and held his mug under the spigot of the big urn. I could almost see the wheels turning in his head. After swallowing deeply, he returned to his desk, which faced his partner's. "Too early to say," Martola muttered, finally responding to Charlene's question regarding possible suspects. "There's a lot of stuff that doesn't fit. What about the Englishman? Comes out of nowhere . . . suddenly cozies up to the victim . . . next thing you know, she's in for the long swim."

"I don't know—haven't got the feel of the thing yet. What's his motive?"

"Motive. Shit—how should I know?"

Not in the least discouraged, Williams leaned across her side of the desk, her dark waves brushing the tops of her shoulders. "What do you make of Agnes Spurgeon?"

"Cold bitch, but think she's too much on the frail side to have pulled this off."

Do think again!

Williams suddenly jerked her head in my direction. Had she heard me? She shook her head, as if to negate the possibility.

"Perhaps," she answered her partner, "but how much strength does it take to push someone into the pool?"

There you go.

Charlene's mouth went slack; her eyes squinting in all directions. She swung around to Martola. "Did you hear anything?"

"Hear what?" He shook his head and blew out some air. "The deceased was what? Thirty, forty years younger? Doesn't fly."

But all I could think of was, she heard me! I know she did.

"Umm," muttered Charlene, "a lot of this doesn't add up."

Martola agreed. Interlacing his hands, he stretched his arms taut above his head. Loud cracks followed as his knuckles popped. "We'll need to talk to the whole bunch—compare their answers with those made Friday night."

Now you're talking!

At this, Charlene developed a sudden coughing spell. "Excuse me," she said, rising abruptly and heading toward the restroom. I knew it was a ploy to get with the good ole girl network, so I tagged along. After ascertaining that the restroom was indeed empty, she backed up against the sink and crossed her arms belligerently. Her eyes swept the empty room, and I realized that she couldn't see me. But she had heard me!

"Okay. Who or what are you?"

You know. It's me—Annie.

I must say, Charlene had even more guts than I gave her credit for. She never panicked. I know I would have, if I'd been in her place. She may have been scared at first, but did a decidedly great job of disguising it. I assured her I meant no harm; that I was as surprised as she was that I was still around.

She shook her head in disbelief. "I've read about such things." Her eyes scanned the room. "Know that some Talk Show hosts have had guests on their shows with so-called special powers, but I've never . . ."

Please don't be afraid. This is new to me, too.

Charlene inhaled deeply but didn't back down. "What do you want?"

To find the bastard who did this to me.

She appeared to think that one over. "Do you have any ideas?"

That's the problem. Strange as it may sound, I have a complete blank of my, uh, last moments, but I'm sure that's just temporary. I damn well will find out who pushed me into that pool! Now, do you want to work with me on this or not?

She appeared to think that one over and nodded her head. (I knew she wasn't stupid.) So, bottom line, we made a deal. I was certain she was gifted; maybe it had something to do with that piece of metal in her head. It didn't matter. All I cared about was that she was the only one who could hear me. If she'd let me, I'd help her find the killer. Five minutes later, Charlene returned to her desk. She held our exchange in the tightest part of her brain, figuring that no one would believe her anyhow. Then she cooly picked up the conversation where her partner had left off.

"I agree. We have to question everyone again, but let's wait until after the pathologist's report."

The what? These last were the most obscene words exchanged that day. Pathologist? Isn't it enough I had nothing to say about when my life would be over? Now I have to suffer even more humiliation? I mean, talk about desecration . . .

I've always been rather modest, so you can imagine my chagrin when I saw my nude body stretched out on top of the medical table *sans* sheet or robe. There I was—naked in front of all those strangers, and mostly men at that. Embarrassing? That's hardly the word.

Well, get on with it! I urged, but of course no one could hear me.

At least one doctor, maybe two—or was that an assistant?—prepared their instruments and slides while a cordon of strangers behind a glass partition stared at the scene, meaning me. One assistant, a dirty old man with an array of slides, began probing my personal cavities for—what?—evidence?

You won't find any traces of semen there, I growled, *no thanks to whoever finished me off.*

But he would not be persuaded. Right then I wished to have my life back if only to shove my knee into his groin. The inability to react was frustrating, and I wondered if, after a reasonable apprentice period, I'd acquire more skills. Suddenly, the light danced off the doctor's scalpel. Now I've always been squeamish about procedures of any kind, and I suddenly realized that this person intended to invade my body without so much as an if-you-please. He placed the weapon at the top of my chest.

Now, wait just a minute! I bellowed. But of course, nobody heard me. It seemed the perfect time to leave.

I'm outta here. The investigation can't go on without me.

Five

I was glad to rejoin the two detectives as they waited outside the main entrance of Agnes Spurgeon's estate, and just in time to hear Louis Martola speak into the gate's intercom. "Yeah, we're here to see Mrs. Agnes Spurgeon."

The voice on the other end inquired politely: "Do you have an appointment?"

"Detectives Williams and Martola," the latter said. "We don't need an appointment."

"Uh . . . one moment, please."

The gate arm lifted up admitting their car, which crunched along the graveled driveway toward the main entrance of the stately residence. I had forgotten how impressive it was. The estate echoed the graceful lines of an old English manor house. I recalled reading an article in the *New York Times* Real Estate section that described how Agnes Spurgeon had interviewed several architects before settling on an Englishman, who she felt was the only one with sufficient credentials to create a house adapted from the old Cotswold estates of Gloucestershire, her family's origin. Our car closed in on the main house, which was set behind vast green lawns that held huge oaks dressed in layers of leaves. The main entrance boasted double-size doors of carved, weathered oak. Agnes's wealth spoke for itself, and I had to give her credit. As much as she irritated me, I was reminded once again that here was a woman of means who did not take the easy way out. No canasta club for this one. She built a business that was the envy of every Manhattan real-estate broker. And even when the doctor gave her an ultimatum to stay at home, reduce her activities and enjoy the life her English manor house afforded, she continued to guide Royal Roosts onto bigger and better things.

Being back at the scene of my sudden demise was not first on my list of things to do for entertainment, but I had to stay on top of the investigation while I waited for Frank. The maid responded to the door chimes and escorted the detectives and me into the library, the room I had come to know so well during my short-lived romance with Michael. Shortly after, the estate's imposing owner herself entered the room.

Something about the majestic appearance of that lady caused these two seasoned professionals to rise from the couch. Their hostess, however, did not extend her hand to either. Arranging herself like a Roman empress, she settled into a stiff-backed chair and nodded, as though to say: *Let the games begin.*

Martola cleared his throat and began (and in a rather gentlemanly manner, I thought): "Thank you for seeing us, Mrs. Spurgeon. We understand your health is not the best."

"My health is no concern of yours."

Now there's a typically gracious comeback.

Charlene swallowed a smile, paving the way for her partner's comment: "We're interested in the events of Friday, July Fourth—the day that one of your guests drowned in the swimming pool during a party you were hosting."

Drowned? That's putting it mildly. I was murdered—annihilated, offed!

"Specifically, what is it you want to know?"

Charlene jumped in. "What can you tell us about the drowning?"

Agnes's chin tilted upward at a thirty-degree angle. She smoothed back some disobedient stray hairs from her forehead and began to recite. It sounded as if her speech had been rehearsed to death: "I was with my guests. There was a commotion. Everyone was talking at once. And that is when I became aware there had been an accident."

You can tell she's really broken up about this.

Charlene covered her mouth.

Ignoring her tone, Martola pressed: "Now, Ms. Dowd worked for your firm for about ten years, I understand."

"About that long, yes." Agnes appeared bored but wary. Nevertheless, the detectives spent a few minutes exploring my history at Royal Roosts.

Ask her where she was when I was going down for the count.

Charlene put my question to the queen, but Agnes stiffened, then unexpectedly rose from her chair. "I don't believe I should answer any more of your questions without my attorney being present. If you will excuse me . . . Bernice will show you out." And the queen swept out of the room not waiting for a response.

So much for noblesse oblige.

The two detectives, now slightly wide-eyed but amused, turned and looked at each other. What was there to say? Plenty. But it wasn't until they were in their car riding back to the station that Charlene spoke. "Well, she's within her rights."

"Yeah, but don't you think it's mighty strange that an *innocent* person would demand to have her lawyer present? I mean, whaddya think she's tryin' to hide?"

"It doesn't necessarily mean she's hiding something," said Charlene. "Maybe she's just a very smart lady. After all, this murder did take place on her property. Between you and me, I don't blame her for being careful."

"Careful—shit! It's fuckin' inconvenient!"

That's the nature of the beast.

Charlene inhaled deeply, signifying she had nothing more to add.

"Who do you want to interview next?" her partner prodded. "Maybe some of the coworkers? How about the bunch the victim rode with to the party?"

That group? I've known them all for years. You're not going to find the killer in that crowd. It's a waste of time.

"Suits me," said Charlene emphatically, going along with her partner anyway.

Since it was past the morning rush hour, it only took us about fifty minutes to get to Midtown. I made myself comfy in the backseat. The car maneuvered along the Long Island Expressway to the Queens Midtown Tunnel, foregoing the Fifty-ninth Street Bridge, my favorite view of Manhattan's skyline, but Charlene was driving, and it was her choice.

She drove like a professional race driver, smoothly dodging potholes and the slower-moving cars. I had complete confidence, astutely aware that even if she made a serious mistake, nothing worse could happen to me. But she was good, and I must say I was rather proud that she was in charge of our vehicle and even prouder that she was in on the case. So I told her that. She responded in my general direction.

"Thanks."

"For what?" asked Martola.

Charlene checked the backseat in the rearview mirror. "Guess I must've been thinking out loud."

But I made a mental note to limit my contacts to safer situations.

On our way over to the office, Charlene wisely pulled into a parking lot on East Forty-third, between Park and Lexington Avenues. Parking spaces in this vicinity were as rare as the South African condor. Anyway, it was only a short walk from there to my former working digs, Royal Roosts, Inc., a.k.a. R. R., Inc. (for Rioting Rentals).

Marian Hingis's voice penetrated the decorous atmosphere like a nail across a blackboard: "DETECTIVES MARTOLA AND WILLIAMS ARE HERE TO SPEAK WITH YOU!" she shouted into the intercom.

Roger Franklin came out as summoned, and moments later the three of them headed down the hall to the conference room. Marian looked like she'd been socked in the stomach.

Yeah. Like you thought you'd be in on this? I, of course, sashayed after them and slipped into a chair next to Roger.

Martola: "How long did you know the deceased?"

There's that word again.

Roger: "Well, let's see now. Annie had been with the company a couple of years before I came—I'd say about seven, eight years."

"You guys date?"

"Oh, no—nothing like that."

Martola raised an eyebrow.

Oh leave him alone. He doesn't know anything . . . I don't think. I realized that I didn't know a damn thing either and decided to keep my mouth shut—or should I say, keep an open mind.

"Well, she was a nice-looking gal," Charlene said.

Why, thank you!

Charlene smiled.

"Yes, but our relationship was strictly business," Roger continued, unaware this was becoming a four-way conversation.

Martola was getting that smart-ass gleam in his eye and didn't try to hide it from Roger, who fidgeted uncomfortably.

Oh, let it go, Louie, he's telling the truth.

Charlene chimed in softly, "I take it you were good friends."

"Yes," came the guarded response, waiting for the next attack.

"Any idea who might have had a reason to kill Annie Dowd?"

A pensive Roger remained quiet for just a beat. "No idea whatsoever. Annie was a decent person. She worked hard, minded her own business and didn't try to cut the next one out of a commission. I trusted Annie, and am truly sorry she's . . . God! I can't believe she's gone. I'm really going to miss her around here. . . ."

This was not just a bunch of words thrown out to cover the moment. Roger's voice caught in his throat, and I thought he would break down at any moment.

"Yeah. It's tough to lose a friend." This last was from Martola, and frankly I was as surprised as Roger.

"By the way, can you remember where you were when Ms. Dowd was discovered in the pool?"

Roger struggled for a minute or so before answering. "Think I was sitting on the patio talking with Marian Hingis."

"Talking. About anything in particular?"

My friend turned suspicious eyes on his interrogator, pressed his lips together and took a breath. "It was a social event. I had no thought of impending tragedy and therefore did not take notes of my every action. Annie was my friend, and I would like to help uncover the truth, but no, I cannot tell you what Marian and I talked about. Maybe she will remember."

Martola stood and cleared his throat, signaling that the meeting was over. Chalk one up for Roger. Next up was Claudia.

She appeared with a large confident smile that seemed to say *I can sell you anything!* and another new outfit. God! That woman was relentless. The two detectives were seated side by side, but Claudia honed in on Martola as if he were all alone.

"Detective." The word rolled out of her mouth like soft toothpaste. "How can I help you?" Like, did he have time to study the menu?

Here's your opportunity, Martola, to see why Harold is willing to risk his whole inheritance for top-of-the-line servicing.

Charlene briefly covered her face with her hands. "Bad headache," she mouthed to her partner after she pulled her hands away and caught his startled look. Still, he shook his head. It's a good bet that if the *femme fatale* had not been there, he'd have had more to say. Now he turned back to Claudia and assumed a perplexed expression.

"Maybe you can help us here. We're trying to figure out who had a reason to kill Ms. Dowd. You being in the same office, maybe you heard something, saw something. . . ." He let his voice trail away, but he never took his eyes off his subject.

"I would certainly like to help, but I just don't have any idea at all."

"Did Ms. Dowd ever talk with you about her personal life? Was anything going on with her that you might now recall as being different—or suspicious?" asked Charlene.

Are you for real? I just about managed to be civil with the bitch, but I never discussed word one about my personal life with her.

"Uh-huh." This from Charlene, but Claudia thought she was adding incentive.

"Please understand, my life is hugely busy. Between business obligations and my fiancé, I have little or no time for distractions."

Well, that was opening the door for a barrage on my part, but I figured I'd distracted Charlene enough already.

"It doesn't make sense," Martola said, "that people working in the same office don't kick around the news of the day. Like, did you know who she was dating?"

"No, and I didn't care," came the sensitive response. "Oh, I knew enough that when her ex-husband was in town, they'd get together." She brushed off some imaginary speck from her Ralph Lauren scarf and smiled in Charlene's direction.

Don't you just feel a kinship growing?

"Sure."

Naturally, the Mrs. Harold Spurgeon-wannabe thought Charlene was actually bonding, so she nodded her approval. Guess Martola didn't see any good coming out of this, so he tried another tract.

"There was some talk of a thing between the deceased and the Englishman . . . uh, the Rheims guy."

Claudia's eyes lit up like the high beams on a Mercedes-Benz. "Yes, I noticed. We all did. One would think he'd have better taste."

Bitch! What did I tell you?

"Stay calm."

Of course, Charlene was talking to me, but Martola threw his partner a worried look.

"I have no reason to get upset!" Claudia huffed. "It's her life, or at least it was. Come to think of it, that gentleman, if he is a gentleman, was the only one at the party I'd never met before. You asked for suspicious persons? I'd start there."

Matt was just passing down the hall when Claudia finished. Charlene motioned for him to come in, and he glanced up and down the hall first like he was hoping the detective meant someone else. To make sure he got the message, she smiled at him and crooked her finger. That, of course, triggered a blush that spread across his cheeks like the petals of an azalea bush in a high wind.

"Have a seat." Martola gestured to the recently vacated chair opposite. "You know why we're here. We're looking for some answers. What can you tell us?"

The kid looked perplexed. I'd known Matt for at least three years and watched him mature from a part-time summer aide to a rookie real-estate agent. He was smart, hard-working and probably had a great future, if he could only get over his shyness, and various other office distractions. For instance, if Claudia would only stop swishing her Eau de Paris under his nose, maybe he'd get more work done. Anyway, I knew he couldn't possibly have had anything to do with my exit from this life. But Martola was in a mood to explore.

"What do you think happened on the Fourth, pal?"

"Huh?"

Martola launched an exasperated glance toward Charlene, shook his head from side to side and began again, enunciating each word: "DO YOU HAVE ANY IDEA WHO KILLED ANNIE DOWD?

"No, sir, none whatsoever."

Tell your partner to take it easy.

Charlene glared at Martola.

"How did you get along with Ms. Dowd?"

"Terrific! I mean, she was cool. We got along great. She helped me out a lot when I started working summers. Encouraging. Know what I mean?"

"Yeah, I know what you mean. Everybody loved Annie." (This last was said with an extra heaping tablespoon of sarcasm.) Martola was running out of patience.

"Thanks for your time," Charlene said, taking over, "I'm sure we'll be talking with you again soon."

Marian Hingis was summoned next. Roger volunteered to answer the phone while she was away from her desk. She patted her hair and smoothed her dress as she walked back to the conference room, sitting down in the chair held for her by Detective Martola and wiggling importantly. "Any way I can help with your investigation, Detectives, you can count on me."

"Well, now that's very cooperative of you, Miss—uh—*Ms.* Hingis," said Martola. "To begin with, what can you tell me about Ms. Dowd?"

He might as well have asked what she knew about the telephone directory. Where to begin?

"Well," she confided, "I know she was once married to this very well known reporter person—Fred, er, Franklin, uh, *FRANK*—that's it! Frank Dowd."

Charlene nodded. "Frank Dowd, huh?"

"Yes, and they would still see each other from time to time."

"From time to time? How often would that be?"

Marian smiled; she was warming to the occasion. "Whenever Mr. Dowd returned from an assignment, I believe."

There was a short pause, and Marian lowered her voice to a conspiratorial hum. "Of course, I don't know if she would have been that anxious to see Mr. Dowd after Friday night, if you know what I mean."

"Oh?"

"Yes, there was that nice Mr. Rheims—from England, you know—Mrs. Spurgeon's nephew. Handsome fellow."

There's an understatement.

"Ah . . ."

"Yes," Marian emphasized, feeling herself a part of the team. "The two of them—well, the two of them were carrying on . . ."

"What do you mean—'carrying on'?" asked Charlene.

You should ask such a question!

Charlene cleared her throat.

"Well, they were holding hands, looking up into each other's eyes and all that."

Oh, baby, you don't know the half of it.

Now my detective was smiling openly. Marian took this as a sign of encouragement and expanded on her report.

"—acting as though there was nobody else around. Everybody noticed."

"Had they known each other long?"

"That's just it. They'd just met for the first time!"

And that was long enough to know what we wanted.

A cough here from Charlene, who inquired, "Can you think of anyone who would want to kill Ms. Dowd?"

I moved closer. Dammit, if anyone knew, it would be Marian.

For the first time, Marian looked bewildered. "To tell you the truth, I can't."

Now, you're at a loss for words?

"Thank you. You've been very helpful. Oh, just one more

thing. Do you recall where you were when Ms. Dowd was discovered?"

"Let's see . . . I was, um, just getting a few more of those delicious snacks. Roger was nearby, and, oh, yes—my feet hurt, so we sat down at one of the tables on the lanai."

"Thank you." Charlene indicated the interview was finished, and Marian stood, somewhat disappointed. "If there's anything else I can help you with, just let me know."

Martola smiled. "Is Harold Spurgeon in the office?"

Marian nodded. "Yes, he and Claudia—" She lowered her voice. "He and Claudia Harmon came in a little while ago."

"Together?"

"Yes." Marian's face split into that oh-so-happy smile. "They're sort of an item around here."

"Tell me about it," invited Martola, and motioned for Marian to resume her seat.

"Well," she confided, lowering her voice again, "ever since Claudia came to work here, she and Harold have become—uh, very close, if you know what I mean."

Yeah, sweetie, they know what you mean.

Charlene rolled her eyes, but leaned in toward the subject. They extended her interview another fifteen minutes, passing along stories about Claudia and Harold.

And I was on the sidelines, cheering her on. *Go, girl, go!*

I must say, I found this part of the afternoon the most fun. I felt like the cheering section. Let 'er rip, Marian, this is what you do best. She did a fine job of informing the two detectives of the relationship between Claudia and Harold. I must admit, I couldn't have done it better.

Harold was on the phone when Marian tapped on his door. Since I didn't have to observe protocol, I left her waiting outside and entered.

"Yes?"

"The detectives want to speak with you."

He looked annoyed. "Tell them I'm on the telephone."

"I did. But they want to talk with you anyhow. They sent me to tell you."

"Oh, all right . . . tell them I'll be right out."

He rolled a finger inside his shirt collar in a weak attempt to let the sun in and went to the sideboard where he poured some water into the crystal glass that sat on a tray next to a silver decanter. None of this did anything to alleviate his flushed and sweaty face.

Of course, Agnes reared her only child in a manner befitting an English prince, but nothing could change the truth: In spite of the fact that Harold was born with the proverbial silver spoon in his mouth (knife, fork and complete tea service for twenty-four), he still had the presence of a jitney driver. *Jeez!* Even for the potential wealth, how could Claudia stand it?

I could see it would take awhile for Mr. Poise to gather his courage, so I ambled down the hall for a quick look around at my former office. Of course, everything was just as I'd left it last Thursday. Admittedly, the ten-by-twelve space was small, but I'd garnered some pretty nice commissions in spite of it. And I was especially nostalgic about the furnishings. The Oriental rug was a gift from Frank, one of his overseas remembrances that, if memory serves, took a full three hours to christen. I sincerely hoped he would reclaim it—the rug, not the night session. My desk, which I'd picked up in a ratty, secondhand store on Second, stood along the wall that formed a right angle with the door. I'd relied on my reference books on the shelf above: my *Webster's*, *Roget's Thesaurus* and the two language dictionaries, French and Spanish, that covered most of my non-English-speaking clients. But they were so enthused about their firms assigning them to the Big Apple, they paid little or no attention to my dumb accents. On the wall opposite my desk hung an Annie Dowd original, a charcoal nude I'd drawn more than ten years before at the Art Student's League on Fifty-seventh. If memory serves, I thought fleetingly about moving to a garret in Greenwich Village and living out my Bohemian dreams. Maybe if I'd gone with that thought I'd still be there today. On that note, I rejoined my detectives.

While waiting for Harold, Charlene and Martola had passed the time reviewing their notes. Martola took a gulp of coffee that Marian had provided and jerked his finger toward the hall. "Slow going, huh?"

Charlene shrugged her shoulders, like, what can you do about it?

Martola glanced at his watch for the umpteenth time. "If he doesn't get his ass in here soon, I'll drag him out. God's sake, we haven't got all day."

"Take a deep breath, Lou. Maybe you should consider yoga or meditation."

He threw her a look. "Yeah, right." He reached for a doughnut just as Harold, with his suit jacket back on and buttoned, entered. Martola didn't miss a beat. Gesturing toward a chair, he said, "Have a seat."

Yeah, Harold, sit! You've kept us long enough.

Charlene grinned. Harold thought she was being extra friendly, so he smiled back at her.

Martola cleared his throat and began drumming on the table. "We're looking to fill in some of the blanks from yesterday," he began. "Help us out here."

My former boss stared back.

Hello, Harold. That's your cue.

Charlene pressed her lips together and took a deep breath. "Can you recall what led up to Annie Dowd's drowning?"

"Uh, no."

We sat waiting for a follow-up, but none was forthcoming. The detectives exchanged quick glances.

"No?" Martola fed him. "How's that?"

"Well . . . I was talking to Ms. Harmon. I, uh. . . ."

I guess what the jerk is trying to say is that his tiny mind can only hold so much, and Claudia was occupying that space while I was dying.

Charlene covered her mouth and coughed. She and Martola wasted another ten minutes trying to glean information from the lovesick dork to no avail. I could have told them they'd have better hunting at Disney World.

It was clear to me that Charlene was the only one capable of hearing me. Whether it had something to do with the piece of metal in her head didn't matter. The important thing was, I had a receiver and needed to figure out the best way to use her talent. Additionally, I'm thinking, maybe that's not all there is. Maybe I can do more. This is sort of fun and scary at the same time. It increases the possibilities and makes the game more enjoyable.

I checked the wall clock and realized that Frank's flight was due to land shortly. One of the benefits of my new status was that I didn't have to observe protocol. I left the office quickly. Unfortunately, no one missed me.

Six

Frank was just finishing with Customs when I arrived at JFK International Airport. He walked like a man burdened with much more than the battered luggage he dragged along after him. Drawn, unshaven and rumpled, he climbed into a taxi and lit a cigarette. I snuggled up as close as my present ethereal condition permitted. The driver, of course, did not speak English, which is normal in the Big Apple these days. It's an old story, the scenario of which goes this way: Refugee escapes from a country torn with political and economic hardships, gains entrée into the United States and feels compelled to fulfill his destiny behind the wheel of a New York cab.

How does one communicate? Here are some tips: Shout NO if the driver heads the wrong way into a one-way street. Then grab your heart and wave your free arm frantically. To indicate a turn at the next corner (if he didn't already pass your street), grunt and point simultaneously toward the desired direction. Last, to acknowledge that he has actually brought you to your destination, extend both hands, palm forward, and yell STOP! Smile and nod your head at the same time, so the driver will understand you do not have a gun.

Frank did not have to resort to any of these, of course. He picked up our driver's accent (Croatian), barked the necessary directions in the guy's own language, and we arrived fairly close to Frank's place, a very desirable two-and-a-half-room apartment, with elevator and doorman, on West Eighty-eighth off Amsterdam, rent-controlled. Yeah, my mind still worked like a real-estate agent.

Upstairs in Frank's apartment, memories flooded over me, and I felt at once nostalgic and sad about what might have been, but I couldn't give in to that now. When Frank headed toward the shower, I meandered around trying to figure out the best way to break through the fog. I really needed his help.

I cooed through the shower curtains: *Frankie, would you like me to scrub your back like in the old days?* But his whistling drowned out my message.

When he stepped out of the shower, toweled off and prepared to shave, I tried again: *Listen, can we talk?* It was my old opening gambit when we were married, and I used to pop down the seat of the john and park myself during the aforementioned man-thing. There's something about the shaving process that opens a man's mind to deep discussion. I learned this when I was quite young. My father and I had the best talks while he was shaving, and I deeply missed his presence in my life.

"Annie," he might begin. "Whenever you have a serious discussion with someone, always look him in the eye, and make sure you get the same in return. An honest person has nothing to hide."

I would nod distractedly while studying the bathroom tiles, wondering if Ma had notified him yet of my less-than-perfect report card. Minutes later, my transgression would be out in the open. For, with one turn of his head in my direction, my father's gaze would have secured the truth. That look-me-straight-in-the-eye speech got me every time. Now I struggled to find a way to translate that experience to my present dilemma.

So, whaddya say? I urged. *Think maybe you could concentrate a little harder?*

Next, I resorted to tickling. I knew all the vulnerable places. Uh, did I detect a smile? No, just of those strange facial contortions men employ when presenting a section of cheek or chin to the razor.

How about mental telepathy?

Foiled again; this time by the telephone.

With shaving cream squishing out from his cheek onto the receiver, Frank took a call from—let me guess—Detective Louis Martola?

From Frank's end, I hear: "Speaking. Yeah, a little while ago. Sure, when and where? Today's no good; I'm leaving for Mrs. Edelstein's—that's Annie's mother—in a little while."

That was comforting to hear.

"How about tomorrow morning? Mineola Precinct? Sure, I know where that is. Around ten? Right. See ya." He wiped off most of the shaving cream from the receiver and replaced it in the cradle.

After a couple more futile tries to make Frank aware of my presence, I gave up and contented myself with accompanying him to Ma's. Snuggling close to him during our cab ride, I tried to prepare him for what he was about to face.

Ma's in bad shape, hon. Your strength will be comforting. But as usual, no response. I had to face the truth: My ex was not receiving.

When Ma heard Frank's voice, she elbowed Herbie out of the way and headed toward the foyer. Frank gathered her up in his arms, their muffled sobs striking the air like waves against rocks during a fierce storm. They rode the crest of pain, the two of them, blindly, without words, but as one in their shared misery. Miriam and Herbie stood by, gawking, unable to cope with the spectacle of raw emotion set before them. It was Frank, finally, who led Ma to the living room and sat beside her on the couch patting her hands. The other two followed. When Ma composed herself, Frank shook hands with Herb and gave Miriam a brotherly peck on the cheek.

"Tell me what you know," Frank said, stroking Ma's cheek.

Ma reached for the box of tissues. In fits and starts, she gasped out the words. "The police—they came Friday night. *Gotteniu!* They told me Annie—my little Annie—oy. . . ."

"Don't make yourself sick, Ma," warned Miriam, who backed down quickly when Frank gave her a hard stare.

"Go on," he urged.

"They said—they said she had drowned! But . . ." She looked up at Frank, her eyes suddenly wide. "But we know that Annie could swim! She swam good, didn't she?" Ma was talking to everyone now, sweeping the room with her remembrance, and I saw the spark of old coming back into her tired eyes. She was demanding confirmation from the group and nodding fiercely as each one acknowledged the fact.

Damned straight I could swim. Good for you, Ma. And no one can say I fell into the pool by accident. Ma didn't flinch, so she wasn't on my list of contacts either.

Miriam and Herb were buzzing together.

"What are you nuzzling about, you two?" Ma demanded.

"Nothing."

But Ma would have none of it. "Speak up!"

"We do know that Annie had been drinking wine," said Miriam. "Maybe . . ."

"So? A glass or two of wine. What does that mean?" Ma sounded belligerent.

"Nothing."

I had a feeling Miriam was going to bring up the subject of Michael Rheims; the police had already spoken to them about him. But Ma's eyes locked on to her daughter's, and the message sent would have shut the devil's mouth. Of course Frank caught the sparks. I could see him making mental notes to follow up during his meeting with the detectives tomorrow. Hey! Neither Miriam nor my mother should have worried. Frank and I agreed long ago that we were each entitled to a life.

"Oy! what am I thinking of?" Ma jumped up and, to everyone's questioning expression shouted, "Tea? Some strudel? We have so much cake and fruit in the house."

It was true, the neighbors, not to mention friends and family, had been bringing a steady supply of goodies to Ma ever since hearing the news. She now had enough food to supply a regiment.

My sister had been neglecting her "Mrs. Stepford" role but now, seeing her mother standing and acting more human than she had in days, Miriam obliged by pushing her back against the pillows and proclaiming, "I'll take care of it!" Smartly, Ma did not argue.

Don't leave just yet! I cautioned Frank. Hell, what was I whispering for? If he hadn't heard me up until now, I needn't worry. I knew he was thinking about his meeting tomorrow with Martola and also feeling exhausted after his long trip, but I prayed he'd remember the importance of "breaking bread" at Ma's—under any circumstances. I saw the familiar twitch, that caught-in-between struggle that acknowledged duty and the itch to leave.

Stay, dammit! I hissed, and wonder of wonders, he sat down and allowed his shoulders to lower themselves from his ears. He reached for Ma's hand again, and she smiled back at him. Following it all, Herbie looked lost.

A half an hour more wasn't so bad, Frankie, I said when we left, accepting our now one-sided conversations. I still didn't like it, and wondered if, before I moved on to the next plateau (whatever that was) Frank and I might experience some real contact. For now, though, I was just grateful he was here. With my help, he'll get to the bottom of this. Of course, I didn't have all the facts myself. No. And I would have been mightily surprised at some of them.

I had no idea, for instance, that in another part of the City, an unsavory character was deeply engrossed in a telephone conversation, and the subject under discussion was—me.

"So whaddya worried about? I did my part and you did yours. Everyone's happy, except of course, the deceased, but somebody had to lose. . . . Nah, stay cool. Nothing to worry about." He held the phone, listening for another minute or so, and an observer would have seen his jaw tense with anger. "I don't want to hear any of that crap! Understand? *All right!* Stay cool." He studied the phone after hanging up, and a wry grimace crossed his face, not an encouraging expression. If I had been privy to the exchange, I would have been morbidly interested.

Seven

Frank and I entered the Mineola Precinct about nine-fifteen Tuesday morning. The inside was a sea of scratched wooden surfaces and bored seen-it-all faces. Detectives Martola and Williams were waiting for us, or rather, Frank, in an interview room: a sparsely furnished work space containing a large, beverage-stained table with slightly uneven legs, six wooden straight-back chairs and a coffee urn, from which emanated a dank, overboiled aroma.

Frank took a not-too-subtle appraisal of Charlene's attributes. I could imagine his brain's calculator running up the statistics: good-looking broad, mid-thirties, 36-24-36, five foot six; warm, honey-toned skin—hot!

With Martola, however, Frank chose the more formal route of male ritual: handshakes, grip-strength test, eyeball contact and the like, all calculated to elicit valuable information for both contenders. From my perspective, it was a humorous affair, and I wondered who was to be the interviewer, who the subject. Knowing Frank and his years of training, this promised to be a memorable session.

A few minutes later, the four of us sat down at the table. Frank passed on the coffee but pulled out a pack of Marlboros and looked challengingly at the other two before lighting one. Smoke streamed out of his mouth like an engine primed to race.

"Heard about you," Martola began, receiving no more than a polite nod from Frank. "Talked to anyone since you returned?"

"Just came from Mrs. Edelstein's, saw the mother, sister and brother-in-law. What I want to know is, do you have any suspects?" He added the last quickly, upping the volume. The tactic worked.

"We've got some flags and, um, questions," said Charlene. "For instance, for someone so universally liked, we're finding it difficult to determine a motive, much less a suspect."

Precisely where I'm at.

Charlene nodded.

Frank squinted his eyes, remembering. "She was a good kid. Never stepped on anyone's toes that I know of."

Thanks, hon.

Frank was responding to Charlene's reasonable approach, but I also noticed he was taking a second look at her pretty eyes and generous mouth. The ash at the end of his cigarette was gaining ground.

Let's concentrate on business first, Frankie—okay?

Charlene tried to suppress a grin.

Frank turned back to Martola. "By the way, did you know that Annie was an excellent swimmer?"

"No, I didn't . . . uh, thanks." Martola scribbled a note on his pad, then looked back at Frank with something resembling sympathy. "Guess this is difficult for you."

My guy just offered a nondescript *"hmm."* They were circling the campfire now.

Charlene hastily slipped an old saucer on the table near Frank's smoldering cigarette, seeking to fill the uncomfortable pause. "Getting back to motive," she said, "would you have any suggestions as to who or what inspired this event?"

That's exactly what I'd like to know!

"None whatsoever. But you can bet I'll be looking for answers."

Martola threw out his chest. "As long as we keep to the rules."

Uh-oh, not very smart, Detective. You don't know my guy's temper.

In one motion, Frank mashed his cigarette into the saucer, pushed his chair back and was on his feet.

Settle down, hon. Nothing's going to get resolved if you lose it. It was an honest attempt to ward off the inevitable, but my Irishman had a short fuse.

"Let's get one thing straight. There are no rules. My wife—er, ex-wife—was murdered! And I'm not going to la-dee-dah down the road at any damned snail's pace. I'm gonna follow the leads, whatever they are and wherever they lead, and I'm gonna get whoever it is who killed her." The timbre of his voice increased as he pointed his finger at the detective, adding, "And I *ain't* interested in any of your freakin' rules!"

By this time, Martola had risen to his feet, and I was beginning to get nervous.

Guys, guys, I pleaded. But why should my faulty communication system begin to work now? Desperate, I focused on Martola's coffee, willing it to tip over. It did! And no one was more surprised than I. Then I turned to Charlene. *Do something!* And I wasn't thinking "clean up."

In a flash, she was on her feet. "Hey!" she interjected. "Will you two remember we're on the same team? We all want to find the killer."

I saw shoulders give an inch or two, but Martola's eyes trained on Frank, whose hands were still balled into fists.

"Maybe we could pool our energy," continued Charlene, throwing some paper towels on the coffee puddle, "*and* our brains and remember what the goal is here."

The contenders glanced in her direction, then eyeballed each other again. Martola was the first to speak. "Okay, so maybe we can forget about the rule thing."

Frank nodded and pushed himself back in the chair. Having had only six hours sleep in the last thirty accounted for part of the strain, but I also realized he was having a genuine reaction to my passing. I tried to smooth his forehead and massage the back of his neck, but I still hadn't figured out how to make honest-to-God physical contact. Was I just limited just to "willing" coffee mugs to overturn? There must be more to this, I figured, and vowed to take extended courses.

In the meantime, try to feel my love, sweetie.

With Charlene's help, the gladiators managed to get past

the confrontation and begin to address the real problem: Who had done me in and why?

Frank scratched the back of his neck absentmindedly (the aftereffects of my soothing touch, no doubt) and said, "It's hard to believe that anyone in Annie's normal circle of business or personal acquaintances had a motive. Seems to me we need to explore whoever stepped into her life in recent times."

Why did I have the feeling he was angling for Michael Rheims? *Honest, Frankie, we never even did it!* Charlene glanced in my direction.

Martola said, "I suppose you know about the Englishman?"

Well, the safe's open now.

"What Englishman?"

Charlene frowned at her partner, but Martola continued. "Fella by the name of Michael Rheims, Agnes Spurgeon's nephew."

"And you say he's a Brit?"

"Yeah. Arrived here a couple of weeks ago—some kind of big shot with Marks and Spencer."

Frank raised his eyebrows. "Annie was a big girl. She didn't have to report to me."

Martola grunted. "The guy's been here a few weeks. He and the deceased only met the day of the . . . incident. We talked with him, but can't come up with any kind of motive. Some of the witnesses report they seemed pretty lovey-dovey during the afternoon—holding hands, one-on-one eye locks and the like."

Charlene's eyes began searching the room.

Don't worry. I'm cool.

Frank nodded at Martola, seemingly unimpressed by his comments, but I knew his curiosity was piqued. "Who else looks good?"

The detectives exchanged glances. "We're still working on preliminary interviews with the deceased's co-workers," Charlene said, "but can't say we've hit on anyone with a motive."

Frank was holding his own here. Not exactly in charge, but also not subject to the detectives' directions. I could see he was frustrated, though. Frank was an action kind of guy, not used to crawling along without a definite plan. He lit another cigarette, exhaling thoughtfully.

"Listen, somebody killed Annie. I don't know who yet, but somewhere, someplace, this person exists. Maybe *we're* not looking in the right places." Frank emphasized the word, and those present didn't need a translator to interpret his annoyance.

Martola raised an eyebrow. "So whaddya sayin'? That we don't know our business?"

Fearing another showdown at the ole corral, I made an attempt at calming Frank: *"Listen, hon, they're doing the best they can . . ."* But I might as well have been talking to the deaf.

"I'm saying that maybe we're taking the wrong approach or neglecting an area of Annie's life that holds some answers."

Even I thought that was brilliant, although I couldn't for the life of me think of anything substantial to suggest. Still, something about the notion got me to ruminating; something I couldn't quite put my finger on. I got this sudden flash, which turned out to be the first of many. It was like trying to recall a dream, so vivid during the night but so difficult to pin down the following morning. *Yes,* I thought, *there is an answer here, something I'm not paying enough attention to. Frank has a point.*

Charlene agreed. "Let's take a fresh look at the deceased's—at Annie's life." Her partner slid her an annoyed look, which she ignored. Instead, she went over to the blackboard and picked up a piece of chalk. "What do we know?" She printed the words WORK and PERSONAL, underlining them and separating them into two columns. Under WORK, she began listing my co-workers: Harold Spurgeon, Marian Hingis, Claudia Harmon, Roger Franklin, Matt Sterling. Under the other heading, she printed the names of my mother, sister, brother-in-law, my best friend, Hannah Green, and even my neighbors Carrie Walker and Mark Gobel. Now she added a third column headed by a question mark.

Neither Frank nor Martola asked what it meant, but Charlene volunteered. "This is for the category of folks who do not belong in either of the other groups—Michael Rheims, for instance. We'll keep an open mind, though, and add some names, or at least the one name that matters."

Way to go! I shouted enthusiastically. *But there's something else that's missing here. Maybe we ought to go over some of my business dealings.*

Charlene nodded. "Like, for instance," she picked up where I left off, "what about her clients?"

"Yeah!" agreed Frank. "What about her clients?"

The meeting ended with the two detectives and me headed to the office in Manhattan. Frankie was off on some unknown mission but said he'd catch up with us later. Frankly, I didn't know whom to follow. I finally chose the detectives, so I could be certain they'd share any information they uncovered with Frank. You might say I was watching out for my guy's interest.

Less than an hour later, Martola, Charlene and I settled into the conference room at Royal Roosts. The detectives were studying the records of my business dealings of the past six months, and they were pretty impressive, if I do say so myself. There was the East Fifty-fourth duplex I rented to Mrs. Myron Thomasville and her Best-of-Show Pekinese, Princess Chen Li—fourteen rooms and a butler's pantry. I certainly hope they're happy. Mrs. Thomasville, as I recall, was having her Fifth Avenue palace completely renovated, and Princess was allergic to dust.

"Nothing unusual about this one," Charlene announced, tossing Mrs. Thomasville aside.

"Or this one," answered her partner, holding up another folder, "except if you consider it features Mack Williams, lead singer for the Desperadoes. Apparently, Williams subleased his place on Riverside Drive to a Mr. and Mrs. Harry Larkings, of the Dallas Larkings. And you should hear what those Texas bigwigs drop a month for the privilege."

Oh, yeah! I remember: oil-rich, money to burn but not the slightest idea what the Four Seasons Restaurant was all about or what the place charges for dinner. "Make a reservation, Margie-babes," *this tycoon says,* "and I'll have the limo pick us up." Charlene was rolling her eyes.

I had only one problem before the lease was signed. Mr. Williams's apartment contained a locked closet (talk about Pandora's Box . . .) that was his, um . . . dungeon. Should I try to explain that their landlord was a sadomasochist? Nah. I finally settled on a version of the truth. Williams kept some of his "equipment" there and, for insurance purposes, required the stuff be kept under lock and key. I was *sure* the Larkings would want to protect their landlord's privacy, even as far as not mentioning a thing to anyone about the closet. That problem solved, the Larkings moved in, I collected my commission and no one was the wiser. I just hoped curiosity wouldn't get the better of them.

The detectives continued rummaging through the pile while I stood patiently by, hoping to catch the sound of something amiss. Alas, I was left with only the knowledge that I'd departed a pretty lucrative job—with no notice—and now Claudia stood to wallow in my commissions.

"Hell-o!" Martola sang out. "Here's a goodie. Show Biz producer Oscar Shine and his wife sublet their place recently for a year. Heading for California, it says here in Annie's notes, but she never got to close the deal, and it was a big one. Claudia Harmon took over."

"Who'd the Shines sublease to?" Charlene called out, not sounding too interested.

"Some geek by the name of Franklin Biddly-Smythe, if you can believe it." Martola shrugged and threw the folder on the pile of no interest.

Hold on a sec, guys. There's something about that deal that strikes a chord. Of course Martola never broke stride, but Charlene hesitated.

Listen, if you want some help, you gotta pay attention! Okay, I'm gonna have to kick up some dust. I mean it now! In my fury, I felt a new strength. I focused on the pile of discarded folders and whooshed them onto the floor. Martola ran to close the window while Charlene stifled a giggle.

"Maybe we ought to go over those again," she suggested.

"Be my guest," Martola offered.

Charlene riffled through them politely. "Let's keep an open mind about these," she said, tapping the pile. I was glad someone was paying attention.

While Charlene riffled through the folders, I wondered what it was about the Shine apartment that begged to be remembered? I strained at my fading memory while the detectives mulled over other properties ranging from Trump Towers to the West Eighties. Yep, I covered them all. Mostly, my clientele consisted of recommendations from previously satisfied or returning customers. I always tried to match the properties with the prospective tenants, at the same time securing a clean, noncomplicated deal for the owners. Duplicity was not my game. I'd leave that sort of stuff to Claudia.

The way it worked was, the owner contacted Royal Roosts, Inc., to negotiate subleasing his or her place for a year or more. Maybe the owner was being transferred across the country or overseas or just taking time off from the good life. Same thing in reverse. Many of my clients were connected with the film industry, television or theater and needed to relocate to Manhattan for a few months or a year or more. What I did was pure matchmaking. What could be more natural? It wasn't that difficult, except if you consider *shmoozing* up a total stranger repulsive. I'll admit that some of those folks were difficult to relate to, but that made it even more of a challenge. The reward was always that signed lease, followed by a trip (for me) to Bloomies or the Red Door at Elizabeth Arden's where I lined up a day that included facial, massage and makeover. Come to think of it, it really was a sweet deal while it lasted. Which reminds me, I need to help Charlene and Martola find out just why the good life had to end.

Charlene was making some notations in her notebook when the door opened suddenly and Frank entered. The perfunctory greetings were polite enough, but the tension in the room increased discernibly.

I hope you'll remember we need to work together, hon, I offered. Frank ignored me completely.

"How's it going?" He gestured at the piles of folders.

"You know this is just the grunt work," answered Martola, a little too quickly.

"Sure."

Frank had something on his mind. I could always tell. His face took on the concentration of a hunting dog: nose lifted to the scent, eyes focused on a point no one but he could see. He smiled winningly at the other two—a dead giveaway. Something else. He was standing in the room, purposefully filling it with his disruptive presence. The ploy worked. The detectives accelerated the pace, hurriedly bundling several folders together for their trip back to Long Island.

"We were just finishing," said Charlene.

"Too bad," said Frank, "I was hoping to go over some of those with you." But his voice lacked enthusiasm.

"Nothing much to talk about so far," mumbled Martola. "We'll be in touch."

"Yeah. You do that."

Frank's grin split his face as soon as they left.

You're onto something, Frankie, I can tell. I felt a strong desire to ruffle his hair, but he reversed his steps quickly as soon as Charlene and Martola left, and made his way to Marian Hingis's desk. Perching himself on the edge, he leaned over in a confidential manner, his craggy face exuding charm.

"Sorry for the interruption, Marian." He leaned in. "You were saying?"

Marian flushed. Frank's close proximity was an unaccustomed intimacy, though not necessarily unwanted. Hope spread across her face like a bird gliding in for a landing after a long flight. She lifted her eyes toward the source of the light. "Uh, Annie's clients were mostly repeats, you know." Marian's normally brassy voice was subdued. "If they were happy the first time, they usually asked for her again. In other instances, friends recommended friends. She wasn't a high-pressure type, and a lot of people appreciated that."

"I see," Frank crooned, zeroing in as if Marian were the most important person in the world. His attention was beyond anything in her normal scope. Her flush deepened, and she dropped her gaze momentarily.

Bring it down a notch, Frankie. Can't you see she's already wetting her pants? But my pleas were in vain; Lothario had launched his campaign.

He pulled a serious expression and was nodding like a therapist, avid interest filling his face, letting only an occasional *"Hmm, hmm"* escape.

Marian warmed to her task, citing various tidbits regarding my work of the past couple of months. There was the Sultan of Sarawak who, along with his entourage, was here for six months on United Nations business. "He brought at least one wife and snapped up a gorgeous penthouse on Sutton Place overlooking the East River and right near the U.N.—just perfect, Frank." (Marian graduated to his first name now, inferring she could be more than just a friend.)

Then Miss Entertainment began name-dropping: a famous film couple, in New York for a year's run on Broadway. "I really wanted their autographs, but Annie nixed the idea."

"Hmm, hmm," went the doctor.

"And then there was that Frenchman, uh, Monsieur Chardin—kissed my hand, he did!" Frank allowed a smile and winked to show how much he agreed with that gesture. Marian's fluster was his reward. "Oh, well, it never came to anything!"

Too bad, sweetie, I well remember that jerk from Paris. Had his brains in his pants, and even though "no" sounds the same in any language, he pretended he didn't understand.

In the middle of Marian's dissertation, a strange thing happened. I had a sudden flash—difficult to explain—a thread of remembrance! But what? I tried to grab onto it, but it flew away. *Oh, please . . . come back!* But my mind allowed no reruns.

The telephone interrupted, and Marian looked surprised. "It's for you," she said, handing the instrument over to Frank. He looked annoyed.

"Dowd here." He sighed. "Maggio." The facade of cultured gentleman faded, and a hardened expression crossed his face. "No. Sorry, pal. Send someone else. Listen, I told you—right now, this is my top priority." Gripping the phone until his knuckles turned white, he hissed, "Yeah, that's the way it goes. I know, you gotta do what you gotta do. See ya."

Now I know you still love me, hon. We'll get this thing figured out. Then you can go back to covering important world events and I can go on to—I don't know—whatever I'm supposed to go on to.

Frank took a minute to compose himself. "Sorry for the interruption."

Marian fluttered her lashes. "I'm sure you must be a very busy man."

Back on track, the good therapist smiled. "Right now, nothing could be more important than the time I'm spending with you. . . . "

Meaningful stares were exchanged before the killer in Frank took aim. "You see, Marian, I have the feeling that, of all the people who knew Annie, you alone possess some important piece of information that will lead us to the solution of this awful crime." His voice dropped to a low, intimate whisper; his eyes narrowed, then widened, opening to reveal blue orbs alive with passion. Frank at his best.

"Wh—what can I say? I mean, of course I'll tell you anything you want to know, but—"

Frank interrupted her. "Sometimes, the stuff we know may not seem important to us. Trust me. I know what I'm talking about."

"You know I'll be glad to help. I mean . . . I really liked Annie. She was okay."

What Marian was trying to say was, we didn't give each other a hard time. I think Frank got the picture.

He nodded and smiled some encouragement, the reporter in him gearing up for the big interview. "I'm going to ask you some questions. Just relax. You don't have to answer quickly. Wait a beat or two before responding."

The subject nodded assent. One would have thought Frank had asked her to remove all her clothes. "I'm ready," she gushed, but just at that moment, the intercom buzzed, and Marian reached for it, an audible sigh of frustration escaping. "Yes, okay. I'll be right there."

She looked up at Frank apologetically. "Harold needs me in his office now. I'm sorry. Can we continue this later?"

He tried to hide his annoyance. "Let's try again tomorrow, Marian. I have an appointment anyhow."

Frank hailed a cab, and we headed toward Ma's. I wanted to help him shake off his disappointment—and mine, too, I guess. Frank was good. I believed he was right about Marian. Say what you like, but she was a source of all kinds of information. If she couldn't sift through the pile herself, Frank was more than capable of arranging the pieces in a sequence that would make sense. It wasn't just Marian who believed he would solve this crime; I'd been affected by the intensity of the moment as well—and something else not quite explainable. Those strange flashes and chills had started coming on, and I distinctly felt that something was about to be revealed. Just what, I wasn't sure, but I had faith.

Eight

Miriam and Herbie were sitting with Ma in the kitchen waiting for the rabbi when we arrived. Turns out they were planning my funeral, at last, which was to take place the next day. Ma looked dazed. Frank took in the scene, frowned, then turned toward Miriam, seeking an answer.

"I gave her one of my Valiums," she offered, by way of explanation. He stiffened but said nothing, just continued walking over to the table.

Ma tried to rise, but Frank gestured her back into the seat and kissed the top of her head. She turned her face up, allowing the tears to roll slowly down her cheeks.

Guilt and sorrow swept across me. *Ma, Ma, I'm so sorry. I never meant for you to be hurt.*

Frank sat next to her, holding both her hands. She seemed to draw strength from his presence, but as soon as the rabbi arrived, she began trembling.

"So, Mrs. Edelstein," he began, nodding and smiling his kosher stamp of approval.

This really irritated me because I could never understand how rabbis could keep smiling under even the raunchiest of circumstances. And, let's face it, these were raunchy circumstances.

"I understand we will be at the Schwartz Brothers Chapel on Queens Boulevard?"

Why was that a question? Another thing was that *we* business. Doctors seem to do that too, especially when dealing with something painful.

Ma looked up at him, struggling with her response when the volume of the living room TV escalated. Mother Miriam jumped up and headed toward the offending source.

Ma sighed. "Schwartz Brothers, yes."

Frank massaged her shoulders, willing her to focus, not to give up. Ma wore a glazed expression as though her emotions were wrapped in cellophane, easy to be seen but fragile. Frank crooned in her ear: "We're gonna get through this. Yes, and you're going to be okay." She offered him a half smile.

Then Frank turned to Miriam. "When did Ma eat last?"

"She says she doesn't have any appetite."

"That's ridiculous!" he said, with mock anger. "Since when did appetite count?"

Miriam took the hint and started pulling out plastic-covered bowls and dishes from the refrigerator. "There's plenty of stuff here—some from family, some from neighbors. But Ma—"

Frank cut her off. "Put it on the table, Miriam," he directed, "we'll have a smorgasbord."

My sister began busying herself with the kind of domestic thing she does best, but she was slow at the task. A compulsive neatnik, I knew she'd waste even more time carefully folding the plastic for future use. Frank had set the scene. The least I could do was push the program forward. By now I'd gained the confidence to know that something as light as plastic covers didn't present that much of a problem for me, so when Miriam reached into the drawer for some silverware, I trained my energy on the platters of food and willed their wrappers to fall off. It was worth everything to see her surprised expression when she spun back around, confronted by naked platters sitting next to a small hill of tangled plastic.

Meantime, Rabbi Friedman and Herbie were plotting the next day's scenario. When the rabbi asked who would speak, Frank included himself. I absorbed everything, fascinated how, even in death, life goes on. Of course, I would have preferred a family gathering that had nothing to do with the current discussion, but that was a choice I'd been denied. By whom? And

I started getting anxious again to discover who it was that cut short my life.

With Frank's gentle urging, Ma began to nibble at the food.

"There! You see? I know your stomach better than you do." His reward was a grateful smile. "Do you remember the first time we met? Now, if I had picked at my food that night, I'm sure you would never have permitted Annie to marry me."

"Oy. Do I remember? You ate like a starving child!"

"I'll tell you a secret," he whispered. "My orders were to eat—to fill myself up until I burst."

And that evoked the first laugh from Ma since my rude withdrawal from this life. Not unexpectedly, Miriam looked askance, which made me wonder for the thousandth time if we were really from the same two parents. Although I'd always accepted my sister for whom she was, I'd secretly wondered if maybe she'd been grown in some petri dish, the result of some wild experiment on my parents' parts. Miriam was born old—and sensible, and conservative, and boring, but Herbie hadn't seemed to notice. Maybe that was because they were so much alike. There's an old saying that claims there's a lid for every pot, and there's no doubt that the two of them fit perfectly.

The rabbi replaced his reading glasses in their case and cleared his throat. "So! We're all set for tomorrow then." It was a statement requiring no response, but Herbie squared his shoulders. "All set." And Miriam felt compelled to echo the same. Frank tightened his arm around Ma's shoulders. The men stood, shook hands, and Herbie saw Rabbi Friedman to the door. When he returned, he looked at Miriam with what I would call "the stare" and she nodded. I don't know whether Frank caught the signal, but we didn't have to wait long before all was revealed.

"Ahem," began the big executive, retaining his standing position. Since everyone else was still seated, he had the advantage. "Miriam and I have been talking."

Together? How democratic!

". . . and we have decided it would be a good idea if Ma came back to live with us." He offered this decree while rocking back and forth and smiling broadly in her direction.

The choreography notwithstanding, Ma looked up at her son-in-law like he'd spoken in a foreign tongue. "Oh, dolling, I couldn't."

Then three voices erupted at once. Herbie was "insisting," Miriam was supporting her man, and Ma was protesting. The stronger Herbie got, the more frightened she looked, finally reaching out to Frank for support.

"Kind offer, Herb, but let's hear from Ma about it." His reassuring smile covered her like a cozy blanket on a chilly night. To add emphasis to his support, Frank began patting her hands.

"I lived here for so long," she said, looking around her kitchen, "I wouldn't know what to do in Ohio."

Miriam took up her husband's platform. "Oh you'll just love it where we are. It's so much more . . . suburban. I'll introduce you to everyone. You can come with us to synagogue—yes, and even join the singles group." Her enthusiasm was nauseating.

Look at Ma, Frank. She looks like she's drowning. Do something! I waited a beat, but there was no reaction other than the sad shaking of his head.

"All my friends are here!" Ma protested.

"You'll make new friends," chirped my sensitive sister.

"I don't want new friends. . . ." Ma's voice trailed away on a sad river of tears.

"Maybe this is a little too much and a little too soon?" offered Frank.

"I believe in striking while the iron's hot!" boasted the sensitive executive from Rosen Plumbing Supplies.

What iron, you jerk? The one you're using to burn through Ma's heart?

Ma hung her head. I couldn't stand to see her so defeated. She was getting dangerously low in conviction, so I decided to take matters in hand. Herbie's eyeglass case sat on the table. When he sat down to what he thought was the triumphant conclusion of his argument, I whooshed the case off the edge and far enough away from the table that he had to get out of his chair to pick it up. When he bent over to retrieve the case, I focused on his generous rear and strained for all I was worth.

Zzzlitt! The back seam of his trousers split open on command. He jerked himself to a vertical position, slapping the flat of his hand to the newly created air duct, the flush of his embarrassment decorating the moment with a hearty crimson. Miriam gasped, Frank stifled a laugh, and Ma looked shocked, but she was the first to respond.

"Put them on my bed, dolling. There's a large robe in back of the bathroom door. I'll fix them in no time."

Ma was in charge again, and Herbie slunk away like the schmuck he was. The event certainly took the spotlight off the earlier discussion and gave everyone a chance to regroup. Plans for next day were finalized, and Frank prepared to take his leave.

I figured the police had given the go-ahead for the funeral because the autopsy results were in. Frank was thinking along the same lines and was only waiting for an opportunity to discuss this with the detectives. After Miriam cajoled Ma into taking a nap, Frank and I headed out toward Mineola.

Thinking about the big event was weird, and if I weren't already dead, I'd have certainly felt chills. Five days had passed. The weather was about the same as that fateful Friday, and even though I tried to focus on what had occurred, my mind was still blocked. Would I ever remember? I thought of Michael Rheims and the missed opportunities and wondered how things might have turned out. There were infinite possibilities, but of course I'd never know about those. He was so . . . so sexy, especially when he spoke. That British accent just knocked me out. Double-oh-seven, I'd called him. D'you suppose he really had the capacity to kill? Nah. I just don't want to believe that. On the other hand, he was the only stranger at the party. I'd known everybody else for years, and let's face it, nobody ever tried to remove me from the guest list before. Still, I kept coming back to the other big question: Why?

Frank was staring out the taxi window, but I had a feeling he wasn't looking at the scenery.

Listen, hon, I prodded, *I know we could help each other if you'd only open your mind to receive.* Instead, he tugged out his pack of Marlboros and tapped out a cigarette.

"D'ya have to light that now?" mouthed the driver.

Frank didn't answer until he'd sucked in the first long drag. "Yeah." Something in his tone plainly indicated he was not interested in further discussion. And there was none forthcoming. Smoke and silence filled the vehicle's interior, and the rest of the ride was spent in contemplation, at least by me.

After days of trying to cope with my new circumstances, flashes of that last day began tapping at my memory. I'd see a segment of frolicking—a scene with Michael, for instance—but sitting next to Frank while remembering such a thing caused untold ambivalence. Not that there needed to be. I'd always love Frank, but long ago we'd settled the practical matter of how we'd spend our time and with whom. I knew he didn't live the life of a priest, and he didn't expect me to sit around waiting for him either.

I concentrated on Agnes Spurgeon's party, the activities, the other guests. I was sure I didn't drink more than two glasses of wine, and I certainly would not choose to take a dip in the pool wearing my new silk Liz Claiborne. So what happened? I took stock of the big-shot reporter next to me and tapped him on the shoulder. *I'm telling you, Frankie, I've gone over this a hundred times and still haven't a clue.* The nicotine cloud thickened, but there was no other response.

I glanced out of the window and, without warning, another fragment flicked across the silent screen. Lightheaded—that was the sensation. I'd been feeling lightheaded! But from two glasses of wine?

Hey, Frankie, pay attention! Think something's coming back. I tried to bang my fists against his shoulder but, like a useless insurance policy, my powers did not cover this movement. My frustration knew no end, but it also pointed me in the right direction: the autopsy results. What in the heck did those bozos discover? And what was I waiting for?

See you later, hon. I've got an errand to do. It sure was depressing that he didn't show at least some curiosity.

I headed on over to the morgue anyway to find out what I could. After the humiliation they'd put me through, the least those guys could do was share. I wasn't disappointed. A big fat file with my name on it lay on the medical examiner's desk, while three crumpled white-coats sat around discussing the results.

"Shame," said the guy behind the desk. One of his assistants nodded and shrugged his shoulders; the other one grunted in a manner I translated as agreement. I waited a beat or two, hoping for something more illuminating, but all I heard was the ugly sound of cracking knuckles.

Is that all you've got to say?

The grunter stretched.

Hey, guys—if you're not too busy, would you mind telling me what the heck I died of?

"Looks as if someone was over-the-top horny, if you ask me," said the big shot behind the desk. The others nodded.

"Yeah," laughed the grunter. "And after seeing the possibilities, I can believe the perpetrator planned a fun night."

You're disgusting, you know that?

I looked around for something to smack him with, but he had picked up my file and was leafing through it, muttering, "Rohypnol . . . Jeez!"

Rohypnol? The "date-rape" drug? I leaned closer. The rest of their conversation was enlightening and oh! so disturbing.

Shortly after, I joined the detectives in one of the interview rooms at the Mineola Station. Their conversation stopped the minute Frankie turned the corner, but the bomb had not yet exploded. I sensed we were writing another chapter of *War and Peace*. Charlene's dark eyes flashed fire at her partner whose jaw pointed toward the ceiling like a two-year-old about to say "no." She locked in on her target like a cruise missile until Martola unhinged his shoulders from up around his ears.

"Here's the deal," he finally conceded in Frank's direction. "The chemical analysis determined there were enough barbiturates to knock out a horse. She drowned, sure, because her lungs were filled with water, but even before she hit the water, Annie didn't have a chance."

I wanted to tell you myself, hon.

"Are you saying, someone slipped her a 'mickey'?" Frank's surprise was sincere.

"That's the idea—rohypnol, to be specific, otherwise known as 'roofies,' or the 'date rape' drug. And it's tasteless. One or two pills mixed with alcohol renders the victim vulnerable to whatever's on the menu. The coroner says she was zonked out when pushed into the pool." Martola swiveled his eyes back toward his partner, having finally conceded to share the report, and was rewarded with a half smile.

I tried to dredge information from the part of my brain that I feared had calcified. Who was it that brought me the wine? Who, dammit? Michael seemed the most logical, being that we were barely apart the whole day. Also, I kept reminding myself, he was the only stranger in my life. But his role as a killer just didn't gel. And what did he have to gain?

Frank was assimilating the news. "So, one of her so-called friends is responsible for her death?" Suddenly, he straightened his shoulders, all business, and jabbed his finger at Martola. "You interviewed everybody at Royal Roosts!" It was more of an accusation than a statement.

"Hell, yes!"

My guy was bristling. "And what conclusions, *if any,* did you come to?"

Sensing the level of male testosterone rising again, Charlene cut him off. "Keep it zipped, guys, nothing's going to get solved if we start mixing it up here."

"I was under the impression we were gonna share information," Frank snarled.

"So?" challenged Martola, "somebody's not telling the whole truth? It's not the first time that's happened."

"Are you—?"

Charlene slammed her pencil down on the table and glared at Frankie who lowered the volume but punched out his next words with a generous helping of sarcasm: "At least share with me your impressions."

Cut it out, Frankie. This won't get us anywhere.

Charlene nodded.

"Listen, you wanna know what they said?" Martola's muscles were twitching. "Nobody gave up nothing!"

"That's it, fellas," interrupted Charlene. "My job is hard

enough without adding 'referee' to the description. Frank, even you ought to know that a killer or an accessory to murder is not going to advertise."

"Humph."

"So, we've got to go over their stories and try to figure out who's holding back."

Good idea. Let's go over their stories, Charlene. I'm curious to see who said what.

In spite of her partner's dirty looks, Charlene pulled out a folder and started fingering through the contents. She volunteered that they'd done thorough background checks on everyone present that evening. "No priors or suspicious events involving any of the participants." With an eye cast in Frank's direction, she added, "I'm guessing we're all interested in hearing what Mr. Michael Rheims had to say." Not a soul disagreed.

"Sorry," she murmured in my general direction. Frank thought she was trying to spare his feelings and shrugged his shoulders. If this weren't so serious, it could be entertaining.

I was totally attentive as Charlene began to read: "Michael Rheims, forty-seven, in charge of Mergers and Acquisitions for Marks and Spencer . . . been with the company for twelve years . . . lives just outside London, unmarried . . . will be in the States at least six months. Says his aunt had sent him to the front gate to disperse a noisy group that apparently mistook the Spurgeon Estate for the nearby country club."

I parked this bit of intelligence into my ever-growing files and whispered to Charlene, *This is very familiar to me. I do remember the racket, although I'm fuzzy about what happened after.*

"That's important," Charlene said. The two guys looked at her curiously.

"You got a special feeling about that?" Martola asked.

Charlene stifled a smile. "You might say."

Then I trained my eyes on Frank to see how he was reacting to Michael's account of the event. No surprise here. My guy had the monopoly on poker faces when he wanted—never gave an inch on whatever emotions were brewing behind those sharp blue eyes. But I knew the man better than anyone in this room. He was fighting for control over his own feelings, listening for clues while trying to stay fair to a stranger. The professional in him was determined to win.

Martola sneaked a peek at Frank a couple of times but could not read past those icy orbs. Frank was focused.

Charlene read on. "No, Rheims did not dispute the observations of most of the guests present at the party. Yes, he was impressed with Ms. Dowd. No, he'd never met her before last Friday. Yes, it was true they'd been holding hands, staring into each other's eyes and all the rest of it." She looked up from the page. "In other words, the guy was smitten and doesn't deny it."

Frank was nodding as if to say, what else is new?

Thinking back, I vaguely remembered the disturbance at the gate, but every time I tried to recall the events just before or after the main event, I was stymied. The drug must have wiped me out. Was it given to me before or after? Whom was I with at that moment? Questions. I wished I could unload some of my frustration. There must be a way to recapture that infamous moment when the murderer slipped me the drug. I will remember, dammit!

Charlene took a deep breath. "Way I see it . . . at this point, the so-called date-rape drug would have been as superfluous as Vaseline for Rheims. Sorry, Frank, but speaking honestly, it looks like condoms were the only accessory required."

It was weird listening to two strangers and an ex-husband evaluating a harmless flirtation between two hormonally charged adults. I wanted to say, *Like, whose business is it anyway?* But I realized it was all part of finding out who did the, uh, dirty deed.

"Any questions?" Charlene was asking. "Obviously, I'm keeping the Rheims statement open—and handy—in case any bright ideas surface, but I think for now, we could push on."

Charlene paused before dumping out the remaining pages from the folder. Was she waiting for a comment from me? None forthcoming, she spread them over the conference table, pushing some toward Martola. They began to study them, calling out the name plus any pertinent or questionable fact. I moved around the table and read over their shoulders.

"Roger Franklin . . . with the firm for eight-plus years," began Martola. "He drove the car that transported the victim, the Hingis broad and the kid, Matt Sterling. Noticed the vic, uh, victim, and this Rheims guy getting cozy during the day. According to Franklin, he and Annie Dowd had never dated. Claims he was at the other end of the patio with the Hingis broad when the victim was discovered in the pool, and Hingis's statement supports this."

Now I always thought of Roger as a decent guy. Knew his market. Didn't step on toes. He'd had a long-term relationship with a woman five years his senior. And he was a quiet man, always aboveboard about sharing leads and commissions. Furthermore, he'd never tried anything funny with me. *You can skip Roger, guys.*

"Possible motive?" asked Martola, glancing from Frank to Charlene, neither one of whom had an answer.

"Let's talk about the others who rode out with them in the car," suggested Charlene.

Her partner nodded. "Here's Marian Hingis. According to these notes, she also observed Annie and this Rheims fellow carrying on during the day. Said she thought there was something fishy about him, although she just *adored* his British accent. What was fishy, she just couldn't put her finger on."

Am I missing something here? Maybe Michael is not the brave knight out of King Arthur's Court. Maybe he's just a lousy killer!

Frank cleared his throat. "Uh, I did exchange a few words with Marian, and I get the impression that she sees plenty. Doesn't have much of a life of her own, so her entertainment is keeping an eye on everyone else. She may have seen more than even she realizes. I got a pretty good start with her. Probably best if I follow up."

Martola nodded reluctantly and Charlene looked pleased. I nudged some papers in her direction.

"Matt Sterling" she announced, grabbing at the documents. "Worked at the firm two summers in a row, running errands and stuff. Evidently made himself useful. Learns fast, makes a good impression on clients. Royal Roosts took him on full-time after he graduated from NYU. He's kind of an apprentice salesman/would-be-broker—and dynamite looking." She grinned and winked her appreciation. "Works out at Gold's Gym. I doubt he has to rely on rohypnol or any other 'artificial means' for satisfaction. Nothing else suspicious at this point. . . . That does it for the carpool."

Ah, Matt. He's just a kid. Began working for the firm when he was just nineteen. Wouldn't hurt a fly. What am I saying? No one gets a free pass here. On the other hand, what would Matt gain by killing me? *Oy,* as Ma would say, *this is not going to be easy.*

Martola eyed the other two. "Now we've got the rest of the players. Obviously, we're going to take a good look at this Rheims guy. Preliminary interview took place the night of the murder, before we knew for sure it was murder—a follow-up on Monday. Nothing one can get a handle on. But before we go off the deep end on the Brit, there are a few others to consider: folks we've already got lots of background on. So let's toss up a few more names and see what we come up with." He nodded at his partner. "For instance, Claudia Harmon."

Yess! Let's hear from the bitch by all means.

"Hmm," began Charlene, winking in my general direction. "Seems she started the holiday a day earlier. Arrived at the Spurgeon digs on Thursday. Says she's engaged to Harold who wouldn't or couldn't confirm. Mama was standing near enough to hear and reacted as if she'd been fed arsenic."

Martola inclined his head. "Why d'you suppose she went out a day earlier?" The others shrugged. "And the Rheims guy was out there too. So, I'm thinking the gathering began at least twenty-four hours before the vic and the others arrived. Enough time to plan something?"

Aha! Claudia and Michael! Nah, that makes about as much sense as a bagel with cream cheese and ham.

"What was the motive?" asked Frank.

Yeah, I echoed. *What was the motive?*

Charlene shrugged, gathered the loose papers together and returned them to the folder. "At this point, we can't say. What we do know is that Mother Spurgeon, cousin Rheims, son Harold and girlfriend Claudia were all more or less in the vicinity of what later became the crime scene. And talking about Harold Spurgeon: He's really a nervous guy, Frank. Anything you know about him that would be of help?"

"Only that he's as addicted to Claudia as a user is to snow. Yeah, she's great looking, sometimes even puts on a good show. But she's as empty a human being as you'll ever meet."

Yess! I tried to give my guy the old high-five, but my hand swayed through the air like an impotent breeze on a sweltering summer night. Evidently, whatever power I possessed was a mind thing. I attempted to explain the relationship between Harold and Claudia:

Like it or not, he'll do most anything to please her because nobody ever made him feel as . . . macho. Ergo, she's got the keys to the kingdom. You're right, Hon, "addicted" is probably the right word.

"Hmm, interesting," mused Charlene. I gathered she was responding to my remarks.

In the middle of this wondrous insight, I started getting flashes again. *Wait a minute . . . There's something missing here. Think you ought to go over this again.*

Charlene excused herself to go to the restroom. I figured that was our signal, so I tagged along.

"What's up?" she asked, after making sure we were alone.

Something about the Claudia-Harold thing. I'm not sure.

"You don't like the woman. That's pretty obvious."

It's more than that. Something else is bothering me. I sense that Claudia influenced the event somehow.

"Influenced?"

Yes. It sounds strange to me, too. I'll let you know as soon as I figure it out.

I wasn't sure just what I meant by that, but I knew I could count on Charlene. It was disappointing that I couldn't connect with Frank, but she certainly was a comforting second.

Frank had declared himself in charge of my wardrobe for the funeral, and even though caskets are closed for Jewish burials, he wanted to make sure that I was wearing something that would have pleased me. Something comfortable for the trip, shall we say? Miriam, of course, frowned and exchanged questioning looks with Herbie, but Ma thought the idea was splendid.

"Yes, dolling, you pick out something my Annie would have wanted to wear." And that was the end of it.

Naturally, I accompanied Frank to my apartment to make sure he selected a winner. My place, on West Eighty-second between Broadway and Amsterdam, was an excellent location. Of course it cost fifteen-hundred bucks monthly for a one-bedroom (and that was a special deal I negotiated through my connections as a broker), but as the well-known hair-care brand would say, I'm worth it—or at least I was. It's going to take awhile before I fully comprehend my early retirement (without benefits, even).

Jake-the-doorman recognized Frank and reached out to shake his hand. "Sorry for your loss."

"Yeah, thanks."

My guy still had a key, so up we went to what used to be my happy sanctuary. I couldn't believe I'd left this place only four days ago, and certainly never imagined it would be my *sayonara!* Frank unlocked the door, and we stepped across a threshold of memories. For me, it was a last look at a life I'd thoroughly enjoyed. I had my independence, my self-respect, all the culture I could ever want and (I thought) good friends. One day soon, I'd find out who took all that away from me. For now, though, I was satisfied that Frank was alongside.

Look around, hon. There's tons of memories attached to this stuff. I pointed out the bookcase. *Remember when you revved me up to go back to school?* I went over to the shelves and reached out to caress the bindings of my beloved books. Oh, well, my touchy-feely wasn't working too well. No matter. Never in my wildest imagination would I have thought I'd develop such a love for the classics. Flaubert's *Madame Bovary,* for instance, drawn from imagination in the nineteenth century by a writer who couldn't have known that one day life would imitate his art. I refer, of course, to *Madame Claudia,* who, let's face it, turned out to be Emma's greedy, spitting image. Ah, *Anna Karenina*, another wasted heroine. Conflicted beyond reason, literally, and could only find solace in throwing herself under the wheels of a train. And what about the artists who created these works? Do today's authors really care about plot and characters the way some of their predecessors did? And, do they make the readers take stock of their own lives and seek ways to improve? The point is—and I could stare at these volumes all day—that the stories these nineteenth-century artists created were about life, real life, the thing I'm going to miss most of all. God! I was growing maudlin. I thought I had moved beyond feeling sorry for myself. It was time to lighten up.

I appeared in the bedroom where Frank was pushing my stuff around the closet like it was a rummage sale.

So whaddya say? Find anything flattering? Something that says, coffin—it's you?

He never paused for a second. Now he pulled out a pale blue, two-piece silk dress, his favorite, if memory serves. We were together when we bought it, and I imagined he was remembering the moment.

He had just returned from two weeks in London and Ireland, covering the bloody riots over there when some bombs exploded near a school and injured some children. Frank's slick, seen-it-all reporter's facade had been penetrated, and it was a large helping of TLC he needed to get it back together again. We spent ten glorious days making love, eating great food and mending injured psyches. His confidence increased with every passing hour. On his last day before returning to "the front," he spotted the blue silk dress in the window of Lord & Taylor. "I want you to have it," he insisted. And over all my protests, he pushed me into the store. Of course, I loved that dress, and I loved the guy who bought it for me. Now Frank shoved aside all the stuff he'd heaped on the bed and stared at the blue silk. I knew he was remembering, too. How I wished he could know what I was feeling.

Even though no one will ever see it on me, Frank, I'm glad this is the outfit you chose for tomorrow's main event.

He swept up the dress and threw it over one arm. Then he looked around the room and stared at the double bed, at the night table and the electronic clock with the huge digital numerals he'd always teased me about: "Do you think the big numbers are going to help if you sleep through the alarm?"

Now he shrugged his shoulders, signifying that it didn't matter anymore and went down the hall to the kitchen.

In the refrigerator, he stared at my supply of fat-free yogurt and shook his head. Well, that was one of the differences between us. I was the health-conscious one; he simply ate and drank whatever he wanted. Come to think of it, maybe he has the right idea. He's still around to complain of indigestion. We left the apartment about ten minutes later with Frank carrying the dress over his arm like some kind of door prize. He looked dazed as he reached for the elevator button.

Maybe you shouldn't have come here alone, hon. I was trying my best to soothe, but the chief in charge of the dress rehearsal was unresponsive. When the elevator doors opened, my neighbors Mark Gobel and Carrie Walker emerged. They embraced Frank warmly, and I only regretted that I couldn't participate in the love-in. Mark and Carrie had been together five years and were terrific neighbors and good friends. Vanilla ice cream with chocolate syrup, that's how I described them. A fun couple, our shared dinners together included the latest in sushi, mouth-watering soul, or traditional Jewish. Sushi was our common barrier; soul food was Carrie's specialty, and Mark and I lined everyone's stomach with poor imitations of our Jewish heritage. But food was not the only thing we celebrated.

Carrie is a writer. She has two murder mysteries to her credit and is working on a biography of Maya Angelou. Bright and funny, she's also blessed with a rich, contralto voice that floats out through open windows whenever she's practicing for Sunday choir. Weather permitting, I always took advantage of the free concert. And Mark—he's so proud of her. Was it serendipity that they met? Mark's not in show business, but he does appreciate good jazz. The two met at the Village Vanguard on Seventh Avenue. As Carrie recalls it, she was enjoying the music with a girlfriend. Despite the fact that Mark was there with a date, his eyes were on Carrie the whole evening. When the date went to use the restroom, Mark came over to her table, introduced himself and insisted they'd known each other in a previous life. In the next two minutes, he threw out half a dozen reasons that they should get together. She blames her receptive reaction on his cocker-spaniel eyes, outrageous sense of humor and down-and-dirty sex appeal. Especially the latter. "Ooh, honey, let me tell YOU. . . ." Mark, of course, would have her repeat the story ad infinitum. Gets him hot every time. Watching them now with Frank, and knowing I can no longer participate in such camaraderie makes me madder 'n hell at whoever is responsible. So, okay, now I'm gunning for the guilty party.

Nine

Heavy storms were predicted the day of my funeral, and somehow it all seemed a fitting finish to a bad movie. Sitting next to Ma in the limousine, I attempted to snuggle against her soft shoulders and wondered if the finality of burial would make a difference in my getting around. I was banking on the optimistic assumption that I'd already proven my spirit had a motor of its own.

Although it was only ten in the morning, thick clouds choked out the sun's light, neutralizing any power it might have had to produce the warmth one expects at this time of year. It was as nasty a July day as I've ever encountered, but somehow appropriate. The dark swollen clouds, the unseasonable chill, the silence that draped itself over all the passengers in our car—all of it reminded me of another July morning more than twenty-six years before.

Acute leukemia, wasn't that something that happened to other people? I mean, my father was such a good man, and his ending so undeserved.

"Listen, *tochterla*"—I can still hear him say, speaking slowly because his breath was labored—"take care of your mother. She's a good woman, your mother is, but . . . she doesn't know how to . . . to handle the big things like you do." I was all of nineteen at the time.

"Pop . . . Poppy, there's no need to worry," I lied. "You're going to be okay. You're going to be just fine!" I wondered if he could see my tears through the haze of his feverish eyes. I held his hand until the nurse insisted impatiently that visiting hours were over.

The next day I awoke at six-thirty in the morning. Did I dream that I heard my father calling? Breakfast could wait. I slipped into a pair of slacks, polo shirt and tennis shoes and drove to Long Beach Memorial Hospital, only a few short blocks from our home at the time. The hospital was located on Long Beach Bay and, unlike today, the air that lazy July morning was just pleasantly cool and without humidity. I remember thinking that we lived in the prettiest city in America. And then the rumbling began. Way off in the distance, dark purple clouds crawled along the horizon like spilled ink.

It was a small-town hospital, adequate for delivering babies and managing most illnesses, but perhaps not sophisticated enough to handle the sneak attack that hit my father. He had not responded to the antibiotics and other medications available at the time and given for what at first was thought to be pneumonia.

"Let's take him to the City," I had urged my mother. "Maybe the doctors there can help him." But the attending physician told us Poppy was too ill to be moved. A day later, his blood tests came back positive for acute leukemia.

My mother was frozen in fear, unable to think beyond the moment. I hired private nurses, and our family doctor arranged for a specialist from Mount Sinai Hospital to come to Long Beach. My sister Miriam clung to Ma, unsure how to handle the drama. We all waited, holding on to each other. I tried to keep things light.

"As soon as Poppy gets his fill of hospital food, he'll come running home to you, Ma." But I was only blowing mist over the fog.

He came from Pop's room, the specialist did, expressionless, his head falling slightly forward. My mother's eyes grew wide with fear. "*Shlecht,*" she hissed. "It's bad."

"I'm sorry, Mrs. Edelstein. I've examined your husband and studied the blood tests . . ." The doctor straightened his shoulders and offered, "We might try a blood transfusion."

"Yes," my mother said quickly, "a transfusion. Do it!"

We remained at the hospital most of the day—my mother, my sister and I—taking turns sitting with Pop. My wisecracks were finally stilled. Already, I felt we were "visiting" at the funeral parlor. The only difference was that now Pop's eyes were open. He couldn't talk much but he seemed to savor our presence, pulling our faces and words into his soul. He was dying. My father was dying and, like my drowning, there wasn't a damned thing I could do about it.

Unknown to my mother and sister, I cornered our family physician in the hospital's corridors, in the parking lot, and whenever I could get him on the phone. "Please do something," I begged. But his frustration was almost as great as mine.

"I'm looking into it, Annie," he lied. "Believe me, if there was anything I could do . . ."

And so it was that I drove to the hospital that very fine morning in July, with the storm clouds threatening in the distance, I found my father fully awake, eyes wide-open and waiting.

"Poppy." I took his hand and we looked fiercely into each other's eyes. "Poppy," I said again, my voice catching. My throat was so swollen with tears, I couldn't articulate another syllable without breaking down.

My father looked directly at me and squeezed my hand, and without another word, he closed his eyes and stopped breathing.

Yis-ga-dal v'yis-ka-dash sh'may ra-bo . . . Almost as a reflex, the ancient Mourner's Kaddish erupted from deep within me, interrupted only by my own choking sobs. Pop—Poppy! Oh, my God, my GOD, OH GOD . . .

Sorrow turned to anger—anger at the Supreme Being. How, I wondered, could a benevolent God take my father? What were we to do without the light of our family? I mean, he was the kindest, wisest most decent person I'd ever known. And he held the entire family together—not just us, but his sisters, brothers, the whole bickering bunch of them. And he helped them resolve their petty arguments. And he found solutions to their problems. And he was always there to help. It didn't make sense to take life away from such a man. His last words echoed in my ears: *Take care of your mother*. And I had complied as best I could, until now. Now . . . who will take care of her?

That was so long ago; yet, the pain is as fresh as yesterday. I looked around me now at our dwindling family: Ma, frightened but stoic. On the other side of her sat Miriam, deep in her own thoughts but blissfully quiet. Next to her huddled her children, about to experience their first encounter with grown-up truth. We all looked toward Frank and Herb, side by side on the jump seats opposite. Our combined thoughts and fears filled the silent vehicle as it inched its way through traffic on Queens Boulevard toward Schwartz Brothers Funeral Home where Rabbi Friedman was waiting. Also at the funeral home we'd meet up with the remainder of our family that now only gathered for these functions and the occasional Bar Mitzvah or wedding. Not so, I reminded myself bitterly, when my father was alive. Family gatherings had been an integral part of our lives then. But when Poppy died, who was left to lead them?

Today, as we entered the funeral home, the sorrowing process began again. An usher directed us toward the sanctuary where my plain pine casket awaited. The men first reached for yarmelkehs and quickly placed them on their heads. Some of the women had donned kerchiefs or small pieces of black veiling. All, including Frank, shuffled slowly toward the chapel with downcast eyes. Ma's legs did not readily accommodate her, and she had to be supported between Herbie and Frank. Many of the pews were already filled, and all eyes turned as our group headed down the aisle toward the front section reserved for the closest family members. Ma's low moaning floated out over the sad gathering like a dark river.

Rabbi Friedman nodded and shook hands with the immediate family, and we slid onto the polished birch benches. The rabbi's eyes covered Ma with pity, but her tears blotted out everything except the casket, plunked down in the front of the somber setting like a boat in dry dock.

Ma, Ma, I'm here with you. It's okay. Honest, I don't hurt at all. But I needn't have worried. The dark mood was about to be broken.

The crowd behind me began rustling, and I turned, along

with the rest of the audience, to see Harold Spurgeon, with Claudia on his arm, hustling themselves into the chapel. Even here, she had to make her entrance, wearing what appeared to be an Emanuel Ungaro two-piece navy suit, across the top of which was draped a conspicuously magnificent scarf by Hermès. Heads turned all right.

Thanks, Claudia, you've managed to upstage me at my own funeral. Just wait till I get my degree in haunting. You'll be my first subject.

Already seated in the rear were Marian, Roger and Matt. Michael Rheims sat across the aisle looking as though the collar of his shirt was just a tad too small. Seeing him there made me want to blush. But let's face it, I wasn't even capable of throwing a sweat. I chucked a quick glance toward Frank, but one look told me his mind was in a different world. When I looked back Claudia was wiggling in beside Matt whose color deepened perceptively at the contact.

I studied the faces of my former co-workers. Marian's oozed curiosity. She couldn't absorb the details fast enough. Roger looked genuinely sad. Poor Roger—he would really miss me. While Claudia garnered admiring glances, Harold's eyes darted about like a pair of mosquitos looking for a place to land. And he twitched as though his undershorts were starched. Hardly poised. If Agnes were here, Heaven forbid, she would be hurling laser-beamed stares at her son. But we were all spared her presence.

I was somewhat surprised to see the appearance of my other relatives because I had not seen many of them in years. I noted they'd all come equipped with their mourning in tact. My aunts, uncles and cousins and their respective spouses sat shoulder-to-shoulder (those who were still talking to each other, that is) sharing the moment. Hannah Green, my friend since grade school, was also there with her husband and children.

Remember our sleepovers when we were kids, Hannah? We talked about lots of stuff, but we neglected this subject entirely.

Hannah was the smart one, the dedicated student who went on to achieve one degree after another until—voilà! She was all at once Dr. Hannah Green, psychologist.

And talking about shrinks, babe, I sure could use a quick session to help sort out some of this confusion. Maybe you could fit me in later, for old time's sake?

Hannah's good-natured countenance bore a troubled expression.

It's okay, sweetie, I'll find a way to make contact. I promise. Hey! Did I ever break a promise?

The murmuring stopped suddenly, and I, along with the rest of the crowd, turned my attention to Rabbi Friedman who was standing at the lectern in front of my casket. He was smiling benignly at the assembled, waiting for the little people to notice his supreme presence, and he was obviously not going to speak until he had complete quiet. With his enormous silk *tallis* draped about his shoulders, he reveled in his rabbinical appearance.

"Dear family and friends, we are gathered here today to pay our last respects to Annie Edelstein—"

Hey, wait a minute! That's Dowd, D-O-W-D.

"—taken from us . . . much too early."

I was reminded of Friedman's penchant for enunciating words. Every syllable had its day in court, so to speak; therefore, two or three sentences took as long as a scene from *Macbeth*. And musical? His voice rose and fell with such color it would have made a virtuoso blush with shame. A respectful quiet settled over the crowd, but instead of buoying him up, the rabbi seemed disheartened. Oh, I remember! He had to relinquish the spotlight temporarily for the others who wanted to speak about their remembrances. Well, this should be interesting.

Herbie strode to the front of the chapel when his name was announced as though he'd just won the grand prize at bingo.

"Annie was not just a good daughter. She was a wonderful sister, sister-in-law and aunt."

One glance at Miriam suggested she might be experiencing orgasm. Uncharitably, I wondered if she knew what that was.

"—She cared about her family, worked hard . . ." (and *blah, blah, blah*).

As much as I appreciated his words, I, along with most of the crowd, tuned out after a while. Herbie was trying to do the right thing, but he had the charisma of yesterday's grits. Rivers flowed from Ma's eyes though, and maybe that was the important thing. My niece and nephew sat next to each other slack-jawed. I didn't wonder whom they took after. Their mother was beaming with pride.

Frank, his voice heavy with strain, spoke next, but as he began, I was transported back in time to our early life together.

Under Frank's tutelage, my exposure to fine foods, wines and world events took on the accomplishments of an Eliza Doolittle. We attended everything together, from Knicks games at Madison Square Garden to Press Club dinners. On my own, I began frequenting museums and galleries. And with Frank's encouragement, I eventually found my way to night classes at New York University, where I finally discovered poetry and literature.

". . . Annie perceived pleasure in the small things," he was saying. "She loved to read, listen to good music and share a fine meal with friends and family. She was an intelligent, curious seeker of knowledge. Her sense of humor always stood her in good stead. But if I talked about Annie's wonderful qualities from now till next week, if I tried with all my might to draw a picture of the woman who deserved life more than anyone else I know, if I used all the words in the English language to list the separate parts that made up the whole, I could never properly draw the composite of one of the finest human beings it has ever been my privilege to know. I'll always love you, Annie Edelstein Dowd . . ."

Ma was crying. Hell, most of the audience was sniveling. Even the rabbi was stunned into temporary silence. But, trooper that he was, Friedman managed to rise to the occasion. Nobody was going to get away without hearing his kosher prayers.

The ride out to the cemetery afterward was the worst part. We were following the hearse, and Ma was shut up in her own misery. Even Frank's attempts to break through were unsuccessful. We all took our same seats, with the rabbi sitting up front with the driver, and for the most part, silence governed.

Protocol took over as soon as we arrived at Washington Cemetery, one of the oldest—and most crowded, I might add—

in the New York area. Just past the entrance, our car slowed and stopped while the hearse moved ahead and out of sight, presumably to unload its packaged passenger. In the interim, the children reminded Miriam of their presence in one way or another, and so we passed the time being treated to Mrs. Stepford's tender cajoling.

Soon we gathered in front of the freshly dug grave in the Edelstein Family plot, a piece of real estate, which my father had seen fit to invest in many years before. Frank and Herbie supported Ma, who was hardly able to stand on her own, while Rabbi Friedman once again took center stage.

It's only a damn box, I insisted, pointing at the casket as the rabbi intoned the final prayers, but who could appreciate my observation? *I tell you, I'm still here! Furthermore, I'm staying until we find out who did this. Get that?*

After the final prayers, Frank draped an arm around Ma, who had picked up a stone and was placing it on my father's grave in the traditional gesture of mourning and remembrance. Then she allowed herself to be led back to the car. The rest followed. Now we had to get ready for the second part of the ordeal—the official mourning period known as *Shiva.*

I knew I could trust Miriam and Herbie to set this in motion while I checked in on Martola and Charlene. Delighted that I still had an unlimited travel pass, I bid all a fond adieu and left.

Ten

I couldn't get over the idea that someone had slipped me this rohypnol stuff. Who and why? Michael? Nah. It still didn't make sense. I mean, I was his for the taking, unless he was into some kinkier stuff that required my being even more willing than we both knew I was. Jeez! I distinctly remember my hormonal level being right up there with YES-anyway-you-want-it! He appeared to enjoy my participation, with the prospect of more to come. No, I can't see where Michael would have had anything to gain by drugging me into a zombie state. However, since the chemical is notoriously tied to seduction, and Michael and I had already been observed nibbling on each other's ears in anticipation of the main course, I could see why he'd be a suspect. Motive? None that made any sense. But why should I leave anything to chance? Perhaps a visit to Michael's place might turn up something. I knew I didn't have to wait for an invitation. The clock on the wall registered 4 P.M. as I headed out.

The Carnegie Hill area was as low-key-elegant as one could get. In the Nineties, off Park, dignified structures posed grandly in their urban landscape. I nodded toward the doorman as I entered Michael's building, but the guy never even tipped his cap, so I went directly to the eighteenth floor. Ignoring the pull of wasted desire, I bypassed the master bedroom and headed toward the study, taking in the wall hangings and elegant old-world flavor of the decor along the way. Furnished in burgundy and gold, the apartment had an inviting, lived-in feeling about it, as if one could easily settle into one of the high-backed chairs in the living room and enjoy a glass of wine, some classical music and suggestive conversation. But what's gone is gone, and there was no use delaying it: I had to go through the stuff in Michael's desk.

Within ten minutes, I came across some strange correspondence from his sister in England. Her letter made some mysterious references to an *incident*. Wading through the convoluted British waters, I gleaned this happenstance pertained to the mysterious disappearance of something valuable. Should I infer that Michael was somehow involved? Perhaps his sojourn in America was merely a cover. Further along, his sister expressed sadness at Michael's recent breakup. She used the term *honorable gesture* and suggested that after a reasonable period, his return to England might be arranged, etc., etc.

So, a broken relationship? What caused the explosion? Cryptic, to say the least, and didn't sound like the Michael I knew. I'm thinking his sister must be a frustrated writer with a poor plot plan. This elegant gentleman is maybe not so wholesome? How do I get myself involved with such characters? And then it hit me: If the gallant Sir Michael is a tad unprincipled or even underhanded, was he also capable of murder? I had to share this information with the rest of the investigating team.

When I returned to the station, I passed on the news to Charlene. She and Martola had been going over some of their notes, but I felt no compunction about interrupting.

Think you should take a deeper look into Michael's background. Maybe he's not so innocent after all.

"Okay," she acknowledged.

Martola looked at her questioningly.

"I've been thinking about this Rheims guy," she said quickly. "He's the only new player in the game. The victim was well acquainted with everyone else."

"So?"

"So maybe we need to take another look."

"You got the hots or something?"

Oh, get off it, Martola. Why do guys have such a one-track mind anyway?

Charlene's eyes narrowed. Her partner recognized the look and assumed an innocent expression.

"Let's just say I'm looking at this from another perspective," she said cooly. "No one gets a free ride."

Her comment struck home. From now on, I affirmed, I'll take a more active role myself. After all, who was better equipped to find the guilty party? In the meantime, I would try to be present at most of the interviews, especially at those whom I considered the lead characters in this farce. I was especially looking forward to their exchange with Claudia Harmon, who had evidently decided that a change of costume was in order. Like, that would make her more people-friendly?

She swept into the Mineola Police Station wearing a go-for-the-gusto two-piece summer suit in melon and beige that reeked of Saks Fifth Avenue. Her dyed-to-match caramel-colored shoes and Coach bag lent just the right touch of nouveau riche. Charlene didn't flinch. Her partner, however, had a little more difficulty maintaining his composure, especially when Claudia, flaunting long acrylic nails, extended her hand in his direction.

Martola shook it awkwardly and motioned back toward Charlene. "Yeah, you remember Detective Williams." Claudia's hand flopped down like a spent phallus. She looked disappointed.

Did you expect him to kiss it, you bozo?

Claudia barely acknowledged Charlene before turning back to Martola. Her eyes swept over his muscular physique and the beast inside began sending signals. "I'll certainly be glad to help in any way I can, Detective." All that was missing was a southern accent, hardly fitting since we all suspected she came from Brooklyn. We'd observed that her Radcliffe delivery slipped on occasion when she became rattled.

Charlene allowed herself a bemused grin and winked at her partner who looked as if he was ready to puke.

Okay, guys, enough of this foreplay; let's get to the nitty-gritty.

Charlene, of course, took my advice. After a few preliminary questions, she asked, "Can you tell us exactly where you were when the deceased was discovered facedown in the pool?"

"Where was I? Let's see. Oh, I remember. I believe I was in the drawing room admiring the paintings. The Matisse is particularly lovely."

I'll just bet! And you were already calculating how much it would go for in a Christie's auction.

Charlene covered her mouth.

Martola, who had collected himself by now, prodded, "And . . . ?"

"I guess it was one of the servants who yelled out that Annie—she had fallen or something—was in the pool and fully dressed!" Claudia made big eyes at Martola, suggesting that was not a nice thing to do. "Then I ran out and saw everyone around the pool . . ."

Nodding sympathetically, Charlene said, "It must have been shocking."

Is that your tongue in your cheek I hear clicking?

My detective smirked.

"Really," agreed Claudia, now looking to Charlene for sympathy and understanding.

Good! Now lead her down the path.

"Do you recall who was standing near you at this time?"

"Difficult to say." She waved her Elizabeth Arden nails through the air. "You know how these parties are."

Resisting the obvious comeback, Charlene nodded sympathetically. "I suppose Harold Spurgeon was not far away . . . I understand you and Mr. Spurgeon are engaged?"

"Well of course he was . . . nearby!"

Like Harold would not be anywhere but in worshiping distance? Now ask her how she felt about me.

"What was your relationship with Ms. Dowd?" asked Charlene.

"Relationship? Um . . . we didn't actually have too much in common."

"So, you were not good friends."

Claudia glanced at Martola with a half-smile, which I interpreted as a call for help, but his eyes returned to his desktop. Charlene tapped her pencil patiently.

"Well," Claudia managed, in her version of a New England

accent, "she and I were colleagues, of course, but we didn't have much opportunity to get together socially."

"You were competitors, you mean," pressed Charlene.

The subject's jaw tightened in obvious annoyance. "I mean we worked at the same firm! Nothing more."

I saw Martola scribbling some notes and ran around to his side of the desk to have a peek. He'd written "no love lost," "a possible" and "motive—accounts?" I repeated these to Charlene, who nodded and extended the session for another ten minutes. When they were finally done, I followed Claudia from the precinct.

Home was a studio apartment on Ninety-fourth and Lexington, small but a good address with doorman service. I'd always suspected that Claudia was not "born to the cloth." Every action, every word she uttered, seemed learned responses. Even her taste in clothes and makeup were projected in what appeared be a self-directed effort toward the top of the mountain. To that end, she deserved some credit. Claudia had invented herself, to be sure, and from wherever she evolved, she was hell-bent on acquiring the last name of Spurgeon. Should I say, "poor Harold"—or—"ha-ha, Agnes, the last laugh's on you"?

There was a Gristide's on the same block, and Claudia stopped to purchase some yogurt, a banana and a can of Slim Fast. How gourmet can you get?

Upstairs at her place, Claudia plunked the package on the counter of the tiny kitchenette, reached for the phone and dialed a number. A busy signal whined, and she slammed the receiver. "Oh, damn!" she said aloud, to what she thought was an empty apartment.

I figured she was trying to reach Harold, but seconds later, she pressed the redial button, and the call went through. The ensuing conversation took me by surprise.

"Yah, Tessie, it's me. Well, I've been busy! So, how is Katya? Good!"

Now I'm listening to this, and suddenly nothing makes any sense. My eyes tell me I'm looking at Claudia, but my ears are arguing against. She sounds like a refugee! Her voice is no longer cultured, but common, like . . . like last month's strudel, as Ma would say. Something's definitely out of sync here. And who the heck is Katya? Hmm . . . nothing is ever as it seems, and Claudia's hiding more than I gave her credit for.

The conversation didn't last long, and while the lady of the house sat down to her sumptuous lunch, I poked around her apartment. Dresser drawers and closets revealed nothing extraordinary. A small desk in the corner of her bedroom held only the barest essentials: writing paraphernalia and some stamps. I felt cheated. Then I spied her Gucci attaché case on the floor next to her desk. I stared at the catch until it popped open, then rifled through the folders inside. Nothing but the specs on her newest clients. Logic dictated that the Dragon Lady had something to do with my murder, but where was the proof, dammit? (I'd figure out the motive later.) I left, finally, feeling infinitely cheated.

Upon my return to the station house, I found Charlene and Martola having a session with their boss, Lieutenant Robert "Bud" Egan. Egan was a thoughtful man in his early fifties, eagerly looking forward to retirement. He'd transferred from the Forty-eighth Precinct in the South Bronx four years before and aimed to keep his life on a steady, safe track until he and his wife could retire to the small house in Pennsylvania they'd purchased three summers before. Egan would permit no interference in his master plan. Any hitch in the operation of the Nassau County Precinct reflected on him. And even though his record was unblemished up to this point, he felt that, as a black man, he had to be twice as good as the next guy.

I slipped in alongside Martola and Charlene to offer what I could.

Wait'll you hear what happened.

The only reaction was a raised eyebrow from Charlene.

The boss was focused on the investigation, and his attention was directed toward his detectives. "Where are we with this thing?" His high, shiny forehead creased with interest.

Frankly, I appreciated his candor. *Yeah,* I echoed, *where are we with this thing?*

"Looks like we have a possible," Martola offered. "One of

the party guests, Claudia Harmon, claims she was inside the house admiring the paintings. But she was alone, so no one can vouch for this."

Well, I checked out her place—a big nothing. No wonder she was cataloging the possibilities in Sands Point. That's her whole agenda, capturing Harold. Sure, she and I weren't exactly friends, but nothing I ever had would make her richer. I'm talking "motive," guys.

My good buddy, Charlene, nodded.

And almost immediately, Egan also asked about motive.

Charlene sat forward. "At the moment, money seems the most logical. Annie Dowd was no threat to anyone." She glanced around quickly. "But she did represent competition."

Wait a minute!

But Martola agreed with his partner. "I've thought all along that was the deal."

Egan studied them both. "Care to elaborate?"

I felt compelled to play devil's advocate. *Listen to me. We all know Claudia is nothing less than an aggressive, gold-digging, second-class piece of work. But isn't murder a little extreme? Even for her?*

"Not really," said Charlene, clamping a hand over her mouth.

Her partner swung around, his face forming a question, and her boss looked puzzled.

"Uh, that is"—Charlene scrambled to recover—"money is one of the obvious motives. There might be some unknown factor we have yet to uncover."

I wondered why I was attempting to defend Claudia. Maybe it had something to do with the vagabond flashes from my last hurrah. Though they refused to stand still long enough to be fully identified, they just didn't seem to point to Claudia as the executioner. My search of her place supported this. On second thought, maybe she was an aide-de-camp to the quarterback. Uh, Claudia play second fiddle? Not likely.

I appealed to my new partner. *I've gone over this thing a hundred times and always come away with the same bottom line: Claudia had absolutely nothing to gain by my death. Maybe I'm too close to the forest?*

"Probably."

"Probably what?" asked Martola, scratching his head.

"Uh, I was just thinking out loud."

Her partner sent her a quizzical look and circled his forefinger in the air next to his temple. "You okay?"

She rolled her eyes. "Why do you ask?"

Her partner shrugged.

"Look, maybe Claudia Harmon wasn't satisfied with just *her* commissions. Maybe she had her sights on Annie Dowd's. After all, Dowd was with the company longer and had a pretty impressive clientele.

"On the other hand, Harmon seems to have the lock on the big guy. He's Agnes Spurgeon's only son and stands to inherit the whole shebang. Why would killing Annie Dowd make life better for her?"

Keep the door open, I say. Didn't find anything when I tossed her apartment, but what does that mean? Maybe she's in cahoots with someone. Also, you might like to know that she dropped her Notting Hill accent when she thought she was alone.

I related Claudia's end of the strange conversation. Charlene wrinkled her forehead as I spoke.

Egan asked if there were any other leads. The detectives hesitated.

"We haven't finished our follow-up interviews," Charlene hedged, more to her partner than Egan.

Their boss nodded. "Well, don't rule out the possibility that more than one might be involved. And get into the money thing. Subpoena bank records, if you need them. Look into the debt situation. Check credit cards. Do I have to draw you a map?"

"No, boss."

Finally, there was a captain at the helm.

Harold's interview did not contribute much more than Claudia's, except I found it amusing that he appeared quite nervous. I chalked it up to the fact that he had the poise of an ant. How disappointed Agnes would have been had she been present! Her efforts to raise the son of a dynasty appeared to have been wasted on a no-talent *shmendrik*, as my mother would say (which, of course, he was since he believed Claudia just adored him).

"Oh, by the way," Martola inquired casually, "do you happen to recall where you were when Ms. Dowd's body was discovered in the pool?"

"Well . . . uh, I was on the lawn with some of the other guests . . . with Ms. Harmon, that is. . . ."

Poor recall, Harold. Get your act together. On second thought, maybe this was not an act but a slipup.

The detectives exchanged raised eyebrows, then turned to stare at their subject. Harold fidgeted uncontrollably.

Charlene ventured, "Would it surprise you to hear that Ms. Harmon claims to have been in the house admiring the paintings when Ms. Dowd was discovered in the pool?"

Silence. Then Harold offered, "Ah, uh, I could be mistaken. There was so much happening at once. . . ." His voice trailed away like a badly warped record, and he began fiddling with his watch band.

Listen, guys, this fella's a zombie, a zero. Not too much up there. Know what I mean?

But Charlene persevered. "Listen, Harold," she breathed, invading his space. "Um, you don't mind that I call you Harold, do you?" I guessed she was pulling her brunette version of Marilyn Monroe.

"Uh, no. That's fine." He hiked up his shoulders a notch or two, under the impression that he was becoming irresistible. As if.

"Annie was with your firm a long time, wasn't she?"

"About nine or ten years, I would say."

"Anything you can tell us about Friday's *tragedy* would be so helpful."

"Yes, but I don't know what I can tell you. I wasn't there . . . at the pool, that is."

After ten more minutes of the same, even Martola was beginning to yawn. It was like being at a boring baseball game, one strike after another when all the home crowd wants are hits. *Put us in scoring position, Charlene!*

Finally, even she gave up, putting an asterisk next to his

name after he left. I assumed the jerk was in for a follow-up interview. Remind me to book a hair-dressing appointment for that occasion.

The detectives agreed to check Harold's financial records. Then they reviewed their notes on the others. Apparently Marian and Roger passed with flying colors, but Matt was not so lucky. Maybe Martola took exception to the fact that the kid was twenty years younger and might be in better shape, or maybe it was because Matt blushed so easily. In any case, an asterisk was affixed next to his name as well.

However, none of that bothered me as much as Claudia's mysterious phone conversation and the peek at what might be under her mask. Had I underestimated her? I recalled seeing her résumé when she first made contact with Royal Roosts. The manager of her previous employer, Sanford Realty, verified that Claudia had worked for them for two years. Sanford was her first foray into the real-estate market after a long career in the garment industry. I figured that was where she apprenticed in how to dress for success. She is smart; I'll give her that. Still, so much about the woman continues to be a mystery, and I wonder how much is yet to be discovered.

I walked along with Charlene when she headed for her car at the end of the day. *Ahem . . .*

"Sheesch! You scared the shit out of me!"

Sorry. I don't know any kind way to get your attention.

"Look, I've had a long, hard day. I don't suppose this could wait until tomorrow?"

In this life or next, who knows when that is?

"I can't believe I'm walking along and talking with a ghost."

How do you think I feel about it?

Charlene ran her fingers through her hair. "You've got a point. Anyhow, what can I do for you?"

It's about Claudia. I overheard her on the telephone today. When she dropped her Park Avenue accent, she sounded just like another person.

"Your point?"

Don't you see? If she can hide her origins, maybe she can hide the fact that she's a killer.

"We're going into this with an open mind. Everyone connected is a possible. Don't worry about your former colleague. No one who was in Sands Point that day gets a free ride."

Okay. Go home and take a load off. I'm going to visit my mother.

Eleven

One thing about my present state that was no different than my previous role was that I still could not be in two places at once. Much as I knew my assistance was needed with the investigation, it was hard to stay away from Ma's. I stopped by to see if I could be of any help, but she was taking a much-needed nap. Miriam and Herbie seemed to have the situation under control. While their children watched mindless television, my sister and brother-in-law were taking inventory on the bonanza of glittery gift baskets of fruit and candy that threatened to overtake the small apartment.

For me? I quipped, with an exaggerated bow. But they were too engrossed in the take to notice.

As I turned to go, Miriam said, "How long do you think it will take Ma to get used to the idea?"

"Hard to say. She's still in shock."

Well, of course she's in shock. And what idea should she get used to?

"It really would make life so much easier," mused my sister.

I didn't like the sound of this. *What would make life easier?*

Herbie began strolling along the bookcases in the living room, pointing. "A lot of this stuff is just junk. I guess some of it could be sold . . . but we'll cross that bridge when we come to it. Look, Ma can have her own room. She can have some of her things, but the rest of this stuff goes."

Say, what, brother? I felt the steam rising, but Mrs. Yes-sir was bobbing her head up and down.

You're not selling any of Ma's possessions. And you can shove your spare room any place it fits. Ma is happy just where she is now.

My brother-in-law was standing near an end table with framed photos of happier times. I concentrated on a five-by-seven frame of Poppy's serene face, the one where he looked like he had the world by the tail. Being new at this, it took a little while to get the momentum going. While my sister's meddling husband espoused the positive points of relocating Ma to the Rosen home in Ohio (so they wouldn't have to inconvenience themselves traveling to New York for their visits), the ornate metal frame finally made its way toward the end of the table. When it plunged over the edge and caught Herbie on his instep, his yelp was all the reward I could ask.

"Are you okay, hon?" asks the little woman.

"Ice! Bring an ice pack!"

When my sister dashed toward the kitchen to fetch for her lord, I let him have it. *Let's get one thing straight, Herb. You are not going to push Ma around. She's happy here. She doesn't need to move to Ohio in order to go to synagogue; she's got her own temple in Forest Hills. Plus, Ma's not looking for activities; she's been playing canasta with the same group for seventeen years. And last but not least, her stuff stays right where it is. Got that?*

I worked myself up into such a frenzy, several other photos on the table overturned, making clattering noises in the supposedly empty room. Herbie began to twitch. He jerked his eyes toward the windows, but the curtains were hardly moving. He frowned, searching the immediate vicinity for an explanation. By the time Miriam returned, he was as docile as a kitten, allowing her to settle him back against the couch cushions and minister to his boo-boo.

So, okay, just tell Ma I stopped by, I quipped, as I headed back to the investigation.

If they'd picked up the trail of anything interesting, the detectives hadn't indicated that to Frank (or me, for that matter). I tried to locate them at the precinct. Their absence suggested they had moved on to more productive areas. But where? And how am I supposed to do my job if they don't leave me a note or something? This is getting complicated. I began to see the necessity of a pager or some similar device. Yes, I would make that suggestion to the higher-ups at my first opportunity. In the meantime, second-guessing was my only option.

After some inconvenience, I finally found the detectives back at Agnes's palatial digs on Sands Point—in the library, to be exact—with the lady herself and her lawyer, a Mr. Thomas McBride. I gathered the interview had been underway for only a few minutes. Apparently, Charlene had won the toss to start the questioning.

"It would be helpful, Mrs. Spurgeon, if you could recall what you were doing at the time Annie Dowd was found to be unconscious in the pool."

By now, I was accustomed to this, their opening gambit.

Agnes's chin tilted upward. "As I recall, I was attempting to get the caterers to serve dessert. It had been a long and extremely tiring day."

Evidently not long enough.

"Attempting?"

"Yes," she frowned, as though Charlene didn't understand English. "The affair was difficult enough to manage. But then there was also that disturbance at the gate."

Martola pushed forward. "Disturbance?"

Lady Agnes swiveled her eyes in his direction.

"How so?" he prodded.

"It was a holiday, after all. The country club is located nearby. People were out and about, celebrating."

Like, wouldn't you know that, Martola?

Charlene cleared her throat. "Could you possibly describe the interruption, Mrs. Spurgeon?"

Lawyer and client exchanged practiced looks.

"A lot of noise. Apparently, some members or their guests had had too much to drink and were attempting to enter the grounds of my home, which is only a short distance from the country club."

Yes. This is very familiar. I can almost remember the hubbub.

"Do you recall the time?"

"I would say it was about ten in the evening."

The detectives continued their questioning for another

twenty minutes before Agnes turned pleading eyes toward her lawyer. "I'm feeling rather tired. Will this take much longer?"

McBride rose on cue. "Sorry, detectives, Mrs. Spurgeon is happy to cooperate, but she is, unfortunately, not well. May we save the rest for another time?" It was more of a statement than a question and required no discussion.

No! Don't stop now—something's coming through, or trying to . . .

Charlene was immediately attentive, but Martola was not interested in my reminiscences. Whatever the thought was, it was gone for now. I was disappointed, but headed back to the precinct with them to meet with Michael Rheims. He had an asterisk next to his name, too. I certainly wanted in on that session.

I'd forgotten how good-looking the guy was. He'd been in casual attire the last time I'd seen him, but he certainly made an impression in his double-breasted Armani suit with color-coordinated shirt and tie. It all looked so custom-made. Had things been different, could I have lived up to his expectations? See, Frank was so easygoing about such things. Whatever I wore, did or cooked was okay with him, as long as we both found time for cuddling. Guess I took a lot for granted. Anyway, back to business . . .

Martola did not disguise his inspection of the man before him. They'd talked before, the day after my, uh, unfortunate mishap, but Michael had not been in his city duds. At this, their second meeting, the two shook hands and looked each other over for a few seconds before Martola began.

"Let's go back to the night of July Fourth. It's no secret that you and Ms. Dowd had gotten pretty friendly during the day—"

That's putting it mildly. Listen, Michael, you don't have to worry about Martola. He's rough but pretty much okay.

"Tell me again where you were when the deceased was discovered facedown in the pool."

Michael's precise British marched forward: "I believe I was just returning from the front gate."

Oh, the beautiful sound of that cultured voice! How could I even think he had anything to do with my death?

"And you were there because . . ."

"There had been a commotion."

"And?"

Take your time, dear.

"My aunt, Mrs. Spurgeon, had dispatched some of the servants to see to it, and I had gone along."

"And?"

"Then Matt Sterling stopped by to chat."

Charlene jerked her head up.

No, Michael. You're mistaken. Matt said he was with Claudia. Don't let Martola intimidate you.

An impatient inflection entered Martola's voice. "And?"

Charlene and I sensed her partner's short fuse was running out, but what could I do about it? Fortunately, she jumped in.

"It would be helpful if you could tell us specifically what you were doing when Annie Dowd was discovered in the pool."

Michael turned his gorgeous gray eyes on Charlene, the very same eyes that had practically charmed the pants off me. With one bold stare, he sent signals of lust in her direction, practically hanging out a sign that read, "Office hours: twenty-four hours a day, Sundays included."

Charlene did not flinch, but I was seething. *What kind of crap is this? Weren't you pretending to melt under my fire only days ago?*

My friend's eyes glistened with amusement, but the subject continued, paying no attention to my snit. "When Matt Sterling joined me, I was coming up the path toward the pool. That's when I heard the screaming and shouting."

As he spoke, Michael's eyes caressed Charlene's face, her throat, and moved down the buttons of her pale blue blouse . . . one at a time . . . *Oooh!* Was this guy horny or what? Still, Charlene stared back, unmoved.

Martola cleared his throat. "So—you're saying when you arrived at the pool, Ms. Dowd was already unconscious?"

"Well, there certainly was a lot of confusion. The way I heard it, she was standing on the coping next to the pool one minute and in the water the next. By the time I got there, I didn't realize she was dead, so I attempted to resuscitate—we're trained in that sort of thing back home—but it didn't work, unfortunately. . . ."

As his voice trailed off, I couldn't help but remember the great time we'd had leading up to the end. But now, watching him practically undress Charlene with his eyes, I wanted to scream: *Tell me the truth, Michael! Did you do this to me?*

Martola pushed forward. "The party was catered, right? Plenty of good food, wine?"

Michael nodded.

"Guests help themselves? Or was it served?"

"Both, actually. There was a long table with assorted foods: meats, side dishes and the like. In addition, waiters carried platters with hot hors d'oeuvres, as well as trays with wine, of course."

"Of course."

Yes, I remember that. Classy and good. Old Agnes didn't hold back on a thing.

"You drink some wine?"

"Naturally."

"Offer some to Ms. Dowd?"

Michael looked angry now, aware he was being challenged, maybe even suspected. "I might have, yes."

Hold it, guys. I'm getting those vibes again.

"This before you went to the gate?" Martola persisted.

Wait a minute, I say!

Charlene jerked her head in my direction. I was straining to remember, but it was like struggling to move against huge ocean waves.

"What are you really asking?" Michael demanded.

Martola's posture spelled bird dog. I knew it and so did Charlene, who interjected, "Someone spiked Ms. Dowd's wine with a drug that rendered her defenseless. We're trying to find out who did this."

"You don't think that I had anything to do with it!" Michael spluttered.

Neither detective responded. Michael's eyes narrowed as he stared back. His jaw tightened.

Charlene asked, "Can you think of anyone present at the party who might have tampered with her drink?"

Michael's face still wore the angry expression of a little boy unjustly accused of fingering the frosting, but he said, "I've only been over here for a fortnight. I truly can't imagine who could have done such a thing. She seemed . . . happy with life . . . carefree—the last person on earth who would have any enemies."

He was striving for a passing grade in sincerity but received no encouragement.

Martola glanced quickly at his partner, exchanging that unspoken language of theirs, then stood. "That's all for now, Mr. Rheims. We'll be in touch if we need to talk with you again."

It was pretty plain that Michael was being summarily dismissed. After he left, the detectives and I analyzed the results of the interview.

I don't know about you two, but the worst Michael is guilty of is having the talent to seduce women. And from my experience, he's sure got what that takes.

Charlene agreed. "From where I sit, it's unlikely that he needs rohypnol to get what he wants. On the other hand, Rheims's recollection of his whereabouts does not jive with Matt Sterling's, who claims he was talking with Claudia Harmon when the vic was discovered. Claudia insists she was alone in the library admiring paintings. One wonders which one has the faulty memory, or which one is lying—or, are a couple of these characters covering for each other?"

A conspiracy?

There was more discussion between the detectives about who else, if it wasn't Rheims, had a reason to slip me the drug.

"I think," Charlene suggested, "we shouldn't focus on the obvious use of rohypnol as a so-called date-rape thing, but rather, that the drug renders the victim helpless. Let's just consider that the person wanting Dowd out of the picture had another reason—other than wild sex, that is—to eliminate resistance."

Eliminate resistance . . . You mean, make it easier to kill me? Hmm . . . but why? I still can't come up with a motive. What the hell did I have that anyone wanted badly enough to kill me for? Bottom line: What or whom are we looking for?

"Okay," Martola agreed. "Like what?"

Charlene smiled wickedly. "Show me the money!"

You're wrong, my friend, and I'm going to prove it.

Twelve

Taking a lead from the film *Field of Dreams*, observant Jews might say, "Follow the customs, and they will come!" *Shiva*: Seven days of reflection by the immediate family of the dearly departed was the event that finally brought the Edelstein clan back together again.

Shiva is the Jewish equivalent of an Irish wake and almost as noisy. Custom requires the front door to remain unlocked from morning until bedtime, so relatives and friends can enter the grieving home without ringing the doorbell. Of course, nobody comes empty-handed. A word to the wise: Calories and cholesterol are particularly uplifting. I vaguely remember accompanying my parents on a few of these journeys. The part I liked best was the abundance of sweets, usually rationed at home, but on these occasions, liberally shared.

Usually, there is a lot of talking, even joking, as friends and family recall their favorite stories about the member no longer here to argue (or defend, as the case may be). Mostly, though, a veritable flood of relatives drift in and out during the process. This was the part I was looking forward to. There were aunts, uncles and cousins I hadn't seen in years.

Uncle Harry, my father's brother, and his wife, Sarah, were the first to arrive. I was concerned about Ma's reaction. They hadn't spoken in years. But the passage of time and sadness for a parent who loses a child reaches even the most stubborn. So on this day came Uncle Harry, the oldest living family member, and Aunt Sarah, the president of his fan club.

Since the head of the clan had given his tacit approval to the visit, other relatives arrived in quick succession, even those whose presence constituted a miracle. Among the latter was Aunt Tillie, Pop's older sister, whose mouth was perpetually pressed into a thin line. Nothing ever pleased her. Eyebrows arched like two suspicious birds, Tillie might have flown in through the window. All conversation stopped as she approached the group clustered around Ma. I moved over there in a flash.

Hold it right there, Aunt Tillie! Don't even think about making trouble, or I'll . . . I'll do something terrible. I'm sure I can if I try hard enough.

My aunt paused. Had I actually reached her? But no. Nodding somberly to one and all, the ghost of Hanukkah Past finally zeroed in on Ma. The air was thick with impending doom as the relative everyone feared finally *k'vetshed* out, "She was a good girl, your Annie."

Besides Ma's sniffled response, there was an audible sigh of relief from the crowd. Tillie was not known for her pleasant nature. Harry had edged nearer during the approaching storm, but his potential threat was unnecessary. Tillie helped herself to a small *ruggeleh* and, not having detected any poison, downed two more in quick succession. I was put in mind of the old commercial that focused on the selection of only the finest Brazilian coffee beans. "When Juan Valdes is happy, everyone can relax." And so it was at Ma's apartment on this day. Only after the *ruggeleh* met with Aunt Tillie's approval, did the talking and buzzing resume.

My father's secrets in settling family disputes went with him to the grave. But I vividly recall the Sunday phone calls: his sisters' complaints about one another; the real and imagined insults that they swore never to forgive; the money difficulties; their older, single daughters, who required husbands. These and more Poppy handled with wisdom, tact and logic. It was ironic therefore, that the event of his death so many years before had caused such a rift in the family. And strange that my passing would be the circumstance that brought them all back together.

Soon Ma's modest apartment was overflowing with family and friends, some of whom drifted out into the hallway to make room for the newcomers. Visit for only a little while? No way. The inherently suspicious Edelstein family members would never leave the field free for the rest of the group to gossip, so they stayed and stayed.

Nostalgia enveloped the small apartment like a cozy shawl, and I was happy for Ma, who, though bewildered about all the fuss, was kept busy and distracted. Miriam flitted about like the Martha Stewart disciple she was, reveling in her role as grand hostess and extolling the achievements of her wonderful Herbert, vice president of Rosen Plumbing Supplies. Her children were trotted out to be introduced and then allowed back to watch their favorite TV show. Rabbi Friedman, supreme leader of our synagogue, took his bows and departed early.

Several cousins drifted in and out during the afternoon, and I found it odd to equate their present matronly demeanor with the shenanigans we used to pull as kids. Wouldn't they, like, *plats*, if they knew I was still here? I was sorely tempted.

Psst, Rachel, Abby! Yoo-hoo, it's me, Annie. . . . Guess what? I'm ba-ack. Haunting is just no fun without audience participation, so I gave up the ghost (you should pardon the pun).

Frank, who had wandered in around two in the afternoon, had a heck of a time even reaching the corner where Ma sat. She grabbed onto him as one does a life preserver, proud to introduce him to those near. She didn't see certain family members giving Frank the once-over. He had *shaigitz* written all over his Irish features. After sipping the requisite glass of Manischewitz, and chomping down on some goodies, he departed. Frank had that on-the-prowl look again that piqued my interest, so I tagged along.

I knew the detectives were doing their best to solve my murder, but something was missing. Charlene thought money was behind it all, but that just didn't make sense. Sure, I made a bunch of the stuff, but nothing that put me in a sky-high tax bracket. The motive wasn't money. Of that I was certain. What nagged at me most were those transient pieces of memory that eluded translation. Trying to sharpen the image only dulled them more. I'd have to find a way to break the code. Maybe hanging out with my favorite investigative journalist would help.

In perfect Spanish, Frank gave the office address of Royal Roosts to the Latino-looking taxi driver and settled back on the seat next to me. He pulled out a small notebook and started scribbling. I tried to read over his shoulder, but he had his own shorthand style that rendered his notes utterly private.

I can tell you're following some lead, hon, and I want you to know I'm right here if you need me. Oh, by the way, that thing between Michael and me? It's over. Don't ask me to explain. The main thing is: I'm all yours again!

Even though he didn't acknowledge my sharing this important bit of information, I felt better.

Marian blushed deeply when we walked into the reception area. Since she couldn't see me, I didn't have to wonder to whom she was reacting so tenderly.

"Why, Frank," she gushed, "what a lovely surprise." Her thin face jerked in anticipation.

My guy put on his happy face and went to work. "Our last talk was so helpful, I wondered if you could spare another few minutes for me."

Puh-leeze. If you asked her to hang out the window, she'd oblige.

"Certainly. How can I help?"

Not in any way you're thinking of.

"If you can remember our last conversation, we were discussing some of Annie's clients. And, incidentally, may I compliment you on your excellent recall?"

The expected happy fluster followed. "Oh, now . . ."

Enough fooling around. She's all yours.

But Frank was not satisfied. He perched on the edge of the desk, assuming once more the dual role of father confessor/therapist. Face aglow with interest, he studied his notebook. "Among Annie's most recent clients, you mentioned a Sultan of Sarawak, a famous film couple, a Monsieur Chardin—"

"Oh, my, you actually wrote all that down?"

"Of course," he cooed, "everything you tell me is important, Marian."

Jeez. What an operator!

"Now I want you to think really hard about the people Annie was doing business with just before the . . . accident."

"Well, I told you about the Frenchman and those others."

"Uh-huh," murmured Father Frank.

"And . . . let's see. Um, there was that TV person—talk show host, or something—but nothing ever came of that."

"Uh-huh . . ."

"And oh, yes, the Shine apartment—"

Having flashes again, Frank. No, not hot flashes. Something familiar is trying to come through. Then I reminded myself that Charlene was the only receiver on my team. But I was suddenly alert. This is exactly what frustrates me: flashes, bits and pieces that don't fit together. Or do they? I shook off my confusion and decided to concentrate on what today's tabloid might be offering.

"What about the Shine apartment?" Frank inquired.

"Well, I remember very well the day Annie showed it to that Belgian couple. Something happened there. That's for sure. Something that was, uh, kind of embarrassing . . . I think."

"Oh?" Frank zeroed in. "Annie told you this?"

"Oh, no! Uh, Annie never discussed—that is, Annie was so busy, she sometimes forgot to share things. But she would have, I'm sure."

Bullshit!

"Of course she would have! Especially with you." He patted her hand.

This is enough to make even a dead person puke.

"What was it that happened?"

"Annie was showing the Shine apartment—or trying to. It was supposed to be empty. Oscar Shine—you know—the producer? He'd gone out to California the week before, and his wife was due to follow him a few days later after she cleared up some stuff?"

I barely heard Marian talking. The memory of that encounter was all at once quite vivid. Johnny Romano! I suddenly knew why my train was delayed. I had a job to do, a job that involves the notorious gangster himself.

Psst, Frankie, I think we have to talk. Fannie Shine was entertaining Johnny Romano.

I offered this juicy piece of information in all sincerity, but Marian was on a roll. "When Annie brought the clients, the place was supposed to have been vacated and available for showing."

"And?"

"It wasn't empty, of people, that is."

"Do tell."

"Really. I gathered that Annie and the clients walked in on Mrs. Shine and, uh . . . some man, uh, doing it." She lowered her head.

It wasn't SOME man; it was Johnny Romano!

"Doing it?" echoed Frank.

I can spell it out for you. . . .

"Yes, you know," continued Marian, her face turning a deeper shade of red.

"Who was the man?"

"I don't know."

I'm telling you. It was—

But Frank was losing his father confessor/therapist facade, and Marian sensed she was in scary territory. "I want to help, Frank, but I just don't know anything else."

Get a grip, Frank, or you'll lose the fish all together.

He must have recognized this, too, because he pulled back from his perch on the desk and allowed a beatific smile to cross his face. "I guess one never knows what one will find when showing one of these apartments." He winked to show Marian he was on her side. She smiled back.

Frankie, there's something about this whole thing . . . It has something to do with what I've been trying to remember. I think.

"I suppose Annie was talking about it afterward."

"Well, not exactly. I overheard—by accident, of course—"

"Of course . . ."

"Annie was discussing it with Roger, and I, uh, just happened by his office."

"I see . . . and when did you say this took place?"

Marian inclined her head, calling upon sacred memories to come forth. "The week before she, uh, died—maybe two or three days."

It was a real yucky situation, hon. I couldn't get out of there fast enough.

Apparently, that was how Frank felt now. He slid off the desk, scribbled something in his notebook and smiled at Marian. "You've been a big help. Is Roger in?"

"I'm afraid he's out showing some property; he should be back later this afternoon. Would you like me to give him a message?"

"That's all right. I'll catch him later."

But Frank intercepted Roger in the lobby downstairs. "How's it going?" he asked.

Roger shrugged his shoulders. "Not the same without Annie."

"Yeah. Listen, I wonder if we could grab a beer. I need to talk with you about something."

Roger glanced at his watch, which showed three-forty-five. "Now? Well, I guess."

With a chummy smile, Frank engineered Roger through a one-hundred-and-eighty-degree turn, and they moved out the front of the building and headed around the corner to Murphy's.

Nostalgia flooded every crevice of Murphy's, a familiar hangout for ending the workday. The high old-fashioned mahogany bar was nearly empty at this hour, awaiting the after-five regulars. Many's the Friday I elbowed my way through the crowd to order a well-deserved Chivas Regal on the rocks. On the lucky days, I even managed to snare a seat on one of the tall, black leather stools. Frank indicated a table against the wall instead and brought back two frosted glasses and a couple of Heinekens. He set them on cardboard coasters and sat facing Roger, who looked a little apprehensive. Though they'd known each other for years, Frank still hadn't gotten it through his head that despite the fact that he lived and worked in the Big Apple, Roger was a gentle guy.

Roger is my friend, Frankie. Take it easy—okay?

Maybe Frankie received my signal or maybe the first cold

glub of the suds calmed him down. His shoulders relaxed and the tension in the air eased. "I'm interested in the episode that took place at the Shine apartment a few days before Annie died. I understand she talked with you about it."

Roger didn't hesitate. "Yes. Annie was a little shaken by the incident."

"Shaken how? Tell me about it."

"Well, she'd taken this Belgian couple, uh, the Foulières, I believe, to see the place. She had the key, of course, and let herself in as is customary."

"So?"

"Apparently, Mrs. Shine had not left for California as supposed. She and a gentleman—not her husband—were, uh, that is, *in flagrante delicto,* if you get my drift."

Stifling a smile, Frank blurted, "You mean they were screwing."

That's my boy. Cut right to the chase.

"Who was the guy?"

Roger eased the collar around his Adam's apple. "Annie said it was Johnny Romano, the mobster."

That's what I've been trying to tell you! I'll never forget that look. Made me feel like the proverbial deer caught in the headlights.

Frank stared at his companion for a number of seconds. Then he nodded at the bartender and held up two fingers, swinging his eyes back to Roger. "He's a piece of work, this Romano."

"So I've heard."

Me too. Listen, guys, if you could have seen that look he gave me . . .

But Frank was on a roll. "Hear he works for Luke Snyder."

"I wouldn't know too much about that."

"Maybe I'll do a little digging," Frank said, talking more to himself than Roger. "Thanks, appreciate your time."

"Anything I can do to help. Annie was a good friend. She didn't deserve . . ."

"Damn straight."

My guy spent a few minutes scribbling in his journal after Roger left. Where was this going? I wondered. My thoughts returned to the exact moment when Romano and I locked eyes. I recognized him instantly, of course, as anyone would who'd ever seen a newspaper article featuring the actor of the same name or heard the sound effects of an explosion. Now the echo of that explosion increased tenfold.

The gangster's name was infamous. For years, Romano had been linked to the dissolute world of drugs and death. Contrary to someone in his line of work, however, this nasty boy loved the limelight and was often photographed with celebrities and starstruck wannabes. Well, no one argued he had the looks, not to mention other attributes. There was a joke going around that his *shlang* was more in demand than box-seat tickets for the World Series. Is that why his photo showed up in publications like *New York* magazine, *The Post* and *The Daily News?* Tell me, what's the thrill of putting out for a known gangster, especially one who parks his marriage in a space called "reserved for when I'm bored"? But the tabloids sucked up to him up like oranges in winter.

One story that made the rounds, though not necessarily in print, claimed that while dining at Le Cirque one evening with a group of friends, Johnny spied a beautiful blonde at the next table surrounded by a crowd of happy people. Next to her sat a heavyset balding man whose loud and commanding manner designated him as the host. The man's possessive gestures toward the gorgeous blonde with the diamond wedding band also tagged him as the husband of a trophy wife. But what's this? The blonde is also giving Johnny the once-over, an interesting if not irresistible combination. Eye contact turned into an evening's entertainment for the two. At one point, the blonde excused herself from the table and headed for the restroom. On the way back, she brushed against Romano's chair, neatly dropping into his lap a piece of paper that contained her name and telephone number. He winked at his companions, and they knew he had scored again.

In retrospect, one could say that the brain power that motivated the pretty young thing into a marriage contract with the fat guy doesn't add much to her résumé as a Phi Beta Kappa. Go one step further: Seeking to be involved with Johnny Romano made as much sense as offering to cohabit with Osama bin Laden.

Thirteen

Frank stepped along briskly after leaving Murphy's Bar and headed toward the taxi stand. It was all I could do to keep up. He told the Haitian driver (in perfect dialect) to take us to Thirtieth and Madison, Frank's home office, then quickly lit up a Marlboro and started scribbling in his notebook.

I know your mind is working in top form now, hon. Do you feel like sharing? I received the usual nonresponse. Nevertheless, it was like old times being together and even more exciting to observe him at his professional best. So absorbed in getting his thoughts down on paper, Frank was not the least bit phased by the Haitian's efforts to prove his manhood on the mean streets of Manhattan. It was nearly five—rush hour—and there was no doubt our driver had a death wish. We were careening through the traffic-clogged streets at a dangerous pace. "Reckless endangerment" was a phrase that kept running through my mind, but neither Frank nor the driver seemed to care. That we arrived at all, I considered an act of charity. Frank flipped some green stuff to the future winner of the Indy 500. The latter flashed a brilliant smile and drove off in search of his next victim.

We took the elevator to the fifth floor and, when the doors opened to the clacking noise of computers, printers and fax machines, Frank looked pleased. Hi-theres and how-are-yas rolled off his tongue like happy oil as we made our way across the expanse of the floor. Frank was clapped on the back, hugged and kissed so many times, I thought we'd never make it to Maggio's corner, which turned out to be our destination. Maggio had been to my funeral, of course, but because of the circumstances, we hadn't had any opportunity to talk. I decided to make the effort now.

Long time no see! I offered, cringing at the cliché. After this brilliant opening, I was glad he didn't respond.

Maggio, the shorter of the two by half a head, had been working with Frank more than twenty years. I noticed the former had put on some weight since I saw him last and had no doubt it was due to his wife Angela's fabulous cooking. As I recall, she made an unforgettable cannelloni with tomato sauce as well as oodles of other high-caloric Italian delights. Ah, but that's another subject, along with the rest of my good memories. I would have enjoyed greeting Maggio more directly but accepted my limitations, such as they were. Instead, I paid close attention to the dialogue that followed.

"Got a lot of good stuff piling up, Frank. Interested?"

Frank shook his head. "No way, and I'm telling you why. Annie didn't just drown. She was murdered."

Maggio's grin disappeared. "No shit. Who the hell would want to do Annie?"

That's what I'd like to know!

"And that's just what I'm gonna find out—with your help maybe."

"Anything. You name it."

Frank lowered his voice. "What can you tell me about Johnny Romano?"

Maggio shook his head slowly. "You don't want to know."

I was getting this weird feeling again. *Psst . . . Frankie, be real careful here.* It wasn't that I didn't trust Maggio. I was clear on that, but Romano, he was not a guy to fool around with. I tried to recall what I'd read about him in a brave *Time magazine* exposé the year before. The piece began with this tidbit:

> When Johnny Romano was baptized, the assembled guests included the heads of two Mafia families, their wives, children and assorted associates—enough to fill St. Francis of Assisi Church on West Thirty-first Street in Manhattan and then some. It wasn't just the

> size of the crowd that distinguished it from the usual baptismal ceremony; it was the celebrity status of so many of the guests. . . .

The author, no longer living by the way, claimed he'd interviewed a close member of Johnny's family who had attended the event. All the facts in the article were purported to be true:

> Salvatore Romano was Johnny's proud father. With his arm around his beautiful apple-cheeked wife, he vowed he would dedicate the rest of his life, and that of his newly baptized son, to the business of "The Family."

As the world found out later, Salvatore's magnanimous offer fell due only three years later when he was shot to death trying to collect on a debt for his boss. That's when young Johnny was invited, along with his attractive mother, of course, to live in the boss's compound, where the two were no doubt welcomed into the day-to-day life of the busy household.

Ensuing gossip grew into a bad fairy tale: The head of the family, having sired four beautiful daughters, yearned for a son. Since it appeared he was to be denied this desire, Mr. Big took young Johnny under his wing and taught him everything he needed to know about the family business.

The article continued for another half a page with more of the same.

Maggio and Frank were reviewing similar background information when I pulled myself out of my reverie.

Suddenly Maggio zoomed in on Frank and asked, "Why are you coming to me?"

His friend stared back at him and after a long pause said, "You know why, pal. Because Romano's your cousin."

If I could have, I would have vomited right there on the spot. *Jeez! Did you say Maggio related to that scumbag?*

Maggio alternated between stammering and shaking his head before turning pleading eyes at Frank. "Guess that's why you're the best in the business," he finally said. Then he drew himself together. "But did you also know that my family doesn't want anything to do with him? Look, despite the money Hollywood's made on the subject, not all Italians are tied to the Mafia!"

"Hell, Maggio, I'm hep to that. I'm not accusing you of anything. I just want to find a way to get to this guy because I think he had something to do with Annie's death." Then he related what he'd learned from Marian and Roger.

Maggio continued to shake his head in disbelief. "Shit! Can the police put Johnny at Sands Point?"

I leaned in, waiting for the answer.

"No. That's just it. There's no mention of Romano being anywhere near the Spurgeon digs the night Annie was murdered."

"So?"

"So maybe he has a longer reach than anyone supposed. . . ."

"You mean, Johnny had Annie killed by using someone at the party?"

Frank nodded, and I felt even sicker than dead.

"Look," Maggio said. "I can't talk to you here. I'll be finished in about half an hour. Your place?"

My guy nodded.

"I'll call Angela and tell her I'll be late."

Frank hailed a cab, and we headed for his apartment. I was too absorbed in Frank's theory to focus on our driver's nationality. It just didn't matter. Could I ever come to grips that someone, possibly one of my co-workers, had something to do with my murder? Once more I wondered who? And why? I started going over the guest list again, this time putting everyone on the suspicious side of the page. I kept coming back to the same point in the circle: Who could have possibly had a connection to Romano? Greedy Claudia? Innocent Matt? Good friend Roger? Schmucky Harold? Silly Marian?

As per Frank's direction, the taxi stopped half a block from the apartment. Frank made an end run to the liquor store where he picked up a fifth of Chivas Regal, a carton of Marlboros and a huge bag of chips.

Perfect diet, right? *Watch your cholesterol, hon! You don't want to go to seed all together.* But he didn't appear interested in my advice.

Frank had plenty of time for a long hot shower before Maggio arrived. After fixing drinks for the two of them, my guy lit a cigarette and gestured toward his friend.

"As I understand it," Maggio began, "Johnny went to work for Luke Snyder after his boss was killed. Rumor has it that it was Snyder who gave the signal. Anyhow, any port in a storm, as the saying goes, so Johnny signed on with Luke. They refer to him as 'the eradicator.' "

"Meaning . . . ?"

Maggio bit his lip. "What do you think that means? He's creative. Has all kinds of ways to make trouble disappear."

Frank just stared into space. "What I'm wondering about is this: If Romano was involved, how the hell did he accomplish it? According to reports, he was nowhere near the Spurgeon place."

That's what I said before, Frankie.

"So who did he get to do his dirty work? And how? By the way, did I mention the autopsy turned up evidence of rohypnol?"

That's the date-rape drug, Maggio, if you can believe it.

Frank was saying almost the same thing at the same time I was.

Just like the old days. Right, hon?

Maggio was scratching his head. "The date-rape drug? I don't get it."

"Simple. One or two capsules in a glass of wine makes the victim a pushover, literally. Someone slipped the stuff into her drink, maneuvered her near the pool, and the rest is history."

"Sonofabitch!"

"Exactly."

I'm in total agreement.

"Okay," Maggio continued. "Given that Johnny is involved, what would be his reason? I mean, Annie . . . How in the hell could she cause trouble for him?"

"Your cousin's married, right?"

Maggio nodded.

"And Annie caught him and a client in the sack. She told Roger Franklin that Romano captured her face in a freeze-frame."

"Yeah, but I hardly think Johnny has to worry about his wife objecting—if she values her life, that is. Hold on! I just remembered something."

"Yeah?"

"About Luke Snyder. As I hear tell, Snyder didn't mind an occasional fling, but Johnny seemed to make a career out of the dames. Maybe Luke thought Johnny's overindulgence might be bad for business."

"Ah." Frank inhaled deeply, and two shafts of smoke streamed from his nostrils like a car's exhaust on a cold morning. "So maybe Johnny decided to cover himself before Annie shared the news?"

Cover himself—like shut me up?

"The only way he could do that, if he couldn't be there himself, was by . . ."

"USING SOMEONE ELSE!" the two finished together.

Oy. Only Ma's most often used outcry could express my shock. *You're saying someone—probably a person I'd known and trusted for years and years—drugged and pushed me into the pool on the orders of Johnny Romano?* This was enough to make a dead person feel even worse.

A large piece of the puzzle fell into place: motive. I was right. It wasn't money; it was self-preservation: Johnny Romano's. A coverup, engineered by Romano to avoid his own extermination by Luke Snyder. I was simply in the wrong place at the wrong time: the Shine apartment. Romano orchestrated the trip, all right, but since he was not at Sands Point that day, who was the designated driver? I vowed to run the names of all those present through my mental Rolodex, this time with a fresh perspective.

Frank and Maggio traded ideas a little longer until Maggio bolted for the door around seven-thirty. "Gotta go. Angela's holding dinner."

Frank waved him off, grabbed his notebook and began scratching some notes.

I waited a couple of minutes before interrupting. *Listen, Frankie, if Romano's behind this thing—and I can buy that—I still can't imagine which one of my so-called friends would or could have gone along with it.* Silence. On the other hand, maybe it wasn't an old acquaintance, but a new entry: Michael Rheims. Why was I always so trusting?

Are you listening? Another stupid question. And then it dawned on me. Maybe Frank was the experienced investigator, but I was the one with the secret weapon.

I caught up with Romano and Fannie Shine in the latter's apartment ten minutes later and wondered for the umpteenth time what excuse Fannie had given her husband about the delay in her joining him in California. At this moment, whatever Fannie had held all of Romano's attention and vice versa. The two of them were in the living room, guzzling wine and noshing on each other's ears. Everything about the man was a cliché, from his jet-black hair and full lips to his piercing, dark eyes. And why do the guys always get the long, thick lashes?

Fannie had on a pair of tiny, tight white shorts and a sleeveless T-shirt, minus bra. Now, I have nothing against a surgically enhanced bosom, but the contrast between her tiny waist and her amply endowed mammary glands was mesmerizing, at least for Johnny. Every time Fanny moved, his eyes followed the rolling hills. When the lovers finally came up for air, Fanny sighed with pleasure; then a frown marred the surface of her otherwise unlined face.

"Johnny," she sighed, "I'm truly worried about Oscar finding out about us."

Now you're worried? Maybe if your brain had responded sooner, I would still be here.

Her lover's eyes responded directly to Fannie's bubbies. "What are you worried about? Told you I'd take care of it, sweetheart."

Sure—"take care of" is the operative phrase.

"But . . ."

"I told you not to worry. I got it covered."

I knew what he meant. I leaned in closer for the name of his messenger, but Lothario had other things on his uh, mind.

"Shhh, not another word."

Fannie's deep sigh of relief sent her undulating anatomy into perpetual motion, and Johnny's whole body closed in on the choice targets. His next words were muffled, but I think he said something like "Would I let anything happen to my best girl?"

Exit time. I couldn't deal with anymore of that shtick. Besides, Romano's remarks vis à vis covering his indiscretions begged to be shared.

Charlene lived on the second floor of a modest two-family house on a quiet street in Hicksville. She was just returning from Waldbaum's Food Market when I arrived and did not take it kindly when I offered to help her carry some bundles.

"A heart attack is what you're likely to give me with that approach," she admonished.

Sorry. I just haven't figured out yet how to get your attention in a quiet way.

"Do you mind if we wait until I get the door open? I don't need to have my neighbors calling the men in the little white coats when they see me talking and no one's in sight."

Right.

When we were safely inside, she turned in my general direction and bravely inquired, "So, what brings you here?"

I told her about Johnny Romano. *I know he's involved in this.*

"Romano, huh? Do you remember seeing him in Sands Point on the Fourth?"

I've drawn a blank about that episode.

Charlene spent the next few minutes trying to help me recall some facts, but my memory would not cooperate, so I shared with her the porno scene I'd just witnessed between Romano and Fannie. She was obviously fascinated by the possibilities.

"I think my partner would be interested in this, but how can I tell him I got it from you? He'll think I've gone completely off the deep end."

I see what you're getting at. I knew she was thinking out loud, not really waiting for me to offer a solution.

". . . and Frank—he shouldn't be the odd-man-out either."

Of course not. *Hey! I just thought of something.* (Not really.)

Maybe you could call him about another matter and sort of lead into it.

Then I fed her the same stuff on Romano that Marian-the-microphone had shared with Frank, adding a warning: *But be creative, my friend, and try to remember you didn't get this from me.* Jeez! I should be getting hardship pay for the extra effort I have to spend in order to get one lousy point across.

Charlene made a move for the telephone directory.

Don't bother; it's unlisted. I shot out the number and shoved the phone in her direction. *See you later,* I tossed, before whooshing myself from her neat place to Frank's rat's nest. After all, who else but me could keep things moving?

Frank sat at a table on which were two legal pads, a laptop and myriad scraps of paper, plus the ever-present ashtray. The big guy was working all right, his signature cigarette smoldering between compressed lips. I parked myself on the edge of the bed, counting the telephone rings.

I hollered at him after the fourth. *Pick up, dammit!* But the genius was hard at work and let his answering machine do the work. In between hunting and pecking on his laptop, Frank kicked up the volume.

"Hi, it's Charlene Williams—"

My guy grabbed for the phone so fast, I thought he was going to swallow his cigarette. "Hello! Charlene? Yeah, I just got out of the shower."

Liar, liar, pants on fire.

"Listen, I'm soaking wet. Give me your number; I'll call you right back." Frank was grinning like a kid as he wrote down the pilfered information. It occurred to me that the great investigative reporter had discovered many avenues to Nirvana. What I suspected was true. His hormones were still intact.

Fourteen

My guy didn't get much in the way of quality sleep that night. I know because I hung around for most of it. He was agitated when he returned from his meeting with Charlene. Yep, he'd talked her into that part of it but had to settle for the corner coffee shop near her place. I found it titillating that he never got to see what color her bedroom carpet was. One smart lady. She was probably the best challenge he'd come up against since Margaret Thatcher. Oh, well, this was only the first act. Stick around.

Frank had been up since around four in the morning, jotting down stuff on legal pads. Evidently his pocket notebook was not big enough to hold all the good news. I knew he was zooming in on Johnny Romano. Now Charlene and I were doing the same. And in the morning after her partner filled him in, Martola would join in.

I'd been asking myself which of my acquaintances would work with that gangster? And why? My list of possibilities shrank to two: Claudia was first on my list. She might share some common attributes with the guy. After all, she was something of a thief herself. And what about that peculiar telephone conversation when her normally polished voice evolved into a *Saturday Night Live* skit of an uneducated foreigner? Now *there's* a part of her life of which Harold is unaware. Maybe that other part of her world also includes Romano. Okay, here's a motive: I'm thinking she and that unsavory character had an affair, and Romano threatened to tell Harold if she didn't do his bidding: Namely, drug me and dunk me in the pool. *Hmm.* I think that flies. Charlene will appreciate that one. My only other possibility is Michael.

In this scenario, Michael is not at all what he appears to be. He's actually part of an international criminal organization with connections in New York. And he's got a record. And he and Romano have worked together before. And his cover is Marks and Spencer, but he's actually here to kill me. And . . . and . . . and I'm beginning to think that death has taken leave of my brains. Talk about a vivid imagination. Okay, okay, let's just try this one again. Michael and Romano have some connection. But what? They're obviously not related. Maybe Johnny is blackmailing Michael. That strange letter from Michael's sister that I found at his apartment. *Hmm . . .*

When I came out of my profound meditation, I realized that Frank was preparing to go out. I wished it were Charlene, but the way he was dressed and the fact that he needed a shave indicated otherwise.

Frankie, please contact Martola and Charlene! This is no time for a solo flight. Listen to me, dammit. Johnny Romano is not a nice person. Look at me! This is what happens when you get on the wrong side of that guy.

I was yelling as loud as circumstance permitted, but so far, my communication system was only connected to Charlene. Ignoring me completely, my guy was collecting his tape recorder, checking batteries and pocketing an extra pack of Marlboros. He was oblivious to all.

This was useless. Did I have to stand by and watch David go against the giant without a slingshot? *I know one thing, mister. You're not going without me.*

We were waiting for the elevator when Frank began patting his pockets again. He turned around and unlocked the door to his apartment.

Don't worry, I growled, *I saw you put the damned cigarettes in your pocket*. But it wasn't cigarettes my guy was fishing for.

Frank slid his hands under a pile of underwear in the bottom drawer of his dresser, and to my utter shock came up with a Colt forty-five revolver.

Oh, no! Please, Frankie. That's crazy. . . .

But he was out of the apartment, me sticking like a shadow, and the two of us slipping into the elevator just before the doors closed. Now he patted his other pocket and nodded with a grimace. I suppose he was satisfied that he, too, had a killing weapon.

In the taxi, Frank used his cell phone to call Maggio's apartment. "Good, you're home. Can I drop by for a sec? Oh, about ten minutes. Right." Frank had already given the driver directions to the modest apartment on Second Avenue and Twenty-third.

After hugging Maggio's youngest daughter and promising Angela he'd come to dinner soon, Frank waited until he was alone with his friend before speaking. "Tell me where I can find your cousin."

"You're crazy, man."

That's what I keep telling him.

"Never mind. I just want to have a conversation."

Maggio scratched his head. "Like, I'm not your friend?"

"C'mon, I'm no amateur. I deal with bigger bums every day and manage to get at the truth. Why shouldn't I have a go at Romano? Never mind. I'm not arguing with you. Just give me the damned address where I can find this guy."

I could see Maggio was struggling with his conscience, but he also knew with whom he was dealing. There was no doubt Frank was aiming to talk to the gangster with or without his friend's help. After some hesitation, Maggio finally gave up the name of a pool hall on a Hundred and Sixty-third off the Grand Concourse. But he warned, "Take it easy, fella. This guy's got no scruples."

Frank nodded. Being a glutton for adventure, he hailed the first available taxi, and we were off. It just so happens that the flavor of the day was jazz, American style. Refreshing, I thought, for Frank to speak to the driver in a language even I could understand.

I had deep forebodings about this plan, though I kept reminding myself there was nothing more that could happen to me than what had already occurred on July Fourth. It was

Frank I was concerned about. If he weren't such a stubborn, pigheaded . . . What was the use? Even if I could get through to him, he wouldn't listen.

Despite the mayor's efforts at cleaning up the City, litter flew around us like crumpled birds when we stepped out of the cab. The sidewalks seemed to say: "This is just the way it is. WANNA DO SOMETHING ABOUT IT?" With me clinging closely to Frank, we headed toward the entrance of Billy's Bowling and Billiards.

A malodorous mist of cigarettes and beer descended upon us when we entered this world of shades. The interior was dark, and it took a minute or so to get accustomed to the selective light in which these afficionados shot pool. Immediately to the left were seven green felt-covered pool tables, each with its own shaded light hanging over the center and casting a bull's-eye of hard yellow below. Farther along, stood a fully equipped bar with a dozen empty stools. The sound of bowling balls brushing smooth wooden alleys could be heard somewhere in the distance. Three of the pool tables were occupied, but all conversation stopped when Frank appeared.

"Help ya?" a gruff disembodied voice boomed in the darkness.

It's still not too late to make a run for it, hon.

"Yeah," my big, dumb brute of an ex-husband answered. I knew he wasn't talking to me.

Stepping out into the half-light was a rough-looking man whose shaved head allowed no distraction from his threatening expression. He came pretty close to Frank, but my guy, half a head taller, didn't give an inch.

"I'm looking for Johnny Romano."

The murmuring around us stopped.

"And who wants to see him?"

"He wouldn't know my name. Is he in?"

"I'll see." The man disappeared behind a door on the far side of the bar.

Maybe we should come back later, Frankie, preferably with two or three squad cars.

A minute or so later, the shaved head reappeared. He motioned to Frank, who headed toward the open door.

Okay, if you insist on doing this crazy thing, I'm going with you. That way, if something happens, we'll be together in eternity.

The mysterious room behind the door turned out to be a spacious, well-lit, air-conditioned office, and stepping out from behind the desk was Johnny Romano. Now that I could again study him up close and personal without losing anything more in the way of life or limb, I stared at the Mediterranean good looks of this six-foot-tall hunk and reminded myself why women were so willing to compromise themselves for a close encounter with Crimedom's best-known crook. Movie-star handsome, I thought, with the only imperfect feature being his nose. And for that, one could easily deduce it had been broken during some earlier altercation, about which smart people would not want to be acquainted.

"You wanted to see me?" Romano asked.

"Yeah. My name is Frank Dowd."

Romano didn't flinch.

"It was my ex-wife who was killed on the Fourth."

Sprouting a sleazy grin, Romano shook his head and shrugged his shoulders. "Should I know anything about that?"

I'll give him credit. This miserable excuse for a human being was cool. *That's it, Frankie. You're not going to get him to admit he had anything to do with it. Please! Let's leave now. The cops will get him sooner or later. Please?*

But my sweetie was on a roll. "I just wanted to see you and to let you know that I don't forget. . . ."

I had to confess that the dialogue sounded like the script from a *Godfather* film.

The easy smile slid off the edge of Romano's face, and two tough-looking guys who had been observing from the couch were suddenly on their feet. Their boss waved them back.

"Are you threatening me?"

Stop it now, Frankie, while you're ahead, and let's get the hell out of here. Please?

My honey stares down the bad guy and gets his shot in anyway. "You'll be seeing me again," he says, and turns toward the door.

"Yeah," Romano answers, and with exaggerated sarcasm, adds, "Sorry for your loss!"

Out on the street, I turned to Frank: *I consider it a fait accompli that Romano left your head on your shoulders, you big dummy! What do you think you achieved with that dumb-ass display of bravado?*

Of course I didn't get a response. My big man was too busy looking for a cab. One came along after a few minutes, and we hopped aboard.

After determining the man's nationality (Hungarian), Frank directed him away from this unsavory neighborhood, and we headed downtown. Our driver, who had been led into this Bronx maze, was just as elated to get back into Manhattan where he would surely be led astray once again after he dropped us off. Why do they do this?

We arrived at Matt Sterling's apartment around eleven-fifteen. Evidently, Frank aimed to use the weekend to interrogate all the folks on his list. I could hardly wait till we caught up with Harold and Claudia. For now, though, it was Matt's turn.

He lived on Sixty-third, between Park and Lexington, a darned good address, too. I'd never been inside his place and always assumed it was because he was a young bachelor involved in yuppie activities who wasn't into entertaining, but the neighborhood was rather plushy for a young guy just starting out. A doorman spoke through an intercom and evidently received an okay. On the fifth floor, Frank rang the doorbell. After a couple of beats, an unfamiliar male voice on the other side of the door asked who was there. Frank identified himself. The process of locks and chains being reversed took a few seconds. Then the door swung open.

I didn't recognize the man standing barefoot just inside the foyer. About forty-five, with light brown hair and moustache, he was wrapped in a pale blue paisley bathrobe the same color as his eyes.

Smiling pleasantly, he extended his hand. "I'm Benjamin Hollis."

My guy didn't hesitate. "Frank Dowd." He smiled easily and shook hands, inquiring after Matt.

"Oh, I recognize your name. I'm sorry about Annie. Matt's still sleeping. Shall I wake him?"

The intimacy with which this guy was sharing this news slapped me in the face like a wet herring, as my mother would say, and resulted in one of the few times I was ever struck dumb. *Who is Benjamin Hollis?* I finally sputtered, knowing full well the answer. Suddenly, it all made sense.

I didn't so much care that the adorable Matt was gay. I wondered why I hadn't caught on before. Maybe (the other half of my brain reasoned) because he wasn't ready to share the news. Well, the cat's out of the closet now, but it won't alter my affection for the kid. However, wait till Claudia finds out. She'd been planning to audition Matt for, shall we say, a higher position?

Frank, in the meantime, never missed a beat. "Sleeping, huh? I was hoping to be able to talk with him. Thought he might be able to help shed some light on Annie's accident. Guess I should have called first. . . ." He allowed his voice to trail away and slumped his shoulders in exaggerated disappointment.

"Oh, I don't think Matt would mind if I woke him. He's been talking of nothing else since it happened. Give me a few minutes."

Benjamin disappeared down the hall, and Frank whipped out a cigarette. Before lighting it, though, he searched around for an ashtray. None being visible, he replaced the cigarette in the pack, frowning.

See? You could really give them up if you tried.

Benjamin returned after a couple of minutes, nodding and smiling. "Matt will be out in just a minute. I'll just get the coffee started." He headed toward the kitchen, whistling.

Psst . . . Frankie, something just occurred to me that I don't really want to believe. But if Matt could keep his gayness secret, maybe he's holding back on something else.

When Mr. Adorable appeared, he was wearing cotton knit gym shorts and a white T-shirt. From bulging biceps to smooth, tight buns, every well-conditioned muscle in Matt's body smiled. His sandy hair was uncombed, and a shy, boyish grin preceded his extended hand.

Nah. Forget what I just said, hon. This boitchick *is too cute to be a rat.*

Frank shook hands heartily and even gave Matt a jockey

punch to the shoulder. "Hey, there, fella. Never got a chance to congratulate you on becoming a full-time member of Royal Roosts's staff. Annie was real proud of you."

While Matt blushed through the acknowledgment, Benjamin was returning from the kitchen carrying a tray with coffee fixings and a plate of muffins. He smiled at the exchange, adding, "Oh, Matt is so modest. I keep telling him he's going to be great."

"That's just what Annie said!" agreed Frank, trying to bring the conversation back to the purpose of his visit. He reached out for the mug of coffee offered by Benjamin, shaking off the milk and sugar.

Matt settled down close to Benjamin. Hell, why not? This was what he needed, after all.

"I, um . . . I feel real bad about Annie," the kid began. "She was very nice to me when I first started working summers at Royal Roosts."

Frank put on a friendly face and just nodded.

"I sure hope you find the guy who did it."

"That's why I'm here, Matt. Thought you might be able to help."

"I don't know what to say. Told the police everything I could remember about the evening."

"I'm sure you did," said Frank, allowing himself to look sad. "But would you mind if I asked a few questions? Maybe the answers would fill in the blanks, just for my own peace of mind."

The young tiger was touched. "Sure thing." He reached for a muffin.

Frankie took out his notebook and after a brief review assumed his therapist pose. "You remember when Annie was discovered in the pool floating facedown?"

I don't like to be reminded of that part, hon.

Matt signaled a yes.

"Who was it that first noticed her?"

The kid swallowed. "I don't really know." His eyes fluttered slightly.

It was obvious that he was not accustomed to lying. But

why? I could think of no possible connection between Matt and the likes of Romano.

"Oh?" Frank prodded. He was probably churning the same waters.

"Yeah . . . I think I was talking to"—he glanced at Benjamin—"to Claudia . . . and, um, I turned around to get my beer. It was on the table, you know? And . . . uh, she—Annie, that is—was just there . . . in the pool, on her stomach, not moving. Oh, it was just awful!"

Benjamin placed his hand on Matt's shoulder in a gesture of support, but Matt was looking less and less confident.

"I see," said Dr. Frank, filling the void.

Something's not right here, Frankie. I distinctly remember Michael telling the detectives he had been sent by Agnes to help disperse the crowd at the gate, and that Matt joined him on the way back. But did my sweetie appreciate this feedback? No, he was totally focused on the kid who continued to ramble.

"Well, everything started happening at once, you know? Some of the women were screaming, 'Get her out, get her out.' It was just, like, awful. . . ."

"I can imagine."

Frankie! I'm getting those flashes again. Something's trying to come through. I can feel it but just can't get hold of . . . whatever it is.

"So, if I understand," Frank continued, completely ignoring me, "you had your back to the pool?"

Matt nodded solemnly.

"I see . . ."

"And . . . and, after that, all hell broke loose."

Matt's eyes began to fill as he recalled the scene, and Benjamin looked desperate to comfort him.

Let's leave now, hon. Maybe they want their privacy.

We did take off a few minutes later, but I felt very unsettled about Matt's report.

Fifteen

I needed to keep myself up to snuff about Johnny Romano's activities. The last thing I wanted was any more surprises. Finding out where he lived was not a problem; stealing myself to visit him required *chutzpeh.* Frank had assured me long ago that I had plenty of that, so I headed out to the gangster's place in Island Park.

Romano's house was a two-story brick and shingle affair of modest proportions, located on a tree-lined street swarming in innocence: the sound of children's laughter as they played catch in the late-afternoon sun; young mothers rocking their carriages while exchanging gossip and recipes, and so forth. Why, the whole scene reeked of Martha Stewart goodness! Was this a déjà vu from the fifties or what? I wouldn't have been surprised to see Donna Reed peeking out her kitchen window or her all-knowing husband arriving home armed with fresh philosophical insight. Typical middle-American family, my eye!

I honed in on the pleasant-looking young woman nearest the door of Romano's house. About thirty, she had dark, shoulder-length hair, a clear complexion and a full mouth, which had recently been treated with lip liner and gloss. Pretty, yes, but she appeared edgy. With the sound of every automobile's motor, her eyes flicked nervously toward the street. I suspected she was anticipating the return of her lord to his castle. At last, a long, dark Cadillac rolled into view. Her smile froze, and I could see her spine stiffen. There's fear here.

Her next words rang out sharply, "Anthony, your father's home."

"In just a minute, Ma," a smaller version of Romano called back.

"No. I'm telling you, now!"

The boy made an unhappy face, mumbled something to his friends and shuffled toward his house. His father emerged from the car, rumpled the top of the boy's head and draped an arm around his shoulders. "How's it going, kiddo?"

The young mother smiled openly now, her husband having given all the outward signs of being in a good mood. Jeez! Imagine having to live one's life never knowing when the bomb will detonate.

Except for his nervous wife, I was witnessing what appeared to be a normal home life. As if anything normal could be attributed to the murderous, unfaithful Romano. I didn't have to wait long to see the other side, though.

While his wife was cleaning up after dinner, the cheat was in the other room, breathing heavily into the phone. "Sure, baby, you know I do."

I imagined the subject being discussed had nothing to do with the stock market.

The little woman called from the other room. "You feel like having coffee tonight, Johnny?" And, after receiving no response, she repeated the question twice more.

"Hold for a sec, will you?" the king whispered into the phone. Covering the mouthpiece, he barked, "How many times have I told you not to bother me when I'm on a business call?"

Yeah, you bum, especially when it's monkey business.

At this point, the party on the other end of the line must have been having privacy problems of her own. Lothario looked crushed. "Yeah, I understand. Well, when ya gotta go, ya gotta go."

How original!

Romano had a short fuse. He picked up an ashtray and threw it against the wall, shattering the peaceful evening with rage. His wife appeared at the doorway of the den, trembling.

"Clean up this mess!" her husband ordered.

She ran to get the broom. Romano glared at her a moment before ripping out his next words: "If you ever interrupt me again when I'm on the phone, I'll give you something you'll never forget. You got that?" She cowered.

I felt sorry for her, so I whooshed some of the ashes and butts toward the dust bin. She glanced toward the open window, grateful for what she thought was the source of the draft.

That miserable husband of hers was as volatile as a bottle of nitroglycerine. If he acts that way toward his wife, it doesn't take a genius to figure out how he treats his enemies, or even his underlings for that matter. I thought of the warning labels attached to potentially dangerous cleaning products: Do not swallow. Avoid getting into your eyes or on your skin. Should any of this product get in your eyes, flush immediately with cold water.

Like that would help?

I had to get rid of the bad taste. What better solution than a visit to Ma's (a return to the womb as it were)? But no one was home. I was about to push the panic button when it dawned on me that today was Saturday—*Shabbes*. Of course! Herb and Miriam must be holding her hostage at temple. When I joined them a few minutes later, Ma's blissful smile complemented her attractive new suit. I didn't remember ever seeing her in this one. Well, good for you, Ma! And your hair, lipstick and accessories are perfect. Miriam's influence? No, she goes for the dowdier look. *Hmm* . . . whazzup?

I sat down next to Ma, partially to pray and partially to get to the bottom of something that didn't quite gel. It was then that I spotted him—this guy across the aisle. He's staring at my mother. In temple, they allow such things? I ought to . . . Now what? She's returning his gaze, but not before rolling her eyes toward Miriam, who is standing next to her. Like, Miriam shouldn't see? Now her admirer is doing a clumsy pantomime, which, even though it's been a long time since I was a teenager, I translate as "I'll call you later." I quickly check Ma's reaction: a shy grin and coy lifting of her shoulders. I'm not out of this world that long that I can't see chemistry in the making. But . . .

my own mother? What's going on here? I swing over to where he's standing and study a possible connection to the worshipers on his left and right. He appears to be alone, but that still doesn't make it right. I was immersed in conflict, almost like drowning all over again. This was turning out to be a bad hair day.

Sixteen

With Frank temporarily detained with some overseas phone calls, I decided to indulge my curiosity vis-à-vis Harold Spurgeon.

Sunday notwithstanding, Harold was hunched over the desk in his apartment reviewing some contracts. I could see that his faded brown hair was thinning at a rapid pace. The emerging bald spot on the crown was sprouting freckles, somewhat like a latter-day Huckleberry Finn, but not nearly as cute. He was dressed in a pair of dark trousers and a button-down Oxford shirt, not exactly casual weekend wear. Well, the sleeves were turned up, but very neatly, of course.

Harold couldn't hear me sigh. *For God's sakes! Lighten up; it's the weekend.* But I'm thinking all those years of private school did nothing more than render the guy a hopeless dork.

I strolled around his bachelor pad and lo and behold! In the closet of the master bedroom, I found evidence of Morticia—well, all right, Claudia. I'll bet Harold rose to the occasion when the bitch slithered around in that lacy stuff. The huge mirrored bathroom (with double-size hot tub) also demonstrated that she had staked out her territory. Assorted bottles and jars claimed most of the shelf space. I found an array of brushes, combs, and one small but very expensive bottle of Givenchy perfume. Altogether, not enough to lay claim to the Spurgeon millions, but a reasonable start. When the phone rang, I hustled into the library to catch what I could from Harold's end of the conversation.

His face paled. "No. I most certainly did not discuss it with anyone." His hands were shaking. Early Parkinson's?

My curiosity was piqued. Could be Agnes raking him over the coals, or Claudia seeing to her future, or who knows? In any event, Harold had the courage of a cow. Within two minutes, however, the phone rang again, and this time there was no doubt it was the ambitious Ms. Harmon herself. A pinkish bloom streaked across Harold's vapid face.

"I thought you'd be here by now, dearest," he whined. "Yes, but . . . I expected you an hour ago. Of course I understand. Another half an hour then." He hung up the phone looking like a child who'd been denied dessert.

And as I couldn't think of anything more boring than hanging out with Harold Spurgeon, I left to check in on Ma where I knew I'd be more appreciated.

Herbie had already left for morning services at the synagogue. He would be reciting the *kaddish* for me, I knew, and I felt strangely grateful. Funny how religion comes to people at the end of their lives. Ma and Miriam were just finishing breakfast, and the children were—where else?—watching television.

"How about the other half bagel?" asked my sister, whose mouth was working on a full load.

I knew she wasn't talking to me.

Ma shook her head. "No, dolling, I couldn't eat another bite."

Miriam countered with the old saw, "You have to keep up your strength."

Personally, I could never understand that one. When someone goes through an emotional upheaval, the brain often turns off the hunger drive. There must be a reason for that. I remember when Poppy died, neither Ma nor I could eat. For others, though, food becomes a solace during stressful times, so we tried to ease the pain with assorted goodies. It didn't work. Our mutual misery outweighed the need, but Miriam's appetite, as I recall, was unaffected. Why should my death be any different? At this very moment, she was happily smearing cream cheese on the bagel half Ma had refused and was soon stabbing at the lox with her fork.

"Well, there's no sense in it going to waste," she said. "Uh, Ma, I wanted to speak with you about something else."

"So? Speak."

"Uh . . . um. . . ."

"What's wrong with you? You're nuzzling again."

"It's just that . . ." My sister took a gulp of air. "Maybe you should give some more thought about moving in with us. You shouldn't decide too hastily."

"Again you're starting?"

"Ma . . ."

"Don't start. You're a good daughter, but I'm not leaving here. I will be happy to visit, but this is my home. *Farshtaist?"*

"Okay, okay, I understand." She shoved the last of the bagel into her mouth and chewed silently.

I added my two cents: *And let that be the end of it!*

Ma looked tired but otherwise okay. Admittedly, I wondered how she would manage when Miriam, Herb and the kids returned to Ohio tomorrow. Perhaps, now that my father's side of the family had reopened the door to her, Ma could once again be a firsthand observer in the ongoing saga of the Edelsteins. That was as good a soap opera as anything on television and would certainly keep her occupied. That and canasta. I planned to keep an eye on her of course, but that could only be a one way dialogue. And, as close as she and Frank were, we all knew he'd soon be returning to his nomadic life. Maybe I could get her interested in a book club.

When Herbie returned, I picked up on the eye contact between him and his chief assistant. Ma didn't notice the quick exchange. Miriam shook her head in defeat, and Herb's shoulders sagged. I knew they meant well, but I was not about to see Ma usurped from her comfortable and independent lifestyle. Maybe somewhere down the road, but not yet. When I was sure the matter lay at rest, at least for the present, I decided to get on with the day's agenda. I had a brilliant idea. Why not take advantage of my present disguise to look in on Johnny Romano to see if (God forbid!) the jerk was still angry with Frankie.

* * *

Entry into Romano's private office proved much easier this time; however, I elected to remain near the door just in case the person in charge of my status decided to revoke my disguise. The man himself was there, along with his silent, ever-present, lackeys. Within minutes after my arrival, there was a rap on the door, and in stepped the mean-looking guy with the shaved head and three men I'd never seen before. Like characters in a play, Romano and his two thugs jumped to attention.

"Luke!" Johnny sputtered. "I wasn't expecting you."

I, too, gulped. So this was the infamous Luke Snyder.

Romano tried to embrace the older man, but the gesture proved awkward on account of it takes two to tango.

Luke Snyder, head honcho of his branch of the Family stepped into the room, anchored on either side by two unsmiling, burly specimens in hand-tailored suits. I could only guess that their clothes were designed to conceal any extraneous bulges their weapons might have otherwise created. And even though I hadn't been able to make contact with anyone up to this point, I feared it was just a matter of time before one of these bozos heard the nervous chattering of my teeth. I tried to concentrate on the big man himself.

Not nearly as good-looking as Romano, Luke Snyder nevertheless carried a certain dignity about him that was compelling. About sixty, but in good shape, the head of the Family was dressed in a pricey looking gray silk suit. The collar points of his white shirt framed the Windsor knot of his tie, a deep burgundy with silver stripes. To complement the picture, the overhead lights emphasized the silver in his well-groomed hair. All told, Luke Snyder seemed taller than his medium frame had at first suggested. But the awed silence that accompanied his arrival was built on fear, I knew.

Romano's bravado disappeared entirely. In a rather submissive gesture, he pulled out a chair for the boss of bosses and beckoned for him to sit down. "Can I get you something to drink?" he offered.

Snyder inclined his head. "A little too early in the day for me."

"Of course."

The clock on Romano's desk registered four o'clock, and if this Mr. Snyder had walked into my parlor at that time in the afternoon, I would have certainly opted for a double scotch. The same thing probably crossed Romano's mind, but it would have been extremely rude for him to indulge if Mr. Big Shot did not, so he settled for shaky hands instead. Oh, yes, I noticed. His boss probably did, too.

Romano inclined his head, waiting for his guest to announce whatever it was that brought him here.

The big man, however, bided his time. During the long pause, one of Romano's guys nervously cracked his knuckles. The look his boss shot him would have sent the stoutest heart running for cover. The noise stopped immediately, and Snyder quickly launched his missile.

"I was distressed to hear about the death of that young lady from the real-estate agency. I believe her name was Dowd."

Oh my God! You know about me?

Romano was equally shocked. His mouth slack, he raised his eyebrows in undisguised surprise and gestured with open hands. Words were unnecessary; he was already traveling the road to ruin. "I . . . well, uh . . ."

A brilliant comeback, no?

"Please don't lie to me or pretend you had nothing to do with it," continued Snyder.

Evidently, this was to be a one-way conversation, and Romano now knew to keep his mouth closed.

"We had an understanding that you would go to Newark to handle that other problem of mine. Instead, you saw fit to send a substitute. If I had wanted someone else to take care of the Newark problem, I would have said so.

"What disturbs me even more, though, is that these *adventures* of yours cause a lot of tongue-wagging. Our business does not need the publicity."

"But—"

Snyder silenced Romano with a hard look.

"And please don't insult my intelligence by telling me that the Shine bitch wouldn't say anything."

Romano blinked. (I took that to mean: How does he know her name?)

"Because (and here the timbre of Snyder's voice suddenly increased) SHE'S ALREADY BOASTING ABOUT YOUR BIG DUMB DICK TO EVERYBODY WHO WILL LISTEN!"

Romano and I gulped in unison.

"And now," he said, dropping his voice to a scary level, "Dowd's husband—I'm assuming you know he is the well-known reporter?—is out there as we speak, searching for answers to his ex-wife's murder. How long do you think it will take before he nails it on you? And how long after that before he tries to pull the rest of us down? And all because you couldn't keep the family jewels where they belong . . . like I asked you a million times." He glared at the frightened man before him to emphasize the point.

Na na na-na nah, you big jerk. See what you get? I slapped my hand over my mouth. But then, who could hear me? It was Romano who was the man of the moment, and in a not very desirable position, judging from his ashen face.

"Anything, Luke, I'll do anything!"

"Of course you will." The countenance of this fine gentleman returned to the actor who had made his entrance only minutes before. He smiled like a father whose son is about to make him proud. "Take care of him, Johnny, and call me after it's over."

No! You can't! I couldn't believe my ears. Luke Snyder had just given Romano an order to kill Frank, and I had to find some way to warn him. Charlene was my only option, but when I zoomed over to her apartment, she was not there. I made a dash for Frank's place only to see him disappearing into a taxi in front of his house. Figured he was on his way to Ma's, so I slipped in beside him.

Boy, have I got news for you! Wait a minute . . . What's this? . . . Aftershave?

As if that were not enough, he was wearing a clean shirt, pressed slacks and relatively neat sport jacket. It didn't take a genius to figure out that Frankie had a date. Um . . . I thought about it for less than ten seconds. Charlene? *Tell me it's Charlene, hon, and my confidence in you is restored.*

I didn't have long to wait. The cab headed toward Hicksville, and as we approached Charlene's neighborhood, Frank began smoothing back his hair. How sweet! *And see that? You didn't smoke one cigarette the whole trip out here!*

Charlene was waiting outside the door of her building talking to neighbors when our cab pulled up. I guessed that's why I'd missed her earlier. Something else. She'd foregone her favorite casual attire for a dress—and what a dress!—two-piece, short sleeve, peach linen. What you'd call the nth degree of feminine. The skirt came just above her knees and showed off previously hidden stunning legs. Charlene broke away from the group as Frank approached, and I would have told him to mop up the drool, but I didn't want to make him feel self-conscious. I made a decision then and there to keep my mouth shut altogether.

"Ready?" he asked.

Charlene looked up at him (shyly?) and smiled. We all moved back to the taxi where, out of deference to the young couple, I squeezed in front with the driver, an older gentleman from Lithuania who nevertheless found his way to the Midtown Tunnel and squeezed through it into Manhattan's unusual Sunday quiet. I didn't have long to wonder where luncheon was being served on this balmy, peaceful day of rest—Café Luxembourg, a hip bistro in the West Seventies. Think I know what Frank's got in mind for dessert. I went browsing around Lincoln Center while Tristan and Isolde went through the motions, telling myself it really didn't matter. Did you ever try lying to yourself? After an hour and a half of useless wandering, I sidled up the street toward the restaurant—just in time to see Frank and Charlene headed for an after-lunch stroll. Since we were still outdoors, tagging along didn't seem too overbearing.

It was worse than I expected. The two ambled along closely, Frank guiding Charlene with just the slightest touch under her elbow. He must have read that somewhere in a "How to Seduce Without Even Trying" manual, and it must be working because Charlene was sporting what looked like a goofy expression. Heck. Come to think of it, I wasn't gone from this world that long that I couldn't remember Frank's law: Touchy-feelies beget sparks. Ah, yes, and when electricity radiates from Frank Dowd, it's not easily forgotten.

It was fall of 1971 when most of my friends would be returning to college, but I'd lost my dad in July, and devotion to studies was the last thing on my mind. I tried a mindless sales job at Bloomingdale's and stood by, bemused, while the rest of New York's elite outfitted themselves for yet another year of pretense. From there, I moved to an assistant buyer's job, tolerating the low pay, but crowing to my former friends about my contacts in the garment industry. After a few years, I watched my contemporaries graduate from college, some even moving toward graduate degrees. And all the while, I told myself it didn't matter, but it wasn't true. The latter didn't become clear to me until I connected with Frank, and that's when my real education began.

Lovemaking orchestrated the background of our relationship, and the music never ended—not even after we married, not even after we divorced, not even though we allowed that we were human and would be seeing other people. Conceivably the only thing that could put a damper on the deal was death. So, it seemed, that's where we had finally arrived. I found out, however, that death doesn't destroy memories. So, was I jealous of Charlene because she was a living, breathing example of hot flesh for the taking? Conflicted might be a better word. I still wanted the best for Frank, and from where I stood, Charlene was a prime example. Guess it was time to pass the gavel.

I eyed the two of them, then pulled alongside expecting to hear their version of "Oh Promise Me," which goes to show that even I can be wrong.

". . . so I'm convinced Romano engineered Annie's murder."

"I don't disagree with that, but I'm curious. What convinced you?"

"I guess you wouldn't believe me if I said Annie told me."

"You're right. I wouldn't believe you."

I clomped a fist over my mouth before shooting any sass. "So, okay, just call it a detective's instinct."

Frank grinned down at her. "Not a woman's instinct?"

(Ah, he didn't forget how the mating dance went.) I knew he was trying to rekindle the flame, so I was glad I'd exercised control. They deserved that much. Charlene managed to keep the spotlight on the gangster-as-murderer for another ten minutes, but it was moot. They were pretty much in agreement on that subject. Anything else my ex had in mind fell to a distant second. Sure, he came close to some serious hand-holding in the cab ride home, but his overall batting average for the afternoon was dismal. The best I can say is that the door was left open. Charlene held out an olive branch when we arrived at her place.

"Frank, I know we've got some chemistry going here, but . . ."

"Yeah, the situation is a bit unusual."

"Yes, you have no idea how unusual." She flicked her eyes around the immediate vicinity. I knew she was trying to ascertain if I was near at hand, but for once, I was keeping my big mouth shut.

"Are you expecting someone?"

"Uh, no."

His grin was widening. "Look, I'm a big boy. A good-looking gal like you must surely be involved with someone."

"No! That's not it at all! Look, I can't explain. Not now, anyhow. This has nothing to do with you—or, actually, it does. I, that is . . ."

Frank cut her off. "You don't have to explain." He was turning to go when Charlene called him back.

"I want to thank you for a lovely afternoon," she blurted out quickly. "I really enjoyed myself." And before either her date or I could react, Charlene reached up and planted a sweet kiss on Frank's cheek. Then she pivoted neatly and headed toward the entrance of her building.

It took Frank several seconds to refocus. By golly! The man is blushing. Now I've seen everything. Frank gave the driver his address and settled back against the well-worn seat. His sweet-assed grin lingered at least ten minutes more, during which, he even forgot to light up a cigarette. But once started, he couldn't smoke just one. He'd had his break of the day. It looked like we were going to spend the rest of Sunday working.

I wasn't wrong. My guy threw himself into his work with a vengeance. Between pots of black coffee and an unending chain of cigarettes, he was wired. If Ma could see him now, she'd be shouting, "*Oy,* do you know what your insides look like?"

I tried to think of some way to warn him about Romano, but all he could focus on were his damned phone calls. With a Marlboro pasted between his lips and ashes dribbling down the front of his T-shirt, he exchanged several long conversations with Maggio and others whose names I didn't recognize. When he finally hung up the phone I figured he was mine at last. But, no, the blasted instrument rang yet again.

I can be patient a little longer, Frankie, but after this call, I want your full attention.

Yeah. He was really impressed with that.

Whap! Frank suddenly smashed out a half-smoked cigarette in the well of an ashtray already overflowing with squashed cancer. The stuff went flying in all directions. "How the hell did you—? Listen, Martola, I don't have to report to anyone." An angry flush flooded his forehead and began to spread across his cheeks.

Uh-oh. When an Irishman's face turns that color (and he's not holding a glass of whiskey) one wants to proceed with extreme caution. Jeez! Why couldn't these guys take a day off from the battle? The two wasted more precious minutes flexing their muscles before they were done. I felt I'd waited long enough for an audience with the pope.

Can't you see you're heading for big trouble? What makes you think you've got diplomatic immunity against the mob? And as if that isn't a problem in itself, how do you feel about long tentacles?

Listen, Frank, one can hardly argue with facts: If Johnny Romano was not present himself at Agnes Spurgeon's on the Fourth, it's a sure bet he got someone else to do his dirty work. Who was Romano's connection? I find it really difficult to believe that someone I've known for a long time did this to me—or worked for Romano, for that matter. What I'm saying is, if he got someone else to kill me, the guy won't have any problem servicing you either.

I tried banging on his shoulders for attention, but my efforts proved ineffectual.

Okay, so now you know about Michael Rheims, but what did he have to gain? Never mind. Let me put it another way: If he was Romano's agent and hadn't carried out orders, what did he have to lose? Does any of this give you any ideas?

His response to these important questions was to step out of his shorts, turn his backside to me and head for the shower.

I stormed after him, sending the wastebasket flying. He turned, frowned and shrugged his shoulders. So much for making an impression.

Seventeen

This whole thing was becoming a delicate balancing act. Like a circus juggler, I had to keep all the china plates in motion at once for fear one would fall and break. On Monday morning, Charlene and Martola were plotting the next step in their investigation. Of course I was standing by ready to help. I reminded Charlene about Luke Snyder's visit to Romano.

Frankie needs protection, for God's sake!

She went into her little coughing fit routine, which allowed us to head for the water fountain where I emphasized the importance of keeping up the pressure on Romano.

We've got to take away all opportunity to carry out Snyder's orders. Another thing, are you aware that four of the main characters' alibis do not fit? Did you get that about Claudia? Admiring the Matisse, she claims. Huh! With no one around to corroborate? She must think we're idiots!

"You've been busy, I see," she managed, just before we returned to her desk.

Almost as though he'd been listening, Martola scratched his head and said, "The Harmon broad can't verify her alibi. Hell, she could've said she was with the president in the Oval Office!"

Happy to see that your partner's not stupid.

I should have had more faith in both of them, for what I heard next was a true revelation. The detectives had checked further into Claudia's background and discovered a treasure trove of lies. She was not without family, as she had claimed, but the daughter of Polish refugees who emigrated here after World War II.

So she's common, like I've been saying all along. And why the subterfuge? Duh. It's the money, honey—Harold's, that is. Or at least it will be one day.

"Maybe Claudia suspected that Annie had found out about her background and killed her to keep her quiet?" Charlene mused.

"It's a motive," Martola acknowledged.

But I disagreed. *What's up with that? There's no connection to Romano. And, for the record, I didn't know anything about Claudia's genealogy.*

Charlene nodded. "On the other hand, if Harmon's guilty, don't you think she'd provide a more believable story?"

"Maybe yeah, maybe no. What about the boyfriend? Spurgeon says he was with her. If they're in cahoots, why in the hell didn't she just say they were together? They could've covered for each other."

Charlene shrugged her shoulders. "What's the motive? I'm not seeing where Harold Spurgeon had anything to gain. Their stories don't match. Is this a case of a really bad memory or deceit?"

I vote for the latter, not necessarily on Harold's part.

Overriding my remark, Charlene continued. "If money's at the bottom of this, we'll turn up something in the credit reports."

You're like a broken record with the money thing.

I think her partner agreed with me because he said, "Let's finish the big picture before we get to those particulars. For example, the kid, Matt Sterling."

That sweet thing? C'mon. I've practically watched him grow up. He wouldn't hurt a fly, much less me!

But Martola wasn't convinced. "Says he was talking with the Harmon broad. It would've been easy enough for her to agree. Again, who's lying?"

"If Sterling's lying, what's his motive?"

Martola threw his partner an accusing look, then grinned. "I thought it was your idea to focus on the money."

And I'm telling you to concentrate on the Romano connection.

"All right," Charlene agreed. "We'll leave him on top with the rest of the sinners."

The focus of their deliberation turned back to me. *Well, hello!* For the umpteenth time, the detectives tried to figure out what I had that was worth killing me for. And once again, Charlene noted that I had no known enemies, appeared to mind my own business and dated only occasionally. The most far-fetched incentive they could come up with was that someone might have been trying to get back at Frank.

Meaning, it could be anyone from Moammar Kaddafi to Idi Amin? Look, we've been running around in circles long enough. Let's get down to business here.

I saw Michael's name on one of the many sheets of papers and gently slid it from the pile and whooshed it across the table. Martola blinked, grabbed the page, then glanced at the ceiling fan accusingly and shook his head.

Charlene giggled. She was catching on to my tricks.

"Okay," Martola said, "let's get back to the British stud. Claims he went to the front gate, met the Sterling kid on the way back, and they returned together."

Personally, I have mixed emotions. My innermost feelings are that Michael could not have done such a thing. At least, I didn't want to believe that. On the other hand, the way he went after Charlene indicates the SOB has no scruples, so . . .

I tapped Charlene's side of the desk. *Woman to woman, what's your opinion?*

"I'm leaving the cell door open for that one," she said, without any hesitation.

Martola thought his partner was referring to his previous remark. "So, whose story do you buy?"

"Uh, about the Englishman? Can't figure out what his motive would be, though. He's got money, position, an easy life." She looked up inquiringly at her partner.

"Yeah, something just doesn't add up in this whole picture. It's like there's a piece missing."

Yes. And I'm still looking for the connection between the gangster and one of my so-called friends.

Martola suggested they clear up some of the loose ends at Royal Roosts, and Charlene and I readily agreed.

Upon entering the office, the detectives found Marian at the front desk, buffing her nails. The voice of the *Clarion* grinned widely. Of course, she would be more than willing to help the police in their quest to find the murderer of her dear friend, Annie.

That's me!

"Confidentially," she cooed, "I've also been working with Frank, poor Annie's ex."

Mop up the drool, sweetie, you're blushing.

If the detectives were annoyed that Frank was sleuthing behind their backs, they never let on. Instead, they donned attentive expressions and pulled up chairs.

No details were omitted. In fact, Marian reached down even farther to recapture scraps of information concerning her knowledge of the Shine deal:

"Of course you know that Annie's contracts went to Claudia," Marian offered, like a line in a script that called for a response.

Martola leaned across the desk. "Oh? And how much would that be?"

Here came a big "Hah!" from Marian, who was pleased the detective was reading his part correctly. "Normally, the commission is split fifty-fifty with the firm. But in this case . . . "—she lowered her voice, sweeping her eyes around the empty reception area like a poor imitation of a secret service agent—" . . . since Claudia and Harold Spurgeon are, you know . . ."

Charlene smiled encouragingly. "You mentioned something about that before."

Happiness seeped from every pore like a leaking blister. "Claudia acts as though they're engaged, but I don't think Harold's mother—Mrs. Spurgeon, that is—likes her. But Harold's in charge now, so Claudia probably gets the whole commission. That's a lot of money."

And we're not talking pocket change.

Then came the stuff about Johnny Romano. "And of course you know about the famous gangster."

Let's hear it for Royal Roosts's Girl Reporter!

"Gangster?" asked Charlene, allowing some interest in her tone.

Whereupon Marian launched into an all-out public relations bulletin on Romano, embellishing as she went along.

You know, kiddo, you would make a great writer. I have to wonder, though, if Johnny Romano would appreciate your imagination.

Charlene was onto the connection, but Martola was hearing this for the first time. Neither had known that the week I was murdered I had an encounter with the gangster at the Shine apartment. Afterward, when they thought they were alone, Martola ventured that Romano might somehow have gotten Claudia's assistance at Sands Point on that fateful day.

Your partner's my kind of guy.

Charlene ignored me, asking instead, "For what? More money?"

"I thought you were the one chasing the money trail."

"True. But there's more than one horse in the race."

Martola waited.

"What about Harold?"

"But he stands to inherit a zillion bucks," her partner argued, then shrugged his shoulders. "Well, okay, it's worth checking into, but first let's knock off the Harmon chick." He gestured down the hallway.

Yes, I'm for that!

Claudia did not seem surprised when the detectives appeared at her office door. She must have heard them enter the reception area earlier because her desk had been neatened up, and her lipstick gloss was slick enough to slide on. I concentrated on the pile of neatly stacked folders that stood near the edge of her desk and thought about the possibilities. Claudia smiled coyly at Martola and gave Charlene a begrudging nod.

"Nice to see you again, Detective*sss*." The plural hissed like a naughty child.

Charlene turned away for just a moment, but I noticed she was rolling her eyes.

We could have been such good friends, Charlene. Now, nail the bitch!

As if on cue, she jumped in to start the questioning. "Did

you know Mr. or Mrs. Shine prior to concluding the sublease arrangements on their apartment?"

Claudia pouted in Martola's direction before responding to Charlene's question. "No."

"Then how was it that you and not one of the others took over that account after Ms. Dowd's death?"

The subject pondered for a moment before quipping, "The luck of the draw."

Personally, I was livid, but Charlene had complete control. "Luck of the draw?" she echoed, lifting her eyebrows. "Or did you request the assignment?"

Claudia looked toward Martola who glared back, leaving no doubt where his loyalties lay.

"I didn't have to ask for the contract. Mr. Spurgeon gave it to me."

Of course he did. Harold knows what side his bed is buttered on.

"Know Johnny Romano?" Martola asked suddenly.

"Romano?" Claudia echoed, caught somehow by surprise. "I know who he is," she purred, "but I don't *know* him."

We spent the next ten minutes doing more of the same, but nothing budged the unflappable Ms. Harmon. She didn't try to dodge any questions, nor did she appear to embellish. The sum total was she didn't give up anything that even smacked of suspicion. Boy, was I disappointed! I aimed for Charlene's attention.

Listen, this woman's got her master's in manipulation. You can't believe she had nothing to do with my death. Dammit! You've got to squeeze the truth out of her. Let's see if I can help.

Charlene nodded, extending the questioning for another five minutes. But the detectives seemed to have run into a wall. Um, it was time for a fresh perspective.

The stack of folders on the side of her desk begged for my attention. I focused all my energy in that direction. Ever so slowly, the pile began to inch closer toward the edge, but conversation between Claudia and the detectives was so intense, no one noticed. Suddenly, the mountain collapsed onto the floor. Oh, happy day! All was mayhem.

Claudia uttered a very uncultured "Shit," Martola's eyes

widened in surprise, and Charlene laughed out loud. More important, Dragon Lady's rehearsed speech fell to ruin as she stooped down to recover her potential commissions. I made sure the pages were thoroughly integrated, thereby ensuring it would take some time to sort out the contents. The best part of it was her loss of poise and prepared script.

In the period that followed, Claudia responded to the detectives's questions fairly honestly. She had no time for games; she couldn't wait for them to finish, so she could get back her life. Unfortunately, Claudia offered no smoking gun. I finally suggested it was time to move on. But Charlene and Martola were already planning their strategy for the next sucker: Mr. Mama's boy himself.

As we moved down the hall toward Harold's office, Martola made a note to double-check Claudia's recent bank deposits for any unusual sums not related to her commissions. Last ray of hope?

I was preparing myself for a boring session with Harold. Was there anything he could possibly say that would add to the equation? I glanced at the detectives and crossed my fingers. Sometimes, one has to have faith, and at the moment, Charlene and Martola were my only hope. A few minutes into the meeting, things got interesting.

If my mother were observing the current head of Royal Roosts, she would inquire, "What's with the *shpilkes*—pins and needles?" I wondered, too.

Sitting with Martola and Charlene in the executive office of the firm, I observed Harold Spurgeon wiggling in his chair like a masturbating adolescent. He was flushed, and his shirt collar threatened to squeeze the life out of his fleshy neck. Both detectives noticed his discomfort, but it was Charlene who spoke first.

"This must surely be a difficult time for you . . . and the other members of your firm."

Harold managed a weak, "Y-yes."

"And I imagine you're as eager to find whoever did this as we are."

"Uh, yes."

Is this a scintillating conversation or what?

Ignoring me, Charlene presented a brilliant smile. "So, any help you can give us will be greatly appreciated." She leaned in close to illustrate the point, and Harold's wiggling increased to a frantic level.

"For example, can you think of anyone who had a reason to want Ms. Dowd out of the way?"

"N-No!"

Fiercely done, Harold. Now, get a grip!

"I understand that Claudia Harmon took over some of Ms. Dowd's accounts."

"Not all . . . some." Harold sounded defensive, but the tranquilizer he'd taken earlier appeared to be kicking in at last. He stopped rocking.

Martola, however, had enough of this pussyfooting around. He moved his chair into Harold's space, the scraping sound clearly announcing his intentions. "Would that include the Shine apartment?"

"Um, er . . . I believe that's correct."

We all noticed his eyes darting from side to side.

"You believe?"

Harold nodded; Martola glowered back.

Look, I could have told you this moron has the communication skills of a third grader.

Charlene flicked her eyes in my general direction, then leaned forward toward Harold. "We understand that Ms. Dowd saw Johnny Romano in the apartment the last time she was there."

Harold looked as if he couldn't breathe.

Okay, now you've got my attention.

Both detectives straightened, but while the three of us awaited his next words, the man of the moment seemed to have been struck dumb.

I motioned to his head. *Hello up there, Harold, anybody home?*

Martola finally broke the silence. "Anything wrong?"

"N-no . . ." Harold's next words came tumbling out. "I knew that Annie, uh, planned on showing the apartment, but I had no idea Mrs. Shine was still there—none of us did! She was thought to have left for California. Then after, I heard about the, ah—mixup—" Perspiration glistened on his forehead.

Obviously, Mr. Private School was unused to such bad manners. *Tsk, tsk.* Imagine that! Two people having illicit sex in the middle of the day! And both participants married to others at that!

Press the Romano button again.

Charlene nodded. "So, you seem surprised to hear that Mrs. Shine was entertaining Johnny Romano."

"Uh, yes . . . Mrs. Shine is—married."

Like he suddenly remembers the Bible.

My detective grinned.

"And Mr. Romano is a . . ." Harold shoved his neck farther down into his shirt collar and mumbled, "He's got a reputation."

What do you make of this?

Martola leaned forward. "What do you know about Romano's reputation?"

"Nothing. I know nothing."

This calls for a line from Hamlet: ". . . doth protest too much, methinks."

Charlene nodded and began making some discreet notes while Martola tried to squeeze some juice out of the dead rind in front of him—to no avail. The rest of the interview didn't produce very much more. I tagged along after they departed Royal Roosts. Apparently, there was more on their afternoon's agenda. Wherever they were headed, I knew they'd need my help.

It was as if the gods were smiling down on me when I realized we were approaching One-hundred Sixty-third Street and Grand Concourse. I'd been pestering Charlene about the urgency regarding Johnny Romano. Finally, she and her partner were responding.

The detectives and I entered Billy's Bowling and Billiards and were welcomed by the familiar stench of cigarettes and beer. All present gave Charlene the once-over while she pretended not to know they were mentally undressing the hell out of her. Martola stared around, and a few wizened citizens dropped their eyes. Out popped the bull with the shaved head.

"Help ya?"

The detectives flashed their badges, and their greeter led the way toward Romano's office without hesitation. Martola, Charlene and I followed closely behind. After a loud rap on the door, the detectives entered, two badges went up and Romano, who was on the phone, replaced the receiver without even saying good-bye. The two stones on the couch stirred, but Romano flashed them a look that effectively froze them in place.

"What can I do for you?" asked Mr. Cool.

"Like to ask you some questions," said Martola.

"Questions about what?"

"Like, what can you tell us about your relationship with Mrs. Fannie Shine?"

I glanced at Charlene to see the reaction to her partner's opening gambit. Nada. Her placid face showed no emotion at all.

Romano spread his hands and grinned. "Fannie Shine?" He winked. "Nice ass."

I steamed at the double entendre. *You're a disgusting son of a bitch. I can't wait to get you on my territory. I'll speak to the guy in charge, and you can bet there'll be a warm reception.*

"Besides that," Martola prodded.

"What can I say, Detective, without my lawyer present?"

Charlene interrupted. "Is there something about these questions that gives you the impression you require an attorney?"

Romano turned his eyes on her, giving Charlene the full benefit of his Italian charm. "We both know you and your partner are investigating a murder. You come here to question me. Why? I'm sure I don't know. Of course, I want my lawyer present. Just name the time and place, and we'll be there."

The urge to squash his irritating grin was gaining on me. *I could have told you. This guy's pure drek.*

But Charlene never missed a beat. "Actually, I think that might be a good idea. Why don't you come on over to the Mineola Precinct with your lawyer—say, tomorrow afternoon?"

She was flipping through a small notebook. "Two o'clock okay for you?"

Romano nodded, his smile lingered, and his gaze continued to crawl across the mounds under her blouse.

Martola didn't speak until after they were in their car headed back toward the precinct, and then he easily summed up his reaction with one word: "Asshole!"

Eighteen

My father taught me a lot. One of the best problem solvers I've ever known, Poppy's favorite expression was, "If you can't get in the front door, try the back." I'd been trying to get this message across to Charlene and Martola ever since they first took on the case. Finally, they took my advice.

After leaving Billy's Bowling and Billiards, the two drove to Agnes Spurgeon's residence in Sands Point, AKA the scene of the crime. Madam Agnes wasn't too thrilled to see them, but the detectives assured her they only wanted to talk with the servants. They made it plain they were not asking for her permission.

Interesting, what one turns up when taking my father's advice. Bernice and Henry, a couple who had been with Agnes for twelve years, provided a wealth of information. Both recall seeing Claudia in the library. Bernice had been particularly concerned because the woman appeared to be pacing out the room, as in calculating the measurements. The trusted domestic was uneasy about possible theft because the library contained a wealth of antiques. "Well, stranger things have happened," she argued, and she did not want to be blamed in that event. Eventually, the problem was resolved when the ruckus developed over my drowning.

Thanks a lot! The outcome was disappointing on both counts.

Henry stated that, to the best of his recollection, I was still alive when Michael was dispatched to the front gate to investigate the disturbance there. Neither he nor Bernice were able to recall where Matt Sterling or Mr. Harold were.

The detectives were about to leave when Martola turned back. "Can you say for sure that Ms. Harmon was still inside the house when Ms. Dowd drowned?"

Bernice strained to recall. "No, I can't say."

I started getting that eerie feeling again. Some scraps of memory trying to break through the fog. Music . . . I could swear I'm hearing music. . . .

I am dancing with Michael, soft Latin tempo. Wine makes me silly. I sway with the rhythm, or is it the wine?

On the drive back to the precinct, I suggested to Charlene that it would be prudent to delve further into Harold's life. *I mean, what do you have to lose?*

It took me awhile to locate Frankie. He'd been at Murphy's, grabbing a beer with Roger and reminiscing about me. How nice! How I wished I could have joined them. Now that would be a party! Afterward, Frank hailed a cab. I hopped in next to him, ready for the next adventure. And oh, "'twas a hint of the ole sod" my Frankie picked up when our driver greeted us. We rode uptown on a blarney-filled balloon before it hit me: We were headed toward the Carnegie Hill area and Michael Rheims!

"Sure and you have a sunny day," Frank sang out as we exited the cab, oblivious of my distress.

The doorman inquired after Frank's business. "I'm here to see Mr. Michael Rheims."

Oy. Are the dead capable of heart attacks? I knew I had to pull myself together, so as we rode up in the elevator, I made an attempt to share the discovery of my earlier foray: *Uh, perhaps Michael is not all I thought he was. Possibly, he's a crook.* (I wasn't ready to suggest he might also be a murderer.)

Undeterred, Frank rapped at the door of apartment 18B.

"Who is it?" inquired a familiar Oxford voice.

Frank identified himself, and the door swung open.

Standing together with Frank and Michael in the same space was weird, and I had to remind myself that, as far as they were concerned, only the two of them were present. After observing for a couple of minutes, I still could not figure out what they were really feeling beneath their cool, civilized exteriors. Frank's demeanor maintained complete neutrality. The professional in him had taken charge. Perhaps unraveling the mystery of my death was taking precedence over any personal feelings. At the same time, Michael's British stoicism kicked in automatically when Frank's identity became clear. All I could think of was how far civilization had evolved since the cave man. My own emotions were mixed. I had accepted Frank's nomadic life long ago. In time, we both moved on. It wasn't necessary if no one else understood this, but Michael was obviously out of the loop. Faced with the former husband of his almost lover, his discomfort was obvious. He stumbled through the introductions and invited Frank inside.

My guy explained his mission. "I'm working with the police," he exaggerated, "and am hoping you can help us out with some details."

Michael readily agreed. (This guy was cool, as I so well recall!) He gestured toward two comfortable chairs in the living room. I hovered nearby, ready to avert a catastrophe.

Never one for the long route, Frank quickly launched into a review regarding the disturbance at the gate, asking Michael to describe his remembrance of the incident.

Yeah. Let's pin it down now. Do you have a legitimate alibi? Or are you more than just a smooth seducer?

Michael started to repeat what he'd told the detectives, but Frank held up his hand. "Let's do this another way. Can you remember what you were doing just before the commotion? Like, where were you exactly? And where was Annie?"

I wondered if he were setting up Michael for an attack, but the latter answered reasonably and, I might add, honestly.

"Annie and I were dancing on the pool deck."

That's true. The music is wonderful—soft, yet sexy. I'm giggling. Michael has to hold me tightly because I am dizzy. I'd almost forgotten that part. . . .

"And?"

"There was a lot of noise at the front gate—nothing nasty—just the sort of thing one hears when people are having a good time."

"So?"

"My aunt, Mrs. Spurgeon, asked me to have a look, so I excused myself and went to the gate." He explained that three persons who had apparently been drinking mistook the estate for the Sands Point Country Club, "actually located about two kilometers farther down the road."

"What did they look like?"

"Oh, ordinary."

"Ordinary, like how?"

"Their clothes, not top quality, you know. That sort of thing."

The devil's in the details, and I was beginning to appreciate Frank's success as an investigative reporter. Before long, he'd gleaned that, while these intruders claimed to have mistaken Agnes Spurgeon's grand home for the country club, they were neither dressed for such a place nor did they act as though they belonged. Possibly they were nothing more than a diversionary tactic for what was apparently the main event back at the pool.

Frank prodded Michael further on the exact sequence of events after he redirected these so-called lost souls.

"As I was walking up the path to the pool, I encountered Matt Sterling. We stopped to chat. He said he'd never been to such an elegant home. He seemed sincerely impressed, and I saw no reason to discount the lad."

Frank was scratching the back of his neck to avoid smiling at Michael's British ways. Well, at least he wasn't balling up his fists, getting primed for a fight. Right about now, I figured he was pondering what it was that I saw in the guy. He should only realize that Michael reads from a different script when on target to seduce a woman. Oh, well.

They went over the sequence twice again, approaching the facts from different vantage points each time. Michael's story never deviated. I don't know about Frank, but I had my doubts that Michael Rheims did me in. A thief possibly—but a murderer? The thing that bothered me now was why did Matt not acknowledge he'd been talking with Michael? Why did he claim he was with Claudia?

Frank must have been wondering the same because after we left, he hailed a taxi and gave the driver Matt's address. The driver was Eastern European. It only took Frank a minute or so to pinpoint the location: Albania. Then, it was smooth sailing.

Benjamin Hollis seemed glad to see Frank, but Matt was less than enthusiastic. I thought that strange, since I never considered Matt a moody guy. Frank accepted Benjamin's offer of an espresso and settled into the chair close to Matt. After some small talk, my guy opened the subject of the investigation, again claiming to be working with the police.

"Sometimes," he began, "when looking back on a traumatic event, it's difficult to recall the details."

Good opening. I knew Frank was on the right track because Matt squirmed and hung his head. Frank was using his priestly voice: kind, tolerant, designed to bring out the truth. He made small talk for a few minutes, then gently introduced the subject of that fateful night.

"I know you were good friends with Annie and want to help us find out who did this awful thing."

Matt looked directly at Frank. "You know I do!"

"Then please understand, only by eliminating the innocent will the police be able to identify the guilty."

A strange quiet settled over the room. Benjamin was studying Matt now. We all were, but no one said anything for a few minutes. I held my breath, as if that were necessary. Matt covered his face with his hands. "I'm so sorry."

I looked at Frank, who maintained his confession-is-good-for-the-soul expression.

What in the world was happening? I wanted to scream. *Get on with it!*

"I lied," Matt finally owned.

There was a collective "WHAT?"

"The truth is, I was on the pool deck when Mrs. Spurgeon sent Michael to the front gate to check on the noise. I, uh, followed partway, pretending to meet him by accident. I just wanted to talk to him for a few minutes, wanted to see if he was . . ."

Gay? Oh, Matt, you thought Michael was cute, too. How sweet!

By now, he was blushing crimson. He hung his head for a minute, then slid his eyes toward Benjamin. "I didn't mean anything by it," he added quickly.

There wasn't anyone in the room who didn't believe him. Benjamin draped an arm around his young companion's shoulder, Father Frank cleared his throat, and I just wanted to go over and give the kid a big hug.

I know you didn't do this to me, Matt. I just didn't know why you lied and said you were with Claudia. Now I understand. You didn't want to hurt Benjamin.

Frank didn't stay very long after that, but his mission was certainly successful. We both knew that Michael was not the culprit. He was nowhere near the pool when I was pushed. Now we could concentrate on the guilty party, or should I say parties?

And talking about guilty parties, my ethnic conscience was on the rise. Miriam, Herb and the children were returning to Ohio today, and Ma would be alone again—this time coping with the additional burden of my absence. I decided a detour to Ma's place would serve two purposes. I could say good-bye to my family and see that Ma was not too depressed at their departure. Unfortunately, I was too late to bid farewell to my family—they'd already headed back—but I was not too late to be shocked out of my newly discarded body.

Sitting across from my mother at her kitchen table was a familiar stranger—ah, yes, the *Shabbes* playboy. On close examination, he appeared to be a man of seventy-something, and he was smiling at Ma. Or was that leering? Worse than that, she was returning his gaze as though they shared a wonderful secret. Disgusting. This guy was putting the moves on my mother? So that's why she turned down Miriam and Herb's invitation to move lock, stock and barrel to Ohio. Ma had a thing going with this usurper? But wait! He speaks.

"I just wanted to tell you again how sorry I am for your loss."

Ma brought her hankie up to her eyes. "Thank you, Manny." She spent a minute or so pressing back the tears. "I'm only sorry you didn't get to meet my Annie. She was a wonderful girl."

That slapped me down in my place. Should I feel lower than shit for eavesdropping?

"If she was anything like you, Selma, she must have been an angel."

Give me a break! This Manny person was a high-caliber shmooze artist if I ever heard one. What's he after? Never mind. I don't even want to imagine it.

"I missed sitting with you at temple last week. . . ."

Sure. And what else did you miss?

"I wanted you to come for dinner, Manny. You could have met my other children."

What? And become one of America's Most Wanted?

"Some other time, Selma. This was a time for family."

Sure, he talks the talk, but I knew that was Ma's cue to invite this freeloader to a sumptuous feast, so I took matters into my own hand. She kept a radio on a small table next to her chair because she liked to listen to the news while she ate her breakfast, so the station was set just where it ought to do some good. I stared at the on/off button, willing it to start, and we were not disappointed. (Naturally, I increased the volume so we could all reap the benefits.)

"THE TEMPERATURES TONIGHT ARE EXPECTED TO BE IN THE MID-SEVENTIES!"

The twosome jumped out of their seats together like synchronized swimmers.

Ma reached over and slapped the radio off. "I don't know why that happened."

"It's okay. I should be getting along now anyhow."

Duh. That's the whole idea!

I kept myself at the ready in case Ma had second thoughts, but she rose from the table like a good hostess and prepared to see this would-be freeloader off.

"Don't forget to double lock the door," Manny-what's-his-name warned, as Ma prepared to close the door behind him.

She nodded, her sunny smile sending us both on our way. I had every intention of making sure this guy headed toward his own place, so I followed along. Home was about eight short blocks away on Jewel Avenue. The pleasant middle-class neighborhood was predominantly Jewish, and almost every house we passed used red brick in its design. Private homes claimed some blocks while apartment buildings rose into the air on others. Still, the neighborhood boasted verdant lawns and lots of old trees. Although my connection with Royal Roosts never extended to Forest Hills, I could vouch that it was an old established section of Queens, accessible to Manhattan and not that far away from the South Shore beaches, should weather warrant. LaGuardia Airport, of course, was another selling point. Be that as it may, my main interest at the moment was in finding out more about this *shnorrer*. Who was this Manny person anyhow?

He stopped off at a small grocery and purchased some milk (no fat) and a small box of Raisin Bran Flakes. All right. Shall I assume that one of his problems was constipation? What else was he suffering from? Clogged arteries? Thinning bank account? I mean, what did he want with Ma anyhow? We went up to his apartment, a dark, three-bedroom job around the corner, and I wandered about, inspecting it all like a potential appraiser from a secondhand store. The furnishings and drapes were of a bygone era but of reasonable quality and style. Ornately framed photographs stood guard over old mahogany tables, the tops of which were hidden from the light under fine films of dust. This guy definitely lived alone. Of course it made sense to cultivate Ma. She kept a clean house. She was also a warm and loving person, a good listener and a fine cook of hearty, traditional dishes. What lonely old geezer wouldn't want to cultivate her and take advantage of all that good stuff? Then a sad realization came over me. Ma was lonely, too. Sure, I argued, but what man on this earth could ever take my father's place? On the other hand, how would I feel if Poppy had been the one left alone? Yeah, but Manny-what's-his-name was no Poppy. I vacillated back and forth. This guy's gonna have to prove he's not out to take advantage of Ma. I'm from Missouri.

Having finally decided to temporarily cut the guy some slack, I headed back to Claudia's place on the odd chance I could fill in some more details on her dossier.

She had a past, all right, I just had to keep digging until I discovered what it was. I didn't bother to ring the doorbell. Just as well; her place was empty anyhow. It was already four-thirty in the afternoon. She was probably still at the office, making calls, following up on the day's showings and plotting her commission-loaded schedule for tomorrow. I couldn't recall which accounts, besides mine, she had on her agenda. If Harold could see past his fly, he would give some thought to hiring an extra salesperson. Because as hungry as Claudia was, she really couldn't handle the double load—hers and mine—indefinitely without showing the strain. And let's face it, anxiety does not go well with her plans.

After ten minutes of searching, I wasn't any more informed than before I started. I was tired of inspecting her closets. Ensembles lined up shoulder to shoulder and filed according to season and color bored me. Row upon row of shoe boxes, stacked and labeled, made me wonder if she'd taken courses from Imelda Marcos. What else counted with this woman besides acquisitions? She must have had some life before Harold and Royal Roosts. Ah, what's in that big box? A carton stashed on the top shelf of the closet offered myriad possibilities, so I concentrated real hard until it fell down on the floor.

On opening the flaps, I discovered an old photo album and realized it offered unlimited information. The pages rotated slowly and in no time, I was walking down memory lane with Claudia and her family, I presume. Did these people, wearing costumes from another lifetime resemble Royal Roosts's most aggressive broker? I studied the photos—sepia replicas of unsmiling faces. In one, a serious-looking man, dressed in an old-fashioned wool suit and beret, stood next to a heavy-set woman whose babushka hid all but her uncertain expression. Her dark, reflective eyes seemed familiar, but I couldn't place where I'd seen them before. The couple stood close together but did not touch. They posed in front of an old house, the kind I'd seen in dark European landscapes. The artist Jan Vermeer came to mind. I browsed through the album, concluding these were Claudia's family from the Old World. Russia? Poland? Lithuania? The photos took on a more contemporary aspect as

I neared the end. Then I came upon the item that made the whole exercise worthwhile—you might call it the pièce de résistance.

Sandwiched between the old pages was an envelope containing a photo of more recent vintage: a young woman with three little girls. I assumed the young woman, who was holding the youngest, was the mother. The resemblance between them could not be mistaken. The child in her arms, who was holding an American flag, could not have been more than two and bore a remarkable likeness to our very own Claudia. I flipped the photo over and read the date: July 14, 1968, Ellis Island. Underneath were printed the words, "Mother, Tessie, Katya and Clara." There wasn't a doubt in my mind that Claudia and Clara were one and the same. I also assumed that the mysterious Tessie she'd been on the phone with was her sister. Let's see—if Claudia was about two in Nineteen sixty-eight, that would mean she's . . . That wasn't the point. What mattered was that Dragon Lady Harmon, AKA Clara Something-or Other, was a refugee. Okay, so that's no crime, but why hide her past? There must be more. What else is she concealing?

It took some effort to raise the photo album to its former place on the shelf, but I gained something in the process. An old shoe box caught my eye, so I hauled it down for a look-see, never realizing that I'd latched onto Pandora's box. Packets of letters secured with rubber bands were crammed into the small space. I checked the postmarks. They were all the same: Ossining, NY. Getouttahere! It's a good thing I was dead; otherwise I'd be leaving pools of drool before I could read the first one. I removed the band from the most recent packet and eased out the contents. The brief message, with all its glorious misspellings, was printed on lined stationery:

> Receeved your letter. It was very funny. Ha ha. You want a divorse? Are you nuts? After all you *did'nt* do for me since I been here? I would not give you change for a quater. Go fuck yourslef.
>
> Love,
> Don

The postmark was one week old. I couldn't take a chance on removing this priceless keepsake from its honored place in the shoe box, but I could share, or should I say "savor" the gem with Charlene. It didn't take a whole lot of talent to memorize. I quickly browsed through other correspondence from "loving Don" but determined that my first selection was the most important. So, how did this impact my untimely demise? Maybe Charlene would have some ideas.

Nineteen

When we assembled at the precinct the next day, Charlene and Martola had already met briefly with Lieutenant Egan and notified him of their expected afternoon appointment with Johnny Romano and his lawyer.

Egan nodded. "Okay. Then what? Nobody puts Romano at the scene."

Martola explained what happened at the Shine apartment when Annie Dowd walked in on the gangster and Fannie Shine. "Evidently, Romano zeroed in on Dowd. She knew he tagged her; he knew she had to go."

Now I learn that their tryst wasn't a one-time happening either. Charlene and Martola showed Romano's photo to the doorman and the concierge. Both were reluctant at first to cooperate, but with a little pressure, they finally acknowledged that the gangster had visited the Shine apartment before.

"So," Egan said, "are you saying you can tie Romano to the murder?"

Charlene nodded. "We're hoping. Romano himself may not have been present when Dowd was drugged and pushed into the pool, but we believe he had an accomplice—one of the party guests."

Egan stared back at her. "Why would one of those upstanding citizens assist a criminal like Romano?"

"Blackmail?" suggested Martola.

Charlene added, "We do know that four of the people present when the crime was committed have given conflicting statements."

"Which four?"

"Matt Sterling, Michael Rheims, Claudia Harmon and Harold Spurgeon."

The detectives hadn't caught up yet with Matt's recent admission. I thought the kid and Michael were out of the spotlight. I moved in closer and whispered the news to Charlene. She turned her head to one side and muttered, "Better to be on the safe side."

Meanwhile, the lieutenant was barking orders. "Find the connection. Look into their bank accounts and do credit checks. Find out who owes what to whom. Blackmail, huh?"

Now you're talking! (Well, it couldn't hurt to have a look.)

"We'll get on it," Martola said, rising from his chair, "while we're waiting for the ex-husband. He's coming in today for another talk."

Egan perked up. "Frank Dowd's coming here?"

Martola nodded.

"Let me know when he arrives."

On the way back to their desks, Charlene and her partner exchanged looks that seemed to say, "What's going on?"

I wondered also, but I parked my curiosity long enough to get Charlene's attention.

We need to talk.

"I'll just be a sec," she told her partner, and headed to the restroom. "What?" she asked, after making sure we were alone.

Listen to this! I just found a motive that makes Claudia the best prospect for accomplice-of-the-year award.

"Let's have it."

You're gonna love this. The bitch is married to a guy in Sing Sing. He won't give her a divorce. I repeated Don's letter, word for schmucky word.

She digested the information, looking thoughtful but not giving me the excited response I expected.

Don't you see? With Romano's connections, he could have found out about Claudia's husband and blackmailed her into drugging me and pushing me into the pool. Plain as the nose—

"Hold it . . . not so fast."

But—

"Slow down. I'm not saying it isn't possible, but you said the name on the return address was Don Bailey. How would Romano tie him to Claudia? She goes by Harmon."

But—

"Yeah, I know. You want it to be Claudia in the worst way. And I'm not saying this is not a possible motive. But we need to look at all the angles. Right now, I'd like to figure out a logical explanation as to how I came up with this news. I don't think Martola will buy a ghost as my source." She moved back to the squad room where her partner was tapping his pencil impatiently.

"Thought you fell in."

"Funny. Actually, I got a call on my cell from one of my snitches. You don't know her."

That's a good one!

"And what words of wisdom may I ask?"

"I was told that Claudia Harmon has a husband in Ossining. Apparently, Harmon's been trying to get him to give her a divorce and he's giving her a hard time. Possible that one of Romano's connections fed him the info, and the big guy used this to pressure Harmon into doing the vic on the Fourth?"

"It's a thought—one of the best we've had."

"Except for one small item. She uses a different last name. How would Romano connect Bailey to Harmon?"

That's only a minor detail.

Martola cracked his knuckles, which I suppose activated his thinking process. "Okay, first let's check out the marriage thing; then we'll do the money stuff."

Charlene volunteered to go after the marriage records, while Martola pulled up Bailey's criminal history. "Yeah," he grunted. "He's a sweetheart all right: long JD history that includes everything from shoplifting to swiping car radios. Graduated to passing bad checks in Ninety-six and got slapped with three months, but he's a slow learner. Six weeks later, he's charged with possession of a controlled substance, enough to share with the neighborhood, class D felony, so he gets sent back up again. This choirboy can't stay out of trouble. Finally makes the big time in Ninety-eight when he was caught robbing a liquor store. Habitual. Nets him a trip to Ossining."

"Here we go," said Charlene. "Donald F. Baily and Clara Horvath? Guess she believes in changing her name from time to time. Married June seventeen, Nineteen hundred and ninety-two. According to this, her birth date is November four, Nineteen hundred and sixty-six."

So, let me get this straight: The prize we now know as Claudia Harmon was born Clara Horvath, then married Donald Bailey, whom she'd like to divorce so she can marry Harold Spurgeon. Would you say her propensity for name change matches her neurotic need for wardrobe acquisitions?

Charlene laughed. Her partner looked puzzled. "Something about the year that strikes you as funny?"

She tried to recover. "Not really . . . just reflecting on all her name changes—seem to go with her wardrobe changes."

Whoa, friend, you're stealing my lines.

"Either that or I'll get carted away."

Martola frowned, said, "Sure," studied his partner and shook his head. "Uh, maybe we should get on with what the boss asked us to take care of."

When he went to refill his coffee mug, Charlene turned in my general direction and muttered, "You're gonna get me in trouble."

Sorry.

Fortunately for today's detectives, the world we live in is guided along by helpful electronic devices, including special databases that provide law enforcement with all kinds of information. Accessing the stuff is only a click away.

Martola dived right into the pool, pulling up facts and figures that would make the average citizen blush. By the time the printer spit out the last page of his inquiry, the detectives had acquired details that included the size and color of Claudia's panties as well as Matt's average monthly bills from Gold's. I tell you, nothing's sacred anymore. More important, however, was who owed the most and to whom?

"What's up with this?" Martola muttered, holding up a sheaf of papers detailing Michael Rheims's credit record.

The printout revealed he had no debts at all. A couple of explanations came to mind. Either he was obscenely wealthy, or he hadn't been in this country long enough to play the healthy American game of living beyond one's means. In any case, being without debt wasn't normal.

Sifting through the pages, Charlene agreed. "He's got a Visa Platinum and an American Express Gold."

Yeah, and a gold Rolex and a cleft in his chin—so, what does it all mean?

Charlene shrugged her shoulders and observed, "He's not shy about spending it either. Still, he seems to pay his bills on time."

As we were to discover, the source of Michael's gold mine was actually twofold. Marks and Spencer compensated him grandly, but that was only part of it. Michael Rheims had inherited a fortune from his grandfather when he turned thirty. That, plus two residences (a country estate in Surrey and an eight-room flat in London's toniest section) kept him from getting bored too easily. No, Mr. Rheims did not have to depend on Johnny Romano, or anyone else for that matter, for anything. And, once again, I clopped myself in the head for what might have been. Cultured, gorgeous and money, too! Oh, the waste! Then I recalled the strange letter from his sister, and I was baffled. Maybe I should leave room for the possibility that his sister was suffering from delusional hysteria?

Martola was already leafing through the next bunch. "The Sterling kid puts most of his money into keeping his bod in shape . . . Gold's Gym . . . Gold's Gym . . . and more of the same. Guess his pal Benjamin keeps the home fires burning. Anyway, no big tabs here."

By now, the detectives had caught up with Matt's gay lifestyle, and it didn't phase them anymore than it had Frank. Poor Matt. Keeping his big secret all this time, and nobody really cared. Or did they?

Charlene looked across the desk at her partner. "Hey, Lou, do you think we're glossing over this gay thing too quickly?"

"Whaddya saying? That the kid killed Dowd because she found out he was gay?"

Oh, c'mon . . . Matt? You couldn't believe such a thing. He wouldn't hurt a fly.

"Well, it's a motive," Charlene insisted, "if he really wanted to stay in the closet badly enough. But I don't see where that would tie in with Johnny Romano."

"We'll talk with the kid about it later."

The rest of the information yielded no surprises. Both Claudia and Harold charged mightily, with Claudia's spending dedicated to clothes and accessories.

Listen, guys, aren't you wondering where Claudia gets the money to cover her rent and telephone—not to mention facials, pedicures and dye jobs? Maybe you should dig a little deeper.

Charlene repeated my concerns. "I know she earns up the ying-yang, but where does she get the money for rent, telephone and the rest of life's niceties? Does it all come from Harold Spurgeon?"

We all know that Claudia's sweetie has been covering that and more for quite some time. Paying for sex is nothing new, although Harold wants to believe she's—you should pardon the expression—just crazy about him. Another question might be—where does HE *get it from?*

I was reading about the big guy's financial map over Charlene's shoulder. *Hmm,* practically unlimited credit, and yet, he's almost maxed out. His gold and platinum cards went mostly toward out-of-sight Manhattan restaurants (with guess whom?) and expensive gifts for (guess again). Something's not right here.

Psst, Charlene. Listen up. The Claudia thing notwithstanding, I've never known Harold to be a lavish spender. Something else you should know: Royal Roosts has a high overhead; it takes a mountain of green to keep it on top. I don't think the business can push enough into Harold's wallet to cover all the expenses you're tabulating. The balance is off. Maybe I'm crazy, but my suggestion is to check the books.

"You're on," she said.

Her partner gave her the eye. "On to what?"

"Oh, nothing," she covered up quickly. "I was just thinking that something's appears off balance with Harold's expenditures."

"Yeah. He must be pulling down a helluva salary for all that and Sutton Place, too."

"Uh-huh," agreed Charlene. "Wonder what kind of arrangement he worked out with his mother when he took over the operation." She then suggested they consult with Assistant District Attorney Richard Sadler and find out if they could subpoena the books for a peek. Sadler was expected to join them later for the Romano interview.

Good job, Charlene. You can use my untimely (not to mention, unpleasant) death as probable cause.

Charlene let that hang in the air a minute before musing, "Wouldn't you think Spurgeon Junior has access to all the money he could ever want?"

"You don't have to convince me," Martola said. "I'm game."

The detectives locked eyes for a few seconds, but before either of them could speak, Frank had sauntered into the precinct. He was wearing his see-ya-and-raise-ya expression, leaving no doubt he was primed for any ongoing confrontation with Martola. I tried rubbing the back of his neck to keep him on an even keel.

Try to remember we're on the same team, hon.

I was thinking about the adversarial reaction he and Martola had exhibited at their first meeting. And while we waited for Charlene, who was making a brief detour to Bud Egan's office, I could only hope she'd rehearsed her partner on the ground rules.

Evidently, he was a slow learner because Martola opened with a careless burst. "We know you've been sniffing around, Dowd. You should have told us about Johnny Romano."

Frank stiffened, but Charlene joined us at that moment and expressed her agreement. He swung around and offered her a big smile, not to mention a look of longing.

I chimed in. *They're right, hon. You can't take this solo.*

If my guy was disappointed that Marian-the-mouth hadn't given him an exclusive on the story, he never let on. He had not the slightest doubt that the gangster was responsible for my murder and so stated to the detectives.

"When Annie caught Romano in bed with Fannie Shine,

you can bet he wouldn't just limp away and lick his wounds. This guy's accustomed to getting his own way."

Charlene tapped her pencil distractedly on the table. "But this—Annie's murder—doesn't seem like a mob thing to me. More like a personal time-out."

The other two were listening.

"The way it plays for me is that Romano and Fannie Shine were having steamy sex when Annie walked in on them."

Steamy is one way to describe it.

"But I'm not sure why he would go to such an extreme to ensure her silence. Surely, he wasn't worried about his wife's reaction. From what I hear, Romano's marriage is one thing, his extra-curricular affairs another. That's a given and, by now, his wife has learned to keep her mouth shut. Johnny has a bad temper. What I haven't figured out yet is why he would want to silence Annie for catching him at what is just an ordinary part of his life."

If that's ordinary, I wonder what the deluxe version is like.

Charlene grinned in a knowing way.

Frank thought the smile was for him. He expanded his chest a bit, tapped out a Marlboro and lit up. "That bothered me, too, but I may have come up with something that fits."

You have our full attention, Frankie. Don't keep us in suspense.

"It's true that Romano is used to having his way, with everybody except Luke Snyder."

I've been trying to tell you this all along. Why don't you guys listen to me?

"Yeah," agreed Martola, "we all know Snyder's the man."

"Well, I did a little scouting, and it seems Snyder was fed up with Romano's afternoon sessions. The string had run out on the big guy's sense of humor." Frank was looking at Charlene. Why? Maybe to give extra emphasis to the term *afternoon sessions.* (A perennial favorite of his own, by the way.)

"I have it on good authority," he went on, "that Snyder was real pissed about it and as much as told Romano if he didn't lower the volume, he could expect trouble."

Martola tilted his head back. "And just how did you come across this gem of information?"

Frank stared back. "You think you're the only one with a license to dig? I've been doing what I'm doing a long time."

Martola thought about that for a moment and challenged, "Okay, so what else do you know?"

I urged my fella to tell the detectives about his visits with Michael and young Matt, but I might just as well have been talking to myself.

"I'm thinking we could get started with this."

Charlene looked disappointed, and that seemed to reach him. Frank broke down and told them about his conversation with Michael Rheims. "He's positive he was talking with Matt Sterling. Funny thing is, I believed him, so I went over to see Matt." Frank then related what followed at Matt's apartment.

Martola nodded. "That explains the conflicting alibis for those two. But does it excuse them from the murder itself?"

Let's get back to the bad guys. Even if Luke Snyder has Romano hanging from the end of a broken fire escape, he, Romano, was STILL *not at Agnes's home the night I was drugged and dumped in the pool. So my question is if Romano engineered the thing, who did he get to do his dirty work? And what hold did he have on this person?*

Charlene conveyed the essence of this to the others. My brilliant journalist smiled approvingly at her, holding the pose for more than the requisite two seconds.

Martola checked the eye contact between his partner and Frank, taking note of the escalating chemistry. He shrugged his shoulders as if to say there was no accounting for taste. I was struggling with my own ambivalence but made an effort to understand. It wasn't long ago that I'd been doing the mating dance with Michael Rheims. This death stuff was becoming very inconvenient, not to mention complicated.

I could see that Frank and Charlene were drawn to each other. So, what was my problem? It wasn't that I could still compete. Guess it boiled down to my annoyance at finding myself out of the loop. Maybe no one else could understand, but Frank was my rock. Although divorce had separated us from our pledge to remain faithful, it had nothing to do with our commitment to each other as friends and, yes, occasional lovers. Now I knew we no longer had either option. On the other hand, who better to fill the gap than Charlene? Smart, independent, a sense of humor, she was the logical person to bolster Frank at this time. Sure, Ma loved him like a son, but she had her own grief to overcome, and besides, Frank had, uh, other needs. On all counts, I couldn't have dreamed up a better person than Charlene to step into the breach. And, if I judged my new friend correctly, law enforcement was her true career, not something to waltz along with until a better proposition like marriage and kids came along. Two individualists. What more could I ask for? Whew! I felt like patting myself on the shoulder for the fine "shrink" job I did on myself, not that I ruled out follow-up sessions!

"So," Martola was saying, "I guess this is where we get out our lists and compare." I guessed he was offering to share information. *About time!*

"Right," Charlene agreed.

There was a shuffling of papers, and Frank took out his coded notebook of scribbled gems as Charlene asked, "Who wants to start?"

Frank inclined his head in her direction. "Why don't you?"

Charlene scanned her notes. "Let's eliminate the obvious. Lou and I have narrowed the field, but for review's sake, let's start at the top."

I'm in agreement with that, but I can't wait for you to get to Claudia.

There was no dissension as Charlene ran through her material. She began with Marian. "No conflict with the statement issued by Hingis. Says she was talking with Roger Franklin, and he doesn't disagree. Hingis lives with her mother—no big lifestyle, no unusual debts."

Charlene moved next to Roger Franklin. "Quiet guy. I believe he and Annie were just friends, and good friends at that. Doesn't appear to have anything to gain by her death."

My guy nodded. "I don't have anything to say against Roger. Lives a quiet life. Has a long-term relationship with a nice woman. Not a gambler. Manages okay on his income." He glanced up at the other two. "Doesn't owe any unusual debts, I take it."

Everybody, including me, voted to skip Roger as a suspect.

"Okay," Martola said, "so we pass on the Franklin guy—and the kid, Matt Sterling." He raised his eyebrows. "The gay part is not news, by the way."

This last surprised Frank. "How long have you known?"

"About four days," Charlene deadpanned. "Did you think you're the only one with talent around here?"

Frank inclined his head. "Touché."

"Hmm . . ." Charlene acknowledged. She turned a couple of pages. "Claudia claims she was in the house—the drawing room, to be exact—checking out the paintings." She eyed her partner, sending a silent message across the table.

Martola cleared his throat. "Yeah. We spoke to the servants—couple by the name of"—he checked his notes—"Barber, Bernice and Henry." Martola described their conversation relating to Claudia's snooping in the library just before all hell broke loose at the pool. "Bernice says Claudia Harmon was alone in the room, but can't swear if she left before or after the ruckus started at the pool."

Frank reminded him that Harold claimed he, too, was in the house talking with Claudia.

No. Wait! Something's all wrong here, and I'm getting flashes and this weird sensation.

Charlene nodded. "Okay. Let's double-check Harold's statement."

But at that point, there was a knock at the door and in walked Bud Egan. Within seconds, the room vibrated with a surprising spectacle.

Frank and the lieutenant stood clasping each other like two lost brothers in a long-delayed reunion, which it turned out to be.

"Sonofabitch!" Frank shouted. His face split into a grin. "What the hell are you doing here?"

"Well, you know," said Egan, gripping Frank's shoulders, "I didn't plan on staying in the Bronx till I died!"

The two of them spent several minutes just hugging, laughing and exchanging half-sentences that only old friends could understand. The rest of us observed the demonstration as if we were watching a tennis match, our heads moving in unison from one to the other as we absorbed the emotional display between two old friends. We gathered that Frank and Egan had known each other since they were kids. As they reminisced, other facts came to light like stickball, Bronx High School of Science—even playing hooky. Their reunion was actually kind of sweet, especially since I saw such a rare glimpse of pleasure on Frankie's face these days.

When the excitement subsided, Egan drew a serious expression. His next words sobered us all: "Frank, you've got to clear out of your place for a while."

Nobody spoke.

"I just got a call from a buddy in the Forty-eighth who passed along some nasty stuff. An informant claims that Romano has put out a contract on you. According to my friend, the snitch is pretty reliable."

I turned toward Charlene. *This is what I've been trying to tell you.*

The detectives were instantly alerted.

Martola asked, "Do you have any place to stay?" It sounded curiously like he was about to invite Frank to come home with him.

Ma. Ma will be glad to have you stay with her, hon.

Almost as though he'd heard me, Frankie said, "Thanks for your concern. I'll probably stay with Annie's mom."

Egan offered to arrange a surveillance team to be posted across the street from Ma's apartment building, but Frank was quite vocal in his refusal.

Anybody else in his position would have made a wild dash for safety, but my Mr. Macho had other ideas. "I hear Romano's coming in soon with his lawyer. I'd like to stay for that session."

Are you nuts? Under no circumstances. And I'm firm on that!

The detectives looked at Bud Egan who shrugged his shoulders. "It's your neck. Stay put in the room next door, though. You can observe through the one-way glass. And keep your mouth shut until they're done and outta here. You know the drill."

I object! That's the same thing as giving him a voucher for suicide. Rethink this, Egan, or your happy reunion with your friend will be short-lived. But Egan was not on my phone list.

Charlene looked dubious, but Martola glanced at his watch and moved quickly. "I'm thinking you may want to settle yourself soon before Romano arrives. He's due in the next few minutes."

Frank nodded and made a move to go. Egan insisted on escorting him.

You can take me too while you're at it. I'm not letting Frankie out of my sight.

We followed the lieutenant down the hallway while the detectives waited for Romano.

God's gift to women appeared with his attorney about twenty minutes later. Martola and Charlene escorted them to Interview Room #2 and offered coffee. Both refused. Martola shrugged his shoulders and placed his own mug on the table. Charlene slipped into a chair alongside.

Frank and I waited in the next room, peering through the one way window. Of course, I could have been in the room with Romano, but elected to keep my guy company instead. Also with us on our side of the wall were Bud Egan and Assistant District Attorney Richard Sadler.

Romano's lawyer introduced himself to the others: "Norman Wasserman."

Martola grunted and extended his hand. Charlene nodded. All very civilized.

He's Jewish? I nudged Frank, who showed no reaction.

"Are you acquainted with a Mrs. Fannie Shine?" This was Martola diving right in.

Romano grinned back. "Sure," he said crisply.

The detective waited.

"Me and Fannie," the other snickered, "have been very good friends for several months."

He emphasized the "very."

"How good?"

Romano laughed but did not elaborate.

Well, they looked like they'd been dancing together for a while.

"You visit her at her apartment on East Sixty-first?"

"You bet."

"And on June twenty-seventh, you were there with her?"

"The twenty-seventh? No."

Lying snake!

Martola leaned forward. "Oh? Are you saying that you were not with Mrs. Shine at her apartment on Friday, June twenty-seventh?"

Norman Wasserman spoke up. "My client has already answered that question."

He's lying, Frankie. Maybe I should go next door and give him a good klop in kop, as Ma would say. Jog his memory. Know what I mean? I slipped into the adjoining room and stood behind Charlene.

He's lying, I hissed.

Charlene nodded. "We have witnesses who will swear they saw you with Mrs. Shine on that day."

That was a bluff, if she was referring to the Belgian couple who accompanied me. They weren't even the ones who wound up subleasing the apartment. Actually, I whisked them out of there so quickly, they never even got to see the rest of the layout, much less Romano and Fannie's grand finale. It is possible, however, they were standing next to me when I walked in on the first act. I can't be sure.

Charlene was regrouping, searching for a hole in the fog that would break down Romano's alibi.

Think again! That oily bastard is grinning back at you like the kid who stole a piece of pie and got away with it.

"Can't help what other people swear to," Romano sneered.

His lawyer put a hand on his arm in an effort to shut him up.

Let me at him. There's nothing I'd like better than to wipe that smile off his face.

Charlene tried again. "We could have Mrs. Shine subpoenaed."

Wasserman sighed and looked at his watch. "If there's nothing else . . ."

I added my two cents and the detectives threw in a few more questions, but nothing that produced any chip in Sir Galahad's armor. The latter left with his lawyer about ten minutes later.

I sat in on the ensuing strategy session with some of the guys on our team.

"Maybe you can squeeze something out of the Belgian couple," Egan suggested to Martola, whose partner was momentarily distracted by something Frank was sharing with her alone. I moved nearer.

"Have dinner with me, Detective," he was whispering.

"I want to, but the timing is bad right now."

"When will the timing be better?" (Did I detect a note of sarcasm?)

"We'll both know when that happens." (Yes, there was a definite bitchiness in her tone.)

Frank dipped his chin and whistled softly. "You've got me on a string, Detective. Call me when my horse comes in."

"I'll raise the checkered flag."

Whoa. Even I was getting turned on, but Egan was clearing his throat impatiently. He glared at Charlene, who turned away from Frank.

Sadler was nodding at something the lieutenant had just said. "In the meantime, I'll look into the subpoena for Fannie Shine."

There was a scraping of chairs. Clearly, this meeting was over, which gave my man-on-the-prowl another opportunity. "May I offer anyone a lift?"

Martola and I knew instinctively we were not the targeted guests.

"No thanks," said Charlene, a little too quickly.

You don't have to worry about me, I lied. *I'm needed at my mother's.*

"Why should I worry?" Charlene tossed out as the others were leaving.

Martola paused on his way out and shook his head at her.

"You have ways of making things awkward," she admonished, after her partner departed. I knew she was talking to me, but Frank took it personally.

"What's awkward about offering you a lift? I'm not asking you to sign a contract."

Charlene opened her mouth to speak, then pressed her lips firmly together. She was annoyed, probably at having lost some control over the situation.

"Hey!" says Frank, like he just thought of it, "there's a great fish restaurant on Franklin Avenue."

It's okay—really. I'm heading to Ma's.

"Come on, Detective, loosen up. Dinner—then I'll drop you off at your place."

Oh, yeah, that'll be the pièce de résistance.

Charlene allowed herself to be led out. Now, who's chasing whom?

Twenty

I thought it was high time someone connected the dots. One of my former acquaintances was lying, but which one? Ah, Claudia. Surely she was guilty of something. And whatever that was, I would find out.

Her Lexington Avenue efficiency was deserted, so I took my time poking around for incriminating evidence. Maybe I missed something the last time, like that neat pile of travel brochures on the corner of her night table, for example. Ah, the Greek Isles—Perchance Romano promised her a luxury cruise in exchange for . . . Nah. I could see that womanizing gangster providing the wherewithal for such an event, but I couldn't see him throwing away Fannie's generous offerings for a bag of bones. Or maybe he wasn't offering escort services. Maybe the cruise included a companion of Claudia's choice. *Hmm* . . . to what lengths would Claudia go to mingle with the jet set? Made a mental note to share this with Charlene and kept on searching, but further investigation only provided an uninterrupted tour of boutique acquisitions. Where in the hell does she get the time to shop? I wondered. Gucci scarves, Hermès perfume and pricey leather accessories crammed her dresser drawers. Bottom line: Harold must have put out a bundle. If only Agnes knew. I'll bet she'd throw that broad out on her skinny ass in a hurry. And talking about skinny behinds, where was this model of haute couture? Harold's apartment at Sutton Place sounded like a good possibility. Oooh, this is gonna be good!

But when I stood just inside the door of Harold's place trying to decide if I really wanted a front row seat to "Frankenstein goes to Paris," I realized that voyeurism was not my forte. Voices drifted out from the bedroom as I debated my options.

"Dearest," Harold was pleading, "you've really got to cut back some on some of your spending."

I gathered they had already done the deed and this was the after-exercise cigarette break.

In a soft, almost unrecognizable whisper, Claudia responded. "But, Harold, dear, I thought you wanted me to have pretty things." I could imagine her mouth had formed the perfect Scarlett O'Hara pout. Perhaps she would even lose herself completely and refer to Harold as Ashley.

"For instance, this apartment. If we're going to live here after we're married, I have some wonderful ideas about redecorating." I could swear I heard her giggle and tried to imagine her blowing gently into Harold's ear.

"It's just that . . . I really don't have an unlimited flow of money—not all the time," he added hastily.

"I hear you, Harold. But after we're married, don't you think your mother will adapt to reality and adjust your income accordingly?"

Sure, Claudia, and the moon is really one big soufflé.

Being the washrag that he is, Harold replied, "I certainly have high hopes."

"Darling," the other cooed, "high hopes are not quite what I had in mind." She was squeezing hard now and didn't intend to let go, but old Agnes still had her grips on the lad.

"Now, my dear, we've been through this before. You have to give Mother time to adjust."

Sure. Eventually, Claudia will grow on your mother like mold.

"Well just how much time would you consider reasonable?"

You're not giving an inch, are you?

But something else bothered me even more. Claudia was never able to hide her ambitions. I just never realized how much pressure she was applying to Harold. His desperation to please her was pitiful. I was getting this eerie, otherworldly feeling and suddenly began to look at Harold in a new light. For all his nerdy ways, the guy was truly obsessed with this woman. To what extremes would he go? Murder? But, how would killing me get him any more than he already had?

The questions started my brain spinning. Flashes. Some snatch of memory breaking through the fog, and I'm once more running the tape of my last night: I am dancing on the pool deck with Michael. The wine makes me heady, but his arms are strong. Silly me. Silver bells in the moonlight . . .

The shrill ring of a telephone interrupted my reverie. I glanced around, surprised to find I was still in Harold's apartment. His voice, cryptic and frightened, whined into the phone.

"Y-yes, I was there, but . . . Of course not. I understand . . . Y-yes."

Now I'm really interested. What could all of this mean? Charlene and Martola should know about it, maybe Frankie, too, although I'm not sure I wanted to jazz up my sweetie any more than he already was. Which reminded me, I needed to make sure Frank was following through on his plan to get over to Ma's.

Earlier rains had cooled down the normally hot and muggy borough of Manhattan, inspiring folks to get out and enjoy this rare and refreshing midsummer break. I noticed some chattering teens giggling together on a corner of the sidewalk near Frank's apartment and felt a pang of envy at their freedom, not only for the moment but for their ability to dream about the future. Couples of various ages strolled by arm-in-arm, innocent of the sadness that lurks around life's corner. And then, in the midst of this peaceful scene, I noticed a dark compact car parked across the street. Inside, barely discernible through tinted windows, were two figures. Could be nothing. But the small alarm inside me disagreed. I hastened upstairs.

Frank had finished packing by the time I arrived. After all, this was the story of his life, always on the go. The shower was running full blast, and his satchel, plopped in the middle of the bedroom floor, probably contained not much more than cigarettes and a change of underwear. I compared him to the wandering Jew. Ironic, no?

As he dressed, I tried to drum some sense into him. *Listen, Frankie, this Johnny Romano is not someone to take lightly. Well, just look at me, and you'll see what I mean. If he can't do the damage directly, he can always get someone else to do his bidding. I'm telling you to stay put at Ma's, and that's final!*

His response to my lecture was to light a cigarette and reach for the phone.

"Yeah, Maggio, it's me. Listen, I'll be on the move for a couple of days. You may not be able to reach me, but I'll call you. No. Nothing concrete as of now. I'll keep you informed."

He clicked off but stared at the phone for some seconds. Then he grabbed his satchel, and we were out the door. The scene downstairs had not altered: the sidewalks were still filled with innocents, and the dark compact had not moved; however, two not-so-wholesome characters were just emerging. They froze as Frank appeared in the doorway. Preoccupied with his own thoughts, Frank hadn't noticed them. He motioned to the driver of a cab, who had just unloaded his passengers. In seconds, we were safely inside.

As our taxi pulled away, I could feel, rather than see, the vehicle following behind us. Dread, like Damocles' sword, shivered above. I struggled to think of a way to avert this impending tragedy. So far, my efforts at warning Frank had no effect.

I won't let them take you, hon, not without a fight anyway.

Twenty-one

Dancing with Michael my feet off the floor/ soft Latin tempo licking my spine/fuses with wine; it rhymes. . . . Shivering synapses join in the play/ like fireworks, unguarded, they've caught hold of a spark/ on your mark; hark. . . .

Oh, don't leave me, Michael! The world is spinning. I need to sit down. An arm. Why, thank you, Harold. How kind . . . whoops!

Harold?

As the detectives began hauling away the company's books, I sensed that Harold was trying to think of some way to explain all this to his mother, the force in his life who was the source of all his terror. Agnes Spurgeon had always prided herself on keeping her private matters just that way—private. Now, the police had arrived with a warrant and were preparing to walk off with the ledgers. How could he ever explain? On second thought, never mind Agnes, some of the pieces of this mess were beginning to take shape for me.

Harold was a true schlemiel—a poor excuse for a human being—weak, gutless, easily swayed. Was it conceivable that his weakness, based on Claudia's demands, led to my end? Maybe they entered into the plan together.

Marian and I watched as the detectives went about their work. Her eyes rolled with excitement, and I could sense her anticipation in sharing the news, possibly even with Frank. I, too, was full of questions. Where would all this lead? Harold as a viable suspect? I tried to look at him in that light, that of a murderer, but the thought was almost laughable. Harold? Nah, there must be some mistake. But Claudia, ah, there's a comfort.

The detectives motioned Harold toward his office. I invited myself along. Marian looked disappointed that she wasn't asked to join us.

Not everyone gets to go to the party. I'll fill you in later.

I caught Charlene before she and Martola began their quest for gold, beginning with my usual *Psst!* She jumped a half a foot in the air.

Sorry. I should have given you some warning.

She pressed her lips together and shook her head in annoyance. I quickly told her about the travel brochures I'd discovered in Claudia's apartment.

Maybe the info will help you when you question this jerk.

She lifted her shoulders. "We'll see . . ."

Martola looked at her with raised eyebrows and muttered, "Damned straight."

Charlene took a couple of seconds to regain her balance, then smoothly offered her partner a smile of encouragement.

As Harold sank into his chair, Martola perched on the edge of his desk and leaned over the trembling man menacingly. "You know, there are some things that just don't add up. Maybe you can help us fill in the blanks."

The guiding light of Royal Roosts raised his weak chin toward the detective. "Wha—what do you want?"

"I want you to tell us what happened on Friday, July fourth."

"I—I don't know what you mean. . . ." His voice trailed away feebly.

"You know everything! And I think you know who killed Annie Dowd."

I didn't think the detectives had that much to go on yet, but I was flabbergasted with Harold's reaction. His face drained of color, and he began to pant.

Great going, Martola!

"What are you saying?" the nerd squeaked.

Yeah, Martola, explain yourself.

Charlene moved her chair closer, soon revealing the tougher side of her personality. "Listen, Harold, we're not fooling around. We're on to the truth," she bluffed. "You and Johnny Romano . . ."

Harold buried his face in his hands. "N-no!"

The detectives exchanged satisfied glances.

Give it to the sonofabitch!

"Maybe you did it, Harold," Charlene bluffed.

The subject took out his handkerchief and began dabbing at his sweaty forehead while moaning, "Oh, God, no . . ."

This is going great! Now, lean on him harder. He must have some answers.

Charlene caught her partner's eyes, giving him the go-for-it signal.

Martola leaned over. "Then maybe you know who did. If you help us with this," he said, almost too softly, "we'll see to it that things go easier."

Now I understood. The detectives had changed places—good cop/bad cop—with a twist designed to throw Harold completely off stride. It worked. The poor shlub looked like he didn't know which end was up. He was clearly confused, a drowning man looking for dry-dock. His gaze swung back and forth between the two detectives as I wondered where this would end. Of course, Harold never majored in brains, so the pressure was working. What the heck, I'd just go along with it too.

Right now, the *shlumperdik* needed a shower. Perspiration glistened above his upper lip like liquid Vaseline.

"I want my lawyer," the creep finally cried.

I learned that Assistant District Attorney Richard Sadler had been patiently awaiting his big break ever since he'd joined the District Attorney's staff more than five years before. In an interview, the hard-working thirty-four-year-old focused on becoming a success, just like his father, the Honorable Judge Harlan K. Sadler. The difference was, Richard hoped to live longer than his dad, who dropped dead of a heart attack at the age of fifty-four while presiding at the embezzlement trial of a well-known bank president. That being the case, Sadler Junior paid close attention to his health. He was known for his strict vegetarian diet and the quantity of vitamins he carted around and consumed daily.

Sadler watched the Spurgeon interview through the one-way glass in the next room. Frank, Bud Egan and I were there as well. By this time, we had all gleaned that a substantial portion of Royal Roosts's proceeds were being detoured elsewhere. But where?

Martola and Charlene took their positions opposite Harold and his attorney, Thomas McBride. The latter was on retainer by Harold's mother, who had thrown a fit when her son finally screwed up the courage to plead for the lawyer's services.

"What *have* you gotten yourself involved in?" she'd exploded, alluding to the fact that there had never been any difficulties *before that woman entered the picture!*

I guess she couldn't bear to mention Claudia by name.

The combination of his mother's wrath, Claudia's demands and accountancy discrepancies appeared to have taken its toll on Harold. I'm sure I was not alone in noticing the pallor of his skin and his shallow breathing.

McBride laid a hand on Harold's arm to calm him when Martola threw out the first question. It didn't help. The subject jumped half out of his chair.

"According to these records, you've been withdrawing funds other than your salary on a regular basis. How do you explain this?"

Yeah, Harold, how do *you explain this?*

The subject shifted in his chair. We all noticed the flush spreading over his cheeks and forehead, overriding the previously ashen surface. Poor slob, he might as well have hung out a sign that said "guilty." But, guilty of what?

He stammered for a few seconds, whispered something in McBride's ear, then mumbled aloud.

Can't hear you, jerk. You'll have to speak up.

Charlene conveyed my message.

The husky response crawled out. "I required some funds for personal use."

"What use?" asked Charlene. "Like maybe you were planning a vacation to the Greek Isles?"

Another huddle with McBride, who interjected, "My client doesn't have to specify."

But the detectives came well prepared. Charlene began to recite from her notes: "Fifteen hundred back on March first of this year, two thousand on April first, another two grand on May first, again on June first . . ." She glared across the table at Harold, who stared at his hands, refusing to return her gaze. "What really piques my interest, though, is that nothing was siphoned off the books on July first, just prior to Ms. Dowd's murder."

At the mention of my name, Harold's head burrowed deeper into his neck.

What's going on upstairs, genius? Are the withered crumbs of your brain having a conference?

Frank, Egan and Sadler had been watching the performance on the other side of the glass. Sadler reached into his pocket distractedly and popped a vitamin into his mouth.

My guy said, "Sounds like blackmail."

"Claudia Harmon?" asked Egan.

"No. She was getting hers already and aiming for a bigger piece of the pie, not crumbs."

On the other side of the glass, Martola was pushing. "Nothing extra withdrawn in July. How do you explain that? Suddenly, you had no need for extra funds for your personal use?"

The subject was sweating profusely.

Martola raised his voice. "Know what? We believe you were in business with Johnny Romano."

"Oh, God!" The words fell out of his mouth like a prayer.

Charlene sighed. "God can't help you, Harold, but you can help yourself. Yes, we think you owed Romano big-time. You borrowed money, couldn't pay it back, and performed another service instead—murder."

Yeah, you bastard, mine.

Suddenly, Harold's eyes appeared to lose focus. His pupils began vibrating, then they rolled up and under his upper lids. The effect was grotesque. His body slammed forward. Martola lurched across the table to prevent Harold from knocking his head. Only then did McBride realize what was happening.

From his position alongside, the lawyer hadn't seen the approaching storm. I just stood there mesmerized. Charlene was already out the door, calling for an ambulance.

Martola pumped rhythmically on Harold's chest. Charlene returned and slid an aspirin under Harold's tongue. Emergency medical technicians arrived within minutes and took over. They started an intravenous, clamped an oxygen mask over his face and took his vitals. I stared at Harold's crumpled body in a new light and looked around carefully to see if he had joined me in my new dimension, but I was still the lone member of the club. As the emergency crew wheeled him out on the stretcher, I detected the faint rise and fall of labored breathing.

So, this is just a respite, Harold. We still have a lot of unfinished business to settle.

Twenty-two

Upon close examination, there was no question that Harold had been cooking the books. Entries dating back to last year traced his metamorphosis from bonehead to embezzler. At first, relatively small sums, weakly labeled "Supplies," were withdrawn in cash. Of course, there were no receipts to support or further explain these disappearances. Sharing this information equally were Martola, Charlene and Frank. Apparently, Egan had decided the more heads, the merrier. Besides, Frank's talent for sniffing out the truth was well known. The precinct's boss was not stupid. He was probably aiming for an early solution of the thing, so he could head toward retirement with the same unblemished record he had before this whole mess invaded his domain. So, over Martola's weak objections, Frank was brought in as an outside "consultant."

As they studied the records, the three sleuths noted that the sums pilfered from the business began to increase in size as time went by. I could imagine Ma describing Harold: "He's nothing but a *goniff,*" which was absolutely true. A thief, but was he also a murderer?

I'd known Harold a long time, long enough to recognize how much he'd changed after Claudia came to work at Royal Roosts. Let's face it, he'd always been a *schlemiel,* but like ordinary, unexciting white bread, you always knew what to expect. After Mata Hari entered the scene, his negative traits escalated. Claudia taught him the true meaning of devious. Trouble was, her teachings were one hundred and eighty degrees opposite those of Harold's mother. Caught between the two strong women, something had to give. Was it his heart?

I stopped by New York University Hospital on First Avenue after leaving the others at the precinct, and let me tell you, Harold did not look well at all.

He was in the Intensive Care Unit, various parts of his body hooked up to machines, with tubes flowing to or from every section—a scary sight. Agnes was pacing the hallway outside, demanding to know why her son wasn't in a private room with personal, round-the-clock nurses. She never inquired about the two uniformed policemen standing in the corner not too far from her son's bedside.

Because, Your Highness, your son may be dying. Private rooms and private nurses can't sustain him like the equipment and personnel in ICU (or a uniformed guard, for that matter).

In the midst of one of her tirades, the elevator doors opened and a cloud of Givenchy perfume announced Claudia Harmon's arrival. The two women glared at each other.

Oh, boy! This is going to be goooood!

"Mrs. Spurgeon," Claudia declared nervously.

Agnes turned to Thomas McBride. "What is *she* doing here?"

I sensed that the lawyer wished he were someplace else. "Now, now . . ." he began.

"I want her *out* of here."

Harold's erstwhile fiancée's nostrils flared, her eyes flashed, but she made a brave effort at control. "Mrs. Spurgeon . . ."

"OUT!"

Way to go, Agnes!

McBride moved toward Claudia with a half smile. "Ms. Harmon, I think perhaps . . ."

There was a brief, icy silence, then Claudia roused herself. "Family rifts can be unpleasant. I don't think Mrs. Spurgeon wants to be on the outside of a relationship with her son."

No one present could mistake the threat. If, however, she had any idea of the unfolding events, Claudia might be plotting a segue to a more detached distance. As it was, she stood her ground for only a minute or so, nostrils flaring, then punched the down button on the elevator in a manner that suggested it served as a substitute for Agnes's face. She disappeared behind the closing doors, but Claudia's wrath as well as the Givenchy hung in the air for many minutes after.

Renown cardiologist, Dr. J. Carter Phillips, sat together with Agnes and her attorney in a far corner of the lounge adjacent to the ICU. The handsome, silver-haired physician wore a pleasant expression, no doubt designed to allay the fears of immediate family members looking to him to pronounce the fate of their nearest and dearest.

"Now, Mrs. Spurgeon," he began, with much authority, "I want you to relax. Your son is not in any danger."

I find that disappointing.

The doctor went on to explain that Harold had suffered a fainting spell, poetically entitled: *neuro depressive vasogenic syncope.* Upon hearing the diagnosis, Agnes's mouth fell open. It turned out to be nowhere as serious as it sounded.

"Merely a temporary deficiency of blood supply to the brain," the doctor assured her, "most likely caused by a stress-induced episode."

Hmm . . . a deficiency of blood to the brain, did you say? That sounds consistent.

The doctor reassured Agnes that her son was expected to make a full recovery.

When she was at last able to speak, Agnes Spurgeon had a number of questions, not the least of which was, when could her son be transferred from this dreadful place into a private room.

"I'd like him to stay in Intensive Care tonight and if there are no changes, Harold can be moved in the morning." He smiled down on Nervous Nellie. "There's no reason your son shouldn't be well enough to go home in a couple of days. We'll schedule an office visit for next week. Harold needs to lose some weight, and get his blood pressure under control."

Yeah. Getting involved with Johnny Romano definitely elevates one's blood pressure.

Detective Lou Martola identified himself to Doctor Phillips as the latter prepared to leave the hospital. Martola explained that Harold had become ill during an interview with himself and one of his colleagues. Further discussion would be helpful, and just when would the patient be able to resume the interview? The doctor looked at the detective then back at the two uniforms, raising his eyebrows. Martola didn't flinch.

"This is beginning to make sense," said Phillips. "So you're asking when the patient will be well enough to continue a conversation that appears to have been so stressful he passed out?"

Martola was not easily intimidated. He smiled pleasantly, leaving the unanswered question hanging in the air.

Dr. Philips started to head to the elevators. "Three days," he tossed back, "if there are no further setbacks."

Agnes Spurgeon was mortified when Thomas McBride described the general events that led up to Harold's collapse. Legal ethics prohibited him from sharing all the details, but one didn't have to draw a picture for Agnes.

"It's that woman!" she concluded.

McBride knew enough to keep quiet during the tirade that followed.

Harold spent one day in a cloud of drug-induced euphoria. Two days later, when he was discharged, Agnes directed that he should come to Sands Point for a few days to recover. Harold started to protest, but his mother's hard eyes bored a hole through his head as neatly as any laser. That ended the discussion but not my curiosity.

After Harold's respite, he allowed himself to be transported to Sands Point where his old room awaited. Since I joined him in the limo for the trip, I had a chance to study my former boss up close and personal. Intravenous solutions and vitamins had substituted for the wine, rich foods and heavy-duty stress Claudia had been pushing on him. In just two days, Harold's weight loss was noticeable. Now his shirt collar actually allowed him to breathe, but the pallor of his complexion was as waxy as a corpse. I got the impression he'd be joining me soon.

So, Harold, is there anything you'd care to share with me? I wasn't expecting an answer, but I figured nothing ventured . . . *I'm convinced you had something to do with my death. I don't know the details yet, but that's only a matter of time. In the meantime, you can't hide from me.* His silence was my only disappointment.

The staff turned out for Mr. Harold's arrival—the crown prince returning to the castle. Bows and curtsies—something like Claudia had been envisioning for her own future—were mine alone to watch. The spectacle made me want to gag.

A little while later, Agnes and I awaited Harold's presence in the library. When he couldn't stall any longer, the prince joined us. Agnes was on her second glass of sherry, while I eyed the twenty-year-old scotch with longing. Harold opted for a two-cents-plain (the doctor's lecture must have been sobering), and the conference began.

"I'm waiting," the queen declared.

"I, ah . . . I'm not feeling well, Mother."

An echo from the Passover service came to mind: *Why should this day be different from all other days?*

"You have not been well ever since that woman came to Royal Roosts. But that's another matter. Now you have some explaining to do vis-à-vis Annie Dowd's death."

Harold's eyes bulged.

Yeah, Harold. Let's have it.

"I, ah . . . I don't think you'd understand."

Maybe you think we should feel sorry for you. I was getting fed up with this pussy. What a wimp! His hand was shaking so hard the bubbles in his club soda were multiplying. Hmm. Why not give them a little extra help? When the glass tipped over, I directed the force toward his crotch. Harold reacted just as I'd expected when the cold stuff struck his jewels. Ah . . . some of the benefits of my new job were immensely satisfying. Of course, Agnes was horrified. Her klutzy offspring was becoming more of a disappointment with every passing day.

Think about it, Your Highness, disowning Harold has many advantages.

My list of responsibilities was increasing, and everything on it screamed top priority. Since my sister and brother-in-law had returned to their quiet life in Ohio, it was left to me to oversee the hazardous material (otherwise known as that Manny fella) appearing in Ma's apartment almost nightly. On the plus side, my new status was not having to wait for transportation.

Yep, like death and toxins, that Miami Beach virus was once more entrenched in Ma's kitchen polishing off a good meal.

"Selma, you make the best pot roast!"

My mother sighs like a teenager, lifts her shoulders, drops her head to one side and opens her hands, palms facing up—like who could deny the truth. "Oy, Manny . . ."

A few more minutes of mutual gazing precede this interloper's real purpose. "So, what do you say? Two tickets to the Mozart concert for the first Friday of next month—Lincoln Center, and the seats are terrific!"

"I would like to go, Manny, but . . . a Friday night? *Shabbes?*"

"So, who's gonna know?"

Well I know, you creep. Friday night is Shabbes. *Ma does not go out on* Shabbes.

"Well . . ." Ma is weakening.

This is how the devil works. He draws you in with promises of goodies, and before you know it, you're breaking the rules.

Listen up, jerk, Ma does not go out to concerts on Shabbes, and that's final!

But, oh! the pain of it all. My mother is smiling back at this leper, and her next words break my heart. "Okay, I'll go."

Whereupon the seducer of fine, previously upstanding, moral, law-abiding women grunts with satisfaction, jumps up from his chair and swings around to Ma's side of the table, where he plants a big, juicy kiss on her cheek. "That's my gal!" he shouts. My mother is tittering like a girl of thirteen.

What am I going to do about this? He's probably after her apartment. After all, how many rent-controlled, pre-war, two-bedroom, eat-in-kitchen apartments are available in Forest Hills? Obviously, the guy is a predator. And let's face it, Ma doesn't have any experience with this kind of beast.

After my tirade abated, and much against my will, I played devil's advocate. Is there any possibility that Manny just plain *likes* Ma? When they're together, Ma seems . . . well, happy. Could I ever accept the idea that Ma finds Manny (you should pardon the expression) attractive? Ugh. Well, I conceded, maybe, but sex is out of the question! Let's call it an "innocent friendship" for now. As for the rest of it, we'll see. . . .

Twenty-three

Romano snatched up the phone nervously, his back straightening like a Marine recruit. I was glad I'd decided to look in on the bastard, otherwise, I'd have missed seeing him get raked over the coals by Luke Snyder, the head of the Family. In an uncharacteristically somber voice, he said, "Yeah, Luke, I know. I sent two of my best guys. Somebody must've warned him." The volume increased. "AND IF I EVER FIND OUT WHO . . ."

I knew he was referring to the missed opportunity at Frank's apartment. Mr. Cool wasn't looking so terrific now that Luke Snyder had raised the flames.

How does it feel to be roasting on an open fire, Mr. Big Shot?

The latter was making a poor effort at sounding outraged, but if he couldn't sell me, I'm sure his boss on the other end wasn't fooled either.

Romano's voice now sunk to a whisper. "Sure, Luke, I'll take care of it." The furrow between his thick brows deepened seriously after hanging up the phone, and he wiped his forehead with the back of his hand. Yeah, I kind of enjoyed seeing the gangster's polish lose its gloss.

Frustration distorted his otherwise handsome face. Romano banged his fist down on the desk, then swept his arm across the top, sending a desk lamp, crystal ashtray, and a heap of pens and pencils onto the floor. But there was something else in his expression I hadn't seen before, fear, and I was impressed.

The dam had broken. Romano looked desperate to plug the gap.

How does it feel to be on the losing end, creep?

One of his underlings from the other room responded to Romano's bellow.

"Clean up this mess," the latter ordered, "and get me Carlos!"

The lackey shot his boss a startled look, repeating sotto voce, "Carlos?" Then he backed out of the office, scraping and bowing like an obsequious servant.

So, another character on the Playbill. Who was this Carlos? *Shlecht,* as Ma would say—this couldn't be good. A minute later, the lackey returned and in a quaking voice announced that Carlos was in Mexico visiting his mother.

Uh-oh. Now you've got to find another way to make things right with Snyder. Unhappily, I realized that one of the items that needed fixing was Frank.

I found Frankie with Charlene and Martola at my previous place of employment, and the first thing I did was relate the aftermath of the conversation between Romano and Luke Snyder.

Think you'd better check on this Carlos person.

Charlene grunted, and Martola looked at her sidewise. "Cramps?"

She shot him a look and went back to her task. The detectives had produced a search warrant, and the now-inseparable trio was about to fine-comb the office for—what?—some original remnant from Sermon on the Mount?

No one disputed that Johnny Romano had engineered my murder. Two big questions loomed: How, and that ever-sticky, whodunit? I was still having a problem giving Harold star billing. Not Frank Dowd, though, the great investigative reporter. Take a heat missile honing in on a target, and you have a wonderful work in progress. Add to that, two sharp detectives and the hunt is on.

I decided to pitch in and offer my help. No one rushed to acknowledge me, so I began riffling through a stack of bank statements. I noticed that the initials appearing on most of the deposit slips were the same: R. B. I called out to Charlene to check it out.

The others had their heads down in their own piles, but she looked over in my general direction.

"Whatcha got?"

"Nothing yet," the other two answered.

Charlene pressed her lips together.

I quickly pushed the deposit slips over to her side of the table. *Check out the initials.*

"Thanks," she whispered, scanning the pile, then called out to the others: "Here's something interesting."

Martola was working next to Frank. He inspected the initials on the slips and shoved the pile toward Frank. "What the hell. It's worth a shot."

When they had satisfied their curiosity on the other office documents, we all trooped over to Gotham Trust where the detectives flashed their badges at the bank officer in charge. Soon they were in a conference room confronting Richard Brackman.

Success had eluded Mr. Brackman who, in his midforties, had only risen as far as assistant vice president in charge of Reverse Mortgages. The title sounded important to the past-middle-aged clients who came in to inquire about such things, but in the banking business, Brackman might just as well have been in charge of the restrooms. Now challenged by the two detectives, Mr. Vice President appeared nervous.

"Why are you questioning me?" he asked.

"Because," Martola said, pushing his face up close, "we need some information that only you can provide. You may be involved in a murder. Hear what I'm saying?"

"A murder?" He looked genuinely shocked.

I was as anxious as anyone to get at the truth, but even I thought Martola's statement was a reach. Which just goes to show how much I don't know about this sort of thing.

In the next few minutes, the investigating committee achieved more than I could have in a year: Richard Brackman was singing like a not-so-happy bird; Frank's mission was nearing completion; and in the offing, I became an educated corpse.

"I didn't mean any harm," the key-to-the-puzzle whined, as

he unknowingly revealed the irrefutable connection between Harold Spurgeon and Johnny Romano! Climbing aboard the safety net of self-preservation, Brackman screeched out all the sordid details.

Ah, here was the smoking gun at last. *Gotcha! Harold, you dumb, nerdy, gullible mama's boy.*

Frank sank back in his chair, absorbing the shock as Charlene, icy calm, pulled out a tape recorder and set it on the table in full view. She recorded the date and the names of all present (except me, of course), then nodded to Brackman to continue. He seemed anxious to cooperate, even going so far as to sign a waiver before Charlene started the machine.

"It all began last April when Mr. Spurgeon explained his problem. He needed a temporary loan, he told me, but it couldn't show on the books. And did I know of anybody who could help him? Said he'd make it worth my while, and he did, at first. As time went on, though, he became real edgy and uptight. Just being around him put a damper on my day. Finally I told him: 'Forget it. This is the end of the line.' "

Frank's knuckles gripped the edge of his chair, and his voice was hard. "Never mind that now. Tell us about your recommendation for this largesse."

"Huh?"

"The money source!"

"Well, ah . . . actually, it was someone who knew someone who knew . . ."

"Yeah, yeah, yeah," snapped Martola. "Give us the name."

"Vinnie Castor."

"One of Romano's lackeys," Frank growled to the others.

Brackman insisted that his connection with this character was purely secondhand, secured quite by accident (according to him) through random conversation with a fellow commuter.

Random conversation . . . oh, sure!

Brackman was allowed to leave fifteen minutes later but not without some parting words from Martola. "So far, you're only on the outside of this. You'd be smart to keep it that way. Don't discuss this with anyone, or we'll have to reevaluate. Am I making myself clear?"

Mr. Vice President looked pained for an instant, then nodded furiously and beat a hasty retreat.

"So, there's the connection," said Charlene.

Got to give you credit. You said all along it was a money thing.

"Yes, it was the money thing all right."

In spite of the "no smoking" sign on the wall, Frank lit up a Marlboro and stared into space, not really seeing anything. Everything went quiet for few minutes, then he began to mutter aloud, mostly to himself. "Spurgeon needed cash, money his mother couldn't know about to spend on his girlfriend, no doubt. He couldn't borrow it legitimately. That would show on the books, so he went to the shady side of the street: Johnny Romano's money shop . . ."

The first part's not news. I just didn't realize how desperate he'd become. Now that I think of it, the word obsessive *comes to mind.*

Frank shook himself and looked at the other two. "Big mistake on his part, but Annie told me long ago, the guy's brains were in his pants."

A loud cackle escaped Martola. "Let's give credit where credit is due. The Harmon broad must be pretty good at what she does."

The guys liked that one.

Charlene rolled her eyes toward the ceiling. "Moving right along . . ."

"Getting back to Romano," Frankie continued, but then he started rubbing his chin and staring off into the distance again.

The detectives exchanged looks, but it was Charlene who spoke. "Sorry, Frank. This can't be easy for you."

"What the hell . . ."

I could see he was struggling, so I offered my number-one, guaranteed-to-work pep talk. *Listen up, hon, you're the best! And since there's nothing you or anyone else can do to change what happened, let's just get this over with. Then you can get back to whatever it is that makes you happy. But for now, pull it together. Uh, Charlene?*

Before my friend could offer some words of her own, we all observed the deep breath and flick of his head as Frank cleared the cobwebs before continuing. Of course he was listening to me. After all, I was good at this.

"We've established that the only person Romano's afraid of is Luke Snyder," Frank continued. "I'm thinking that when Annie interrupted his tryst with the Shine broad, Romano had to find a way to silence Annie before Snyder got wind of it. The Sands Point shindig afforded the perfect opportunity."

Martola looked at Frank with renewed respect. "And Harold Spurgeon was the perfect patsy. His debt to Romano was growing faster than a cancer. Gangster had him by the balls. Now we do. First order of business: a warrant for his arrest."

Frank's jaw was working, a sure sign that anger was replacing sadness. "That so-called disturbance at the front gate was engineered by Romano, I'm willing to bet, and that wimp bastard, Harold, killed Annie because Romano ordered it!"

Yeah, the disturbance. I remember now! I remember everything! I remember the wine, the pool, the water closing over my head, the awful realization that I'd reached the end. I remember it all . . . But especially, I remember Harold. His was the last face I saw.

Charlene was the only one who could appreciate this revelation, but it didn't matter. The roof was about to come down on the bad guys.

After talking with his detectives, Bud Egan contacted Assistant DA Richard Sadler, requesting a warrant for Harold Spurgeon's arrest. About six o'clock that evening, Sadler met with his boss, District Attorney Karl Wagner, and described the situation. And, since I was keeping late hours these days, I was in on the conference. It's a good thing I was, too.

Playing devil's advocate, Wagner pointed out that they might be able to prove that Spurgeon borrowed money from one of Romano's guys, but doing murder for the big man? That was a leap.

Sadler argued that Spurgeon had motive and opportunity. "In fact, everyone present when the victim was pushed into the pool can be accounted for except him!"

Wagner hesitated. I figured he needed some enlightenment. *Look. I'm the proof. That flaccid-brained weakling did it. All you have to do is apply a little pressure.*

And talking about pressure . . . A neatly folded *Wall Street Journal* lay atop his desk with a lead story referring to the upcoming election. I stared at it, concentrating hard, gently pulling it toward the edge. Then I gave him one last chance.

Listen, Mister Big Shot, the next election's not that far off. Bringing Johnny Romano to justice would sure look good on the ballot. Whaddya say?

Wagner appeared unmoved. I had to do something. *Here goes!* Quickly, I whooshed the *Journal* over the edge. It fell open, inviting a quick glance. Headlines talk. Loudest.

"Lean on Spurgeon," Wagner suddenly decided.

Wow! I didn't know the extent of my own talent.

"If you're that convinced," he went on, "have the detectives bring him in and squeeze. Offer Spurgeon's lawyer a deal, man-one, in exchange for solid evidence we can use against Romano. We'll go after the big guy for murder one. Also, bring in Vinnie Castor, the go-between for the money deal. I'm willing to bet his rap sheet against whatever cards he's holding that we've got the advantage"

Now you're talking! And if I can be of any further help, just whistle.

Twenty-four

I left them and headed back to Ma's so I could bring Frankie up-to-date on the latest. But as I approached her building, I noticed the same dark car parked across the street that I'd seen earlier at Frank's. Since my new position in this world comes equipped with a bad-news sensor, I knew right away that something was wrong. And as they exited the vehicle, I recognized two of Romano's goons from the pool hall and rushed upstairs to warn Frankie.

Nostalgia hit hard when I entered the apartment. Frank was seated at the kitchen table, sipping on a scotch. Ma was putting the finishing touches to dinner.

"We're having one of your favorites, dolling," she confided, "stuffed cabbage—the way you like it."

"Every time I sit down to one of your dinners, I have to wonder why the Lord blessed me so."

"Ach . . . you're a regular shmooze artist, you are!" But the flush that graced her cheeks was one of sheer pleasure.

"Never mind," Frank said. "Come and sit with me. The dinner will wait a few minutes."

He'd poured a glass of wine for Ma, which he now pushed across the table.

"To Annie."

Her eyes glistened, but she smiled as she raised her glass.

And again, I hear the music and feel the cool evening breeze brush across my shoulders. The wine, the music, and, incongruously, Har-

old—never more gracious. I'm dancing on the pool deck, but I can hardly feel my feet touching the ground. So lightheaded. Surely, it's the wine. I cling to Michael and feel silly falling against him.

Oh, sounds of celebration, but what an ill-timed interruption! More guests? The world is spinning. Don't leave me, Michael. I feel . . . so strange. Can't believe a glass of wine could make me so dizzy. Truly, I need to sit down. An arm. Why, thank you, Harold. How kind—whoops! Harold, why?

Everything about those last moments now pushed through the fog, beginning with the wine. I remember feeling self-conscious with Michael about my strange reaction. He shouldn't think I'm a drunk, but I literally couldn't seem to hold my head up. Felt like I'd been hit with a strong muscle relaxant. No control over my legs either. Like rubber. Harold had been unusually solicitous, handing me the glass and insisting I drink it all. "A shame to waste" is what he said. "It was a very special year." Will Claudia be angry if she spies her *intended* making gracious gestures toward me? Jeez! It was bad enough working with the bitch. I wouldn't want her to get the impression I'd entered the ring with her. What a thought! Harold? Bite your tongue, as Ma would say. Yet here he was, hanging around like he had big ideas. If I didn't know any better, I'd say he'd been smoking something. But Michael's presence was a definite deterrent, at least until he headed off to the gate to check on all that noise. Then it was me, trying to regain some equilibrium. When Harold approached and offered his arm, I actually thought he meant to help me to a chair, but he maneuvered me to the other side of the pool instead, the side that blocked my view of the other guests, the side that blocked their view of me. Then the motherfucker pushed me! I was too sloshed to resist. The water was cold, and I couldn't move. I fell through the abyss, just like "Alice in Wonderland." How easy it is to remember the ugly part.

So, I succeeded in capturing my elusive last moments, but the recollection was bittersweet. I always knew I'd be able to recall the final moment clearly, but part of me wanted to hold on to life just a little while longer. I'm so afraid this means I'll have to leave soon. Leave for where? Ah, that's the mystery.

Well, I won't go until the bad guys get punished: that means Harold, that sonofabitch, and the engineer of the train, Johnny Romano. In the meantime, it's my job to protect the good guys until the garbage gets collected and processed. That reminds me, those two goons downstairs in the car aren't browsing in the neighborhood just to borrow a cup of sugar.

Listen, hon, now we know it was Harold, and even though I'm mad as hell about what that mealymouthed mama's boy did to me, that's not what I'm here for. You've got company downstairs.

It isn't that I expected a direct response from the big lug, but one would think he'd care a little about this imminent danger.

Say, am I speaking just to hear myself talk? Those poolroom bullies are practically outside the door! Where was Charlene when I needed her?

Ma pushed herself away from the table to answer the phone. "Hello? Yes, this is Mrs. Edelstein. Maggio? Oh, yes, Frankie's friend. One minute, I'll get him," but Frank had already risen from the table and reached out to take the receiver.

"How did you know where to reach me? Oh, yeah? When? Right. Thanks."

Cryptic is hardly the word to describe the exchange.

What's going on, hon?

No response.

I do believe I've got a right to know. After all . . . Soft scraping noises were barely discernible as the elevator doors opened and closed in the hallway outside.

Frank put an arm around Ma and led her out of the kitchen. "Listen, Ma, do you trust me?" It was not really a question because in the same breath, he reached out and turned off the wall switch for the big overhead light.

Just before the room rolled into dusk, I caught the frightened look on Ma's face. Now I heard her whispering, "What's wrong?"

"Maybe nothing," he answered, "but you're better off in the back." He began to lead her down the hallway.

"Oy, Frankie—what?"

"Shhh. Everything's going to be okay."

I've been trying to tell you those guys are out there. Call for help.

In the meantime, I'll do something that will make them wish they'd never gotten out of bed this morning.

This being daylight savings time, there was still plenty of light filtering into the apartment. Frank led Ma along the hallway toward the bedrooms in the rear. He eased her into a comfortable chair in her room, and smiled down at her while pressing his forefinger against his lips. Ma's eyes were wide with fear.

"Lock the bedroom door after I leave, and don't open it until I say it's okay." He kissed the top of her head and slipped out.

It's all right, Ma. I'm right here, and I'm not going to let anything bad happen to you.

I could hear Frank on the other side of the door dialing the detectives from his cell phone. "Hope you can hear me," he whispered. "I can't talk any louder. I'm calling from Mrs. Edelstein's. A couple of uninvited guests are in the hallway outside the apartment. I'm assuming Romano sent them. Get a couple of squad cars here ASAP. I'll start barricading the front door as soon as I hang up and collect whatever weapons I can lay my hands on after that."

Hurry, dammit! I added, mouthing a prayer. I heard some crackling from the other end but couldn't distinguish the words. If I had a working heart, I'm sure it would be beating out of my chest.

The sound of heavy furniture being dragged along the floor toward the front door filled the next few minutes. Ma sat in her chair, one hand on her chest, her eyes looking up toward the ceiling while rocking back and forth. I could hear a soft "oy" with every outgoing breath. I tried rubbing her back. Sadly, I knew she could feel nothing.

I kept repeating, *I'm here, Ma, and I'll take care of you.* I knew she couldn't hear me either. I assumed the clattering in the kitchen was Frankie, arming himself with weapons. If Ma had any idea, she would probably remind him not to mix the meat with the dairy.

My frustration knew no bounds. What's the use of being a

ghost if I can't help those I love in an emergency? I remembered something from long ago. Everything is ordained, Poppy used to remind us at Yom Kippur. Everything that will occur during the upcoming year is written down during the period between Rosh Hashana and Yom Kippur. That's why the good men of our family went to synagogue and prayed like hell at this time. They were trying to ensure that their loved ones would enjoy a year of good health and prosperity. Well, I couldn't rely on last year's ledger. I slipped out of the bedroom and eased toward the front door. I didn't have a plan, but that wouldn't stop me from derailing what I suspected was about to occur.

Sounds in the hallway were easily detected. Taking on Romano's lackeys was going to be a learning experience. What the heck, I'll wing it. With this, I was suddenly in the hallway outside Ma's apartment facing two very mean-looking characters.

I tried to pump myself up. Nothing but cartoon robots. They're used to being told when to sit or where to stand, not self-starters, easily bamboozled. Maybe I can throw a little happy confusion into the mix.

Every apartment door was identified. Ma's was labeled 3G. I pushed my energy toward the *G* until it swivelled on its nail, dangling awkwardly upside down. Surprised at my own success, I whirled around quickly and repeated the mischief on the three other apartment doors.

Hey! I'm pretty good at this.

Encouraged, I stared at the *G* on Ma's door, causing it to swing back and forth. Not even waiting for applause, I did the same on the other dangling letters. *D, E, F* and *G* were now moving too fast to identify. Romano's messengers froze in midstep and were staring open-mouthed at the dancing characters.

Take a good look, jerks. That's how you're going to swing if you try anything. Pretty corny sounding, but I was having fun.

One of them elbowed the other. "Do you see what I think I'm seeing?" His partner remained slack-jawed and disabled. The talker checked the hallway window. It was closed. His brain wasn't conditioned to hold any other possibilities, so he nudged his partner and began backing up toward the elevator, leaving the other standing like a frozen statue. He pushed the button, and when the door opened, he pulled his comatose partner inside after him.

Allow me! I stared at the emergency button until the alarm went off, automatically preventing the elevator from moving. It was *The Sound of Music* for me, beyond deafening for the two culprits, but before they could escape the fray, I willed the doors closed, thus sealing them safely inside.

Uh, should I say, this hurts me more than it hurts you. Just couldn't resist . . . Actually, I was quite pleased with my efforts.

The cavalry, in the form of a SWAT team, arrived shortly after, followed by Martola and Charlene. With the sounds of friendly voices, my guy climbed over the obstacles at the front door and looked through the one-way viewer.

Romano's emissaries were pushed up against the wall, their feet spread, looking as forlorn as three-year-olds who'd just messed their pants. After handcuffing them, the SWAT team trained their weapons on the two while Martola and Charlene read them their rights. When he was sure the situation was contained, Frank lugged the heavy stuff away from the door and stepped out into the hall.

Charlene pushed the two goons back into the elevator, but Frank called to her to wait up. He took stock of the handcuffed duo, branding their faces into his permanent memory. After a quick handshake with Martola and a hurriedly whispered, "Thanks, I owe you," he waved at Charlene and ducked back into the apartment.

Ma was relieved Frankie had returned. She clung to him for fifteen minutes before she could get herself to return to the kitchen. Although Frank stayed over that night, they were never able to recapture the festive mood they had enjoyed earlier.

That was close, hon. I mean, I miss you lots, but there's plenty of time before you need to join my club.

Twenty-five

The net was closing around that wise ass, Romano: Vinnie Castor, his go-between loan shark, was hauled in for questioning and presently sat in an interview room at the Mineola precinct with his lawyer; Harold Spurgeon and entourage were expected shortly. The district attorney's office was abuzz with possibilities as the big boss there looked forward to headline publicity and a landslide reelection victory; and Richard Sadler envisioned himself as the next Clarence Darrow, who felt enriched by the news and increased vitamin supplements. Yes, the case would attract media attention for many, but my latent celebrity held no thrills for me. I would have much preferred to be an ordinary citizen, sharing coffee and a bagel at Royal Roosts. Speaking of which, my curiosity was overflowing vis-à-vis my former place of employment. I decided a catch-up visit was in order.

Marian Hingis's cup runneth over. There was so much to share! Mrs. Spurgeon had informed her that Harold would not be in the office for a couple of days. Actually, the *big* news hadn't become public yet.

Oh, Marian, you have so much to live for!

Harold's mother, the queen herself, had made the announcement personally the previous afternoon when she showed up before quitting time and called everyone together for a meeting.

"She said," Marian oozed over the phone to a friend, "that

Harold was still not recovered from his attack. But we think there's more to it than that because Claudia is not at the office either."

When the details become public, sweetie, you can negotiate for the movie rights.

Of course, Marian was not far from wrong.

Harold had begun to shake uncontrollably when the detectives confronted him at his apartment the previous afternoon. In one motion, Charlene pulled his arms behind his back and neatly snapped on the handcuffs while Martola read him his rights:

"Harold Spurgeon, you're under arrest for the murder of Annie Dowd. You have the right to remain silent and refuse to answer questions. Do you understand?" (A weak nod was his only answer.)

"Anything you say may be used against you in a court of law. Do you understand?" (He accepted the tic in Harold's eye as a weak response.)

"You have the right to consult an attorney . . . If you cannot afford an attorney, one will be provided for you without cost. . . ."

Martola continued reading conscientiously from the card he was holding, the music of his words elevating my soul to greater heights. Harold was so stunned he could only nod weakly. He allowed himself to be led to the detectives' car where he was neatly folded into the rear seat. Every visible pore was sweating. His watery eyes threatened to overflow.

Agnes was livid when her son, with McBride at his side, tearfully confessed his connection with my death.

"You don't know Mr. Romano," Harold whined. "He would have killed me if I didn't do as he said."

I noticed the color fade from his mother's face when the tawdry truth became known. Her silence was more frightening than any verbal abuse she could have launched. Harold began to tremble. McBride placed his hand on the crybaby's shoulder to steady him while Agnes continued to stare with obvious loathing at the faulty product she had created. If I weren't so angry at Harold for cutting short my life, I could have felt sorry for him.

When she finally spoke, the holding room at the jail echoed Agnes's rage. "You worm! You contemptuous, weak, shallow imbecile. You let that woman—that whore!—bring you to this! You've disgraced our family."

Harold opened his mouth as if to reply, but Agnes dismissed him with a wave of her hand and turned to Thomas McBride. Her clipped tones sliced the air like a paper shredder. "Do whatever you think is necessary. I don't care to be any further involved." She turned and left the room. What an exit! I felt like applauding.

McBride had already reminded Agnes that his primary focus was estate law. Harold would need a criminal attorney, a litigator with a great deal of experience, if he were to escape the death penalty. McBride had in mind to recommend Fein Gallagher, whose reputation in the field preceded him. But Gallagher's services came with a price tag. The family matriarch gave McBride carte blanche. As they say, money talks—nobody walks. Well, we'll see about that.

Following an interview with his new client, the famed attorney and an assistant met with Richard Sadler in the district attorney's office on Friday afternoon. And since I was the party of the first part, I thought it fitting to attend. I was not disappointed. Fein Gallagher was about Frank's age, fiftyish. He also possessed an undeniable Gaelic charm that included wit, intelligence and more than a modicum of sexiness. On a scale of one to ten, his attributes were right there at the top.

"Your client is looking at a possible death penalty," began Sadler.

Gallagher produced a serene smile. "Whatever happened to 'innocent until proven guilty'?"

"Oh, come on, Counselor, we've got the motive. He was into the mob, specifically Johnny Romano, for big bucks. Couldn't pay it back fast enough, and was scared of the consequences. When Romano gave him an opportunity to walk out a free man, your client couldn't comply fast enough. His way out from under the hammer? July Fourth, Sands Point. I call it motive and opportunity."

"Hmm . . . interesting, but then, fiction always held a special interest for me." Gallagher appeared to be taking stock of the opposition. Even though his cardinal rule was never to underestimate opposing counsel, one couldn't help but notice the relief that filled his soul. Sadler's ego dominated his brain.

"We're not talking fiction here, Mr. Gallagher. I've got plenty of evidence *and* witnesses."

Yeah. And there's one witness—me—who's not going away until justice is served.

Again, that beatific smile as Fein Gallagher rose to indicate that, as far as he was concerned, the meeting was over. He shook hands with Sadler. "Looking forward to seeing you at the arraignment."

A rumpled, secondhand Harold stood next to Attorney Gallagher at the defense table as the bailiff announced the charge: murder in the second degree. Judge Melanie Krups riffled through some papers and wearily asked, "How do you plead?"

The poor excuse for a human being was too traumatized to answer, so his lawyer responded for him. "Not guilty." The two sat down.

Isn't that just a little careless? I mean, did anybody give any thought to the consequences of lying? We're in a court of law here. Let's show a little respect! My lecture fell way short of the mark. Neither Harold nor his attorney blinked.

Richard Sadler immediately asked for $500,000 bail on behalf of the state. As much as I was rooting for Sadler, I couldn't help but admire Gallagher as he rose to respond. Carefully securing the middle button of his impeccably tailored Saville Row suit, he addressed the judge.

"Your Honor, my client is a respected member of the business community. He has recently been hospitalized, is on medication, and is in no way a flight risk. I ask that he be released in his own recognizance."

The judge looked bored. She hardly paused before declaring bail to be set at $100,000, banging the gavel loudly to emphasize her decision.

Bail? You mean that murderer goes home tonight? Oy!

Harold looked bewildered as his attorney led him out of court to arrange bond. I couldn't help but wonder where Claudia was hiding. Wasn't this the time to "stand by her man"? Should I feel sorry for the guy because both his sweetheart and his mama deserted him? Hell no! He took everything away from me.

This is hell, Harold. How do you like it?

It annoyed me that a murderer was permitted to go back to his apartment where he could enjoy the luxuries of a free man. I wanted him to be miserable, to be deprived of comfort, to have it all taken away, as he took away everything that I held dear. Little did I know I would soon get my wish.

The first thing that bastard did after taking a shower and getting into some clean clothes was to call that other winner, Claudia. I was interested to hear what excuse she would offer for not having been at court with her beloved, but Harold and I were both disappointed. Madam was not at home. Harold left a message on her answering machine and proceeded to fix himself a turkey sandwich. He turned on the television and settled down to watch the news. A few minutes later, the story of his arraignment sent him into the bathroom where he not-so-gently barfed up the first half of his sandwich.

Ha! How do you like being on the losing end, you schlemiel?

He threw himself on the bed, vomit still trickling out of one corner of his mouth, and dialed Claudia again. And again, he got her answering machine.

Do you think it's possible that your former girlfriend doesn't want to know you anymore? Yeah, Harold, I'll bet she's there, listening to your whining voice pleading with her to call you back. I'll bet she's wondering why she ever thought money would compensate for having to put up with drek like you. I'll bet she's wishing you would just go away and crawl back in your hole!

Harold began to sob. I couldn't stand looking at him any longer. *I'm outta here, you big baby. You're on your own now. Jeez, wipe your face.*

* * *

And where was Claudia, the inspiration for Harold's nefarious act? At home, just as I had assumed, monitoring her answering machine and seething with frustration at her own defeat. Out of step? My dears, she was out of sync, stories and ammunition. For the moment, it looked like she was out of ideas. This was turning out to be a great day! Too bad Agnes wasn't here to share.

Harold's ex-fiancée was muttering aloud as she paced. I moved in closer. "Why do I always get stuck with the losers?"

Hah! Better you should ask why others have to suffer fools like you. So, just between us gals, what are *you gonna do now?* I didn't expect an answer, but I thought the prospect was interesting. *Maybe the devil has a spot for you. Like, you could emulate Lorelei. You know, that beauty who tempted sailors to crash onto rocks. Or maybe you take after Claudius's wife, Messalina, known for her, uh, creative ways, or even Delilah, Samson's mistress.*

I was thinking that as long as Claudia remained on this plane, the devil could keep her in the manner she had come to expect. And after? Ah, that was too rich to contemplate. But just as a guess, I figured she could be the recipient of the hot coals others were forced to stoke. *Mmmm* . . . Has a nice sound to it.

"What the hell am I supposed to do now?" moaned Agnes's former nemesis, as she stomped across the floor, arms folded over her bony chest.

You can always apply for reinstatement in your marital status. After loving Don gets out of jail, you and he can go into business. Let's see, there's embezzlement, fraud, larceny. Hell, between the two of you, a buck can be made.

After another few minutes of listening to the "poor me" stuff, I decided to cap off the visit with a gesture only Claudia would appreciate. Ma had an old cookbook with the motto: "A man's heart is through his stomach." Ms. Harmon could be best reached through her possessions, particularly her clothes.

I went into her bedroom and stared at the contents of her closet. Let's see. . . . With one breath, I worked one end of the closet rod out of its niche. The clothes sagged, then gravity took the rest downhill. I whooshed the shoe boxes off the top shelf for good measure. A nice, noisy touch. The black-haired witch appeared, all ladylike demeanor gone out the window:

"Fuck!"

Ah, I'm thinking that now I can rest in peace, at least as far as this part goes.

Twenty-six

I should feel satisfied. Everything seemed to be falling into place. So, why did I have this nagging feeling there was still some unfinished business?

Ma was in the kitchen, humming, watching her "soaps" on the small screen while ironing one of Frank's permanent press shirts, obviously redundant but so typical. And I guessed my sweetie was in for a surprise. The fixings for a brisket dinner were stacked on the drainboard.

She picked up the phone on the second ring. "Frankie, dolling, I was just thinking of you. You will? Good! Because I'm making a nice dinner. You should remember you ate good during your visit with me. A surprise—you'll see."

The humming escalated into the theme from *The Sound of Music,* as Ma went from ironing to cooking. Since the good woman possessed a talent for everything but perfect pitch, it seemed the perfect time for my exit.

I was certain Frank had phoned from the precinct, probably following up on the two jerks who pursued us to Ma's apartment with the express idea of fulfilling Romano's lethal wishes. They were in jail, of course. But if Frank had his way, they'd be halfway to Sing Sing by now. I joined him in Egan's office.

"They're not talking," the latter informed Frank, gesturing toward the interview room next door. "Williams and Martola have been working on them for an hour, but neither has had any luck yet. They're more scared of their boss than whatever the law can do to them."

"Can't say as I blame them. Romano's probably gonna make them wish they were dead anyway."

"It's probably useless for me to suggest this, Frank, but would you consider knocking off for a while and letting my detectives do their job?"

"You're right. It's useless for you to even think about my stepping back. I won't quit till that gangster heads for the Chamber."

"Had a feeling you'd take that tack."

Martola and Charlene returned after a while, their expressions indicating they still hadn't gotten anywhere. Frank waved and nodded as they entered. "Thanks again, guys. I owe you."

Charlene wondered aloud if they could get a warrant for Romano anyway, either for attempted murder (Frank's) or the real deal (mine). Referring to the two goons, she said, "Everybody knows who they work for. They went to Mrs. Edelstein's for the express purpose of killing Frank."

"That's not enough," said Egan. "Anyway, the DA's office is working on Spurgeon to give up Romano."

Frank grunted. "That's probably our best bet anyway, if the guy doesn't have a shit hemorrhage first."

You got that right! I was over to his place earlier and am beginning to wonder how much longer the jerk can hold up. Listen to me. He's crazed. Claudia won't even return his calls! Charlene appeared to appreciate that.

Egan looked thoughtful. "Maybe I'll speak to Sadler about taking Spurgeon into protective custody."

He couldn't possibly be responding to me, probably just thinking out loud. But Frank had other thoughts.

"Yeah, that way you can seal his death warrant. Romano will most probably decide Spurgeon is spilling his guts."

Egan dialed the district attorney's office anyway and offered his suggestion. After he hung up, he told Frank that Sadler would call back as soon as he finished the paperwork. I decided to oversee the operation, so there would be no slipups.

For all his expertise, reputation and experience, Fein Gallagher was not above making a deal if it would save his client from a lethal injection. He was in the assistant district attorney's office discussing the possibilities. Sadler was chewing vitamins (as though that would make him smarter) and pointing out the advantages of cooperation. I tried to stay focused, but, truly, the assistant district attorney had the charisma of a pine tree.

"Save your breath, Richard, and let's get to the nitty-gritty. What does my client get if he gives you Romano?"

"Man-one," Sadler finally *k'vetshed* out, outlining a sentence he thought appropriate: "Eight to twelve, eligible for parole in five years."

"Man-two," Gallagher countered. "Suspended sentence and relocation under the witness protection program. I'll expect round-the-clock coverage for my client to begin immediately."

Bargaining is something one does with a butcher, Ma would say, but haggling over murder? That's a *shandeh!*

"He gives me Romano and the details," Sadler continued, "who gave him the drug that knocked out the victim—plus the names of those involved in the disturbance at the gate."

I felt like I was in an Arabian flea market. *Do you guys understand we're talking about a killer here? This is not an Oriental rug we're dickering over!*

"You know I'll have to discuss this with my client?"

"Yes, of course," Sadler acknowledged, but the headline wannabe couldn't hide the smirk that sneaked across his ambitious face.

After Gallagher left, the assistant DA popped a few vitamins before calling Lieutenant Bud Egan. "Think we've got a deal. Just waiting for a confirmation from Spurgeon's lawyer. I've agreed to round-the-clock protection for his client, so think about who you want to assign for that detail."

There were high-fives all around when Egan shared the news. Frank offered one of his rare smiles. I joined them just as Martola declared his pleasure at the prospect of arresting Johnny Romano.

"Hang on, partner. We get to choose which one of us cuffs him," reminded Charlene.

I was trying to stay in harmony with the others, but I had this nagging feeling. . . .

While they celebrated, I mentally ticked back a couple of weeks to the moment I walked into the Shine apartment with the Belgian couple. That old cliché is so true: Timing is everything. Imagine, if I'd only waited another couple of weeks until Fannie Shine had left for California, none of this would have ever happened. I'd be doing God-only-knows-what with Michael Rheims. Frank would still be overseas in some tent. Miriam, Herbert and the kids would still be worshiping in Ohio. Claudia would still be chasing after her rainbow. Marian would still be in charge of informing the world of everything. But most of all, Ma's heart would still be relatively insulated and calm.

Besides having Harold Spurgeon's pending testimony against Johnny Romano practically laid out on a silver platter, Richard Sadler gloated over his good fortune at having two of the crime boss's henchmen safely behind bars. The jerks who frightened Ma (and almost got Frank) occupied separate holding cells in the Mineola jail. Their rap sheets ensured they would not be checking out of that hotel too soon.

All the police could charge them with so far was concealed weapons with intent to commit bodily harm, but they had records, didn't they? Sadler could threaten them with hard jail time, then soften them up by offering lighter sentences in exchange for their cooperation. He had a chance to get Romano in a double blind. What a sweet deal!

But the ambitious assistant DA's joy would be short-lived.

Romano's attorney, Norman Wasserman, arrived at the jail early the next morning and requested a visit with his other clients, Carmine "The Knife" Pacelli and Fat Sallie Rizzo. Even though lawyers' conversations with their clients are considered privileged, you can bet I was there.

Wasserman studied the reprobates in front of him and took

in their worried expressions and two-day-old beards before speaking. "So, I've got good news and bad news."

They regarded him suspiciously.

"Johnny sends his regards," Wasserman continued, "and wanted me to let you know he's holding on to your bonuses. He appreciates your friendship."

Not surprisingly, Pacelli and Rizzo looked puzzled. They believed Johnny would be angry because they screwed up. (They were correct but also stupid.)

"That's the good news. The bad news is that in order for you to earn your bonuses, Johnny expects you to plead guilty to all charges, and keep your mouths shut. Understand? Do your time, and your bonuses will collect interest, just like the banks!"

Pacelli and Rizzo looked like they'd just discovered the truth about Santa Claus.

So what did you expect? Wasserman would post bail and give you a ride home?

The two returned to their cells suspecting their train would never pull into the station. So much for career opportunities.

Assistant District Attorney Sadler was sure to be disappointed as well. Two pigeons silenced. Only one possibility left. Or was there?

Twenty-seven

Fein Gallagher drummed his manicured finger nails softly on his nineteenth-century Regency desktop. "Please keep trying until you reach him," he said into the intercom.

I was exploring the private office of the famed attorney, completely overwhelmed by the plush interior. The walls alone held an outstanding collection of paintings. One in particular caught my eye. An original Lebadang? I wondered, gazing at a magnificent oil. It depicted a sampan, low in the water, surrounded by vines and overhanging tree mosses, shrouded from view by a dark, almost magical, mist. Other paintings caught my attention, but the Vietnamese-born artist's technique was almost a signature. Classy. If this was Fein Gallagher's taste, my respect inched up another notch.

The man of the moment reached for a folder, but after a few minutes, he punched the intercom again.

"Nothing yet? Okay, get me Agnes Spurgeon's residence."

A few minutes later, his secretary buzzed. "Mr. Spurgeon is not at Sands Point, Mr. Gallagher, and Mrs. Spurgeon is not available. Do you want me to leave a message?"

"No. Uh, see if you can contact Mr. Thomas McBride."

"Yes, sir."

Gallagher picked up the phone on the first ring. "Fein Gallagher, Tom . . . Oh, not too bad, and you? Listen, I'm trying to get hold of Harold Spurgeon. No answer at his apartment, and he's not in Sands Point. Got any ideas? Thanks, I'll give it a try."

Punching the intercom button once more, he asked his secretary to see if she could locate Harold at Claudia Harmon's apartment.

I don't think Claudia wants to play house anymore, Gallagher. Doubt you'll find Harold at her place.

Of course his secretary told him more or less the same thing a minute later, which led to a small furrow between the attorney's brows and more drumming. *Hmm,* so this is how the rich and brilliant reason.

Wanna know what I think, Mr. Big Shot? I think you should hustle yourself over to Sutton Place and ring the doorbell yourself. Harold didn't look that well when I saw him last.

Even I was surprised when the big guy pushed his chair back and reached for his suit jacket. In the outer office, he motioned one of his legal assistants to follow him. I decided to tag along.

The two met with resistance, however, when Bill Mackey, the concierge at Harold's residence, refused them entrance. Mr. Rich-and-Famous was either not at home or not responding to the intercom. "Sorry, sir, but I can't admit you. Yes, sir, I know who you are, but the rules . . ."

"Well, could you tell me what time Mr. Spurgeon left his apartment?"

The concierge consulted his records and shook his head. "I don't believe he's left yet, sir."

Gallagher frowned

I told you he wasn't real happy the last time I saw him. He's probably sulking because his erstwhile fiancée won't talk to him.

Fein Gallagher took his associate aside for a hurried exchange. After receiving his instructions, the young man immediately made a call on his cell phone. I thought about going up to Harold's apartment, but some sixth sense held me off. Within minutes, the flashing lights of a patrol car and an unmarked sedan dominated the scene, assuring all of us a front-row seat.

The concierge blinked and ran for the doors just as four men, two uniforms and two plainclothes detectives, bounded toward the entrance. Everything after that played like a movie out of the Thirties.

The ligature marks around Harold's neck were deep, precise and just as deadly. He lay in a crumbled heap on the floor of his elegant bedroom, his worries in this world completely absolved. He would never again find himself on the wrong end of his mother's temper. He would never again have to concern himself with Claudia Harmon's comforts. And he would never again have to worry about high blood pressure. Twenty-four-hour, round-the-clock protection? Too little and too late. Harold Spurgeon had been strangled by a skilled professional. Now, what makes me think Johnny Romano had something to do with this?

Harold was now the star of the show. Two uniformed policemen were stationed in the hallway outside the apartment. Detectives from the Seventeenth Precinct began going over the crime scene while Fein Gallagher and his assistant observed from the bedroom doorway and the concierge cowered in the living room. A few minutes later, a crew from the medical examiner's office arrived, and Bill Mackey was encouraged to return to his post.

Oh, Harold, you always were a shmuck! I figured he ought to be able to hear me now, so why should I bother keeping my thoughts to myself? But I didn't get any response. Soon the ramifications of this event would echo around the City. And to think it all started with me.

At the district attorney's office, Richard Sadler sat across from his boss's desk, glassy-eyed, all his recent plans for glory gone down the drain. "If only I hadn't waited . . ."

"If I had a dime for all the if-onlys in my life, I'd be a millionaire," Karl Wagner replied.

"It was Romano, of course," persisted Sadler.

"Prove it."

Sadler shook his head and sighed. "That guy's got a cover for every dirty deed."

"Be patient. His luck won't hold up forever."

The atmosphere at the Mineola Precinct was similarly depressing. Only recently the scene of a happy celebration, Frank,

Charlene and Martola sat in Lieutenant Egan's office looking as if they were in mourning.

Oh, pull out of it, fellas! If anyone has a right to complain, it's me.

Charlene sent a nod in the general direction of my voice. After a while, Frank roused himself, reminding the others that Romano was still out there.

"True," agreed Egan, "but our direct link to the gangster just got himself killed."

Frank started to pull out a cigarette, but Egan shook his head. "Do me a favor, will you? Don't make me watch you committing suicide."

Frank made a face but put the pack away. Then he began rubbing his chin absentmindedly. "The concierge—how much of a straight arrow do you think he is?"

The others were attentive.

Charlene said, "According to detectives at the Seventeenth, he refused entrance to Spurgeon's lawyer because Gallagher wasn't *expected*." She emphasized the last word.

Frank leaned forward. "Maybe Gallagher didn't come up with the right admittance ticket, like a twenty?"

Egan nodded at his detectives. "See what you can get out of the concierge."

My guy started to get up, too, but Egan motioned him back into his chair. "Officially, I can't condone your working the case, Frank."

That's within reason, hon. I tried rubbing his shoulders, but Frank was not a happy camper. He and Egan started to have some words about it, so I took the opportunity to slip out with Charlene and Martola. See? That's the one advantage I do have. Nobody can give me orders!

Bill Mackey was not on duty today. After obtaining his home address from their compatriots at the other precinct, Charlene and Martola headed for the guy's apartment on Tenth Avenue and Thirtieth, also known as Hell's Kitchen, a low-rent area with ancient brick tenement buildings that got seriously warm during the summer months. Portable fans only helped move the stale air from one room to the other, so space on the outside stoops was at a premium. In the winter, tenants prayed for the health of the old furnaces that fed the boilers. What the heck, this was New York, wasn't it? Surviving these conditions took skill.

It was three in the afternoon, and Mackey was enjoying a beer while watching the Yankees rip the Texas Rangers. He frowned when the knocking began. "Yeah, whaddya want?" he bellowed from the couch.

"Police, open up!"

"What the hell . . ." The off-duty concierge rolled off the well-worn cushions and made toward the door.

I picked my way through the litter-cluttered room and shuddered. Everybody wears a mask, I thought. Who would have thought the spiffy-looking concierge who worked in the astronomically priced Sutton Place area and this beer-bellied slob were one and the same? Charlene was wrinkling her nose. Can't say I blamed her. It was Martola who began the questioning.

"Getting back to yesterday," he began, but Mackey interrupted.

"I told the detectives who questioned me yesterday, I don't know nothing."

"Yeah," Martola said, putting his face close to the other, "but I'm asking the questions today!"

The concierge shrugged and lowered his voice a notch. "So, whaddya wanna know?"

"You can tell me what happened yesterday—before Mr. Gallagher arrived."

Mackey turned away and sat back down on the couch, clearly indicating his annoyance at being interrupted on his day off. He repeated what he'd told the other detectives. "Nothing happened. Mr. Spurgeon never left his apartment."

"Oh, and you expect us to believe that the victim wrapped a noose around his own neck, strangled himself, then hid the noose somewhere and quietly died?"

"I don't know nothing! Like I told the other detectives, the guy never left his apartment."

Martola grabbed the front of Mackey's T-shirt and twisted

it, pulling him to his feet. The unexpected physicality of the move sobered the guy. "I don't know anything, I tell you!"

His fear was real. Charlene moved forward, tapping her partner on the shoulder. "Let me give it a try, Lou. And if he doesn't cooperate, I'll just step into the hallway for a minute."

They were putting on their usual good-cop/bad-cop routine.

Charlene pulled up a chair and sat down close to Mackey. She studied him, letting a few seconds go by before speaking. "I'm sure a lot of people think your job is easy."

The subject threw Martola a dirty look before answering. "No, it ain't."

"Hmm . . . It's a ritzy place. Bet those people keep you hopping."

"Like you can't believe." Mackey recited a litany of chores he was expected to perform for the privileged, such as responding to owners' special requests, receiving packages, doing unexpected errands—"sometimes even walking their spoiled dogs. I do all of that and more!"

"Sure you do," soothed Charlene, "and you're probably not paid nearly enough." She glanced around the room meaningfully. The unhappy tenant appeared to relax.

"It wouldn't be unreasonable," she continued, "to think of yourself from time to time."

Damn, Charlene, you're good!

She nodded her appreciation.

Mackey shrugged, then averted his eyes. I turned to check Martola's reaction. His expression hadn't changed, but there was a real sparkle in his eyes.

The room fell silent for a few seconds, then the concierge began to twitch nervously. "What do you mean?" he finally asked.

"You know what I'm saying, Bill," she cooed.

The use of his first name took him off-guard, like Charlene was actually treating him like a person instead of an anonymous doorman. His face lit up.

In the next few minutes, she had gotten Mackey to concede he'd granted access to a very persuasive gentleman earlier that morning.

Persuasive like how? Do you mean he knew to grease the old palm?

Mackey protested that he did not know the person's name (which was a lie) and never saw him leave (which was probably true). It was determined later that, once inside, anyone could take the elevator or stairs down to the garage level and exit through there.

The detectives asked Mackey to describe the man.

After a halfhearted attempt to avoid answering, the slob complied. "He was tall, maybe six feet, good-looking, dark hair . . ."

Yeah. Mr. Anonymous. The description could fit a lot of men, but it was also suspiciously familiar—a lot like Johnny Romano, in fact.

"Do you think you'd recognize him if you saw him again?" asked Martola, equally excited.

"I don't know. I don't want to lose my job." He was still trying to wiggle out of a bad situation.

You should have thought of that before, Mackey. It's too late to turn back now.

"If you cooperate with us," Charlene cajoled, "we'll go to bat for you."

"Yeah," her partner growled, "cooperation is always the best policy, especially since you most likely accepted a bribe, in which case your alternative is either to help us or explain to your boss why you admit gangsters to the high-class building you're supposed to be keeping safe for residents."

Mackey hung his head, then meekly followed the detectives downstairs to their car.

At the precinct, he unhesitatingly identified a photo of Johnny Romano as the man who slipped him a hundred bucks earlier that day! Mackey swears he saw Romano enter the elevator but had no idea where the gangster was headed. On questioning him further, however, Martola got him to admit that the light panel indicated the elevator stopped at the fifth floor, which just happened to be the location of Harold Spurgeon's apartment. *Hmm . . .* Isn't it grand the way fate works? Because the mysterious Carlos was not available, Romano had to do his own dirty work.

Lieutenant Egan shared the information with his counterpart at the Seventeenth Precinct, who agreed to compare Romano's fingerprints to those lifted at the crime scene. A half-hour later, Egan gave the go-ahead to his detectives to pick up Romano. Was this an occasion to celebrate or what?

Twenty-eight

When the news reached Luke Snyder, I was glad I was incognito. He was enraged when he learned of Romano's arrest. Evil altered the refined characteristics of the previously distinguished-looking gentleman into those of the mob master he really was. Snyder's mood was now raw and frightening. He called upon the gods—or anyone near enough—to explain how, after he'd ordered "that *pomposo* prick" to clean up his mess, Johnny Romano had actually spread the manure around even farther! He ranted on and on, and I had a front-row seat to this tirade. Couldn't wait until I visited the object of his wrath in jail.

An orange jumpsuit, Romano? Orange is not your color. It's a definite turnoff for the ladies, too. Oh, I forgot . . . where you're going, there won't be any ladies. Aw, what a shame. Tell me, how did it feel when you strangled poor Harold? Man, that must've been a kick. I can see the headlines from here: "Diesel Truck Squashes Ant"—what you'd call an even match, huh?

As I spoke, Romano alternated between pacing the small, smelly cell and sitting on the sagging, unappetizing bunk bed.

Not exactly the Hilton, is it?

In the midst of my soliloquy, one of the guards appeared. "Your lawyer's here," he announced, unlocking the cell and nodding at the prisoner.

"It's about time."

Norm Wasserman greeted his client through the glass shield and picked up the phone. I was sure he was planning a creative defense, but I'd be damned if even Wasserman had a clue about where to start. Romano's fingerprints were discovered on the dresser in Harold's bedroom, and a tiny, dried drop of perspiration—not belonging to Harold—was found on the victim's shirt. Oh, DNA, how I laud your discovery! This was indeed a day for celebrating.

Alone in his office, Richard Sadler agreed. I thought I might be at an old-fashioned revival meeting when he looked up to heaven and began shouting, "Thank you, Lord! Thank you, Lord! Thank you, Lord. . . ."

At the Mineola Precinct, Charlene and Martola were also in a festive mood. Wading through the stack of paperwork in front of her, Charlene smiled across at her partner. "Lucky break, finding Romano's sweat on the victim's clothing."

"Lucky, hell. That jerk was so full of himself, he was bound to make a mistake sooner or later. But, yeah, it was a good break." Martola reached for the phone on the second ring. "Hey, Frank, how's it going?"

It was amusing how the two previously ferocious gladiators had become friends. But then, people who share similar characteristics often do not get along at first. It takes awhile to appreciate the irony. After a rough start they finally learned to trust each other. By God! Martola was now actually smiling!

"Sure. You take care, too. Yeah, hold on a minute." He winked at Charlene and nodded toward her extension.

Don't try to hide the smile, Charlene. I know you're pleased Frank called.

The color rose in her cheeks and her first words were monosyllabic: "Hi. Uh-huh. Well . . . yes."

Martola stood up, waved a sheaf of papers and gestured toward the photocopier at the other end of the room.

Soon as he left, Charlene's sentences got longer. "Yes, I'd like that. When are you leaving? So, that doesn't leave very much time. Um . . ."

She was looking at her watch. I could only imagine what Frankie wanted. Charlene twirled a wisp of hair around her finger distractedly—decisions, decisions—and finally came out with, "Okay, I'll meet you there in an hour."

Yeah, that Irishman will get to you every time, but I don't begrudge you, Charlene. You two should be great together. Besides, I can't give Frankie what he needs anymore. Oh, but a word to the wise: In spite of the fact I got him to the altar once, Frank's not the marrying type.

"Who said I was?" Charlene whispered, checking around to make sure her partner was still out of range. "And, by the way, thanks for all your help. I really mean that, Annie."

All this sentiment was beginning to reach me. I hadn't been cognizant of any deadlines up until now. But some otherworldly sense began to take over. Time. I was getting the impression my window on this plane was about to close, so I gathered my remaining strength and organized my priorities.

Tying up loose ends can be complicated, especially when it comes to Ma, but I knew I couldn't leave without making sure that Manny would not take advantage of her. Miriam and Herbie were not the ones to judge. Hell, they wanted to ship her off to Ohio and assign her permanent baby-sitting chores. Like, hello! She's not entitled to a life, too? Oh, just listen to me! And how was my attitude any different? Okay, okay, I'll give the guy another look, an objective look. If he passes . . . well, dammit, so will I!

Back at his place, Manny was just making his bed. One could see this was not a job he excelled at, but he was exerting a mighty effort. He struggled to smooth out the top blanket, then hauled the bedspread off the closet shelf. I could tell by the creases it hadn't been used in a while, but he smoothed and smoothed until he had it looking decent. Like I should wonder whom he was expecting? He even gave the tables in the living room a halfhearted wipe. I followed him into the kitchen and watched him open a bottle of wine. *Hmm . . . Chateau du Charron* '98. Not a bad year. He removed some stem glasses from the cupboard and held them up to the light. *Scheesh . . .* A suspicious-looking dish towel was called into service. Another check against the light. *Yuck!*

No good, Manny, try some soap and water.

Isn't is amazing what some positive reinforcement will do? The old geezer actually rinsed the glasses with lukewarm water and liquid soap.

Now, make sure you rinse them well, or your efforts will go down the drain.

I could tell he wasn't paying attention because the amount of water he used wouldn't put a dent on a cotton ball, so I turned the hot water on full force. He jerked around and stared at the faucet. Then he shook his head disbelievingly and reached over to turn it off. But I would hear none of it. I tipped over one of the glasses so that it rolled onto a used steel-wool pad. When I say *used,* I'm pulling no punches. The *shmuts* on that pad would turn anyone's stomach. It certainly spread enough rust over the glass to warrant another rinse. Good! Manny took the hint. He shrugged his shoulders and ran both glasses under the faucet. This time, after he finished, I allowed it to stay shut, although the poor guy stood guard just in case. We were both rewarded when he dried the glasses and held them up to the light. Actually, Manny had a pleasant smile.

Okay, so far so good, but it better be Ma you're expecting and not some other broad.

I needn't have worried. Ma rang the bell ten minutes later. She looked fabulous in a dress I'd never seen before *and* she was wearing lipstick and a little rouge.

Manny swung open the door, smiled warmly, and swept his arm toward the living room. "Come in, Selma. Come in. I've been waiting for this moment a long time."

If I could have, I would have cried. Ma was so radiant and her eyes sparkled. Okay, okay, so I was wrong. Maybe he's not such a bad guy after all. If being together with Manny makes Ma feel good, so be it. I left quietly. I shouldn't disturb the happy couple.

I took in the early evening scene outside Manny's apartment building. Some would consider it corny, but I found it nostalgic and satisfying. A cool breeze drifted over the urban landscape, lifting the leaves of the old trees that had been dying and returning to life for as many years as I could remember. I used to wonder about that when I was a kid.

"Are you sure," I'd prod Ma when fall stripped the

branches of their foliage, "that the trees are not dead?" And she would promise me that they were just going to sleep for the winter. "And will they come back in the spring?" *Of course,* she'd assured me, but I always wanted proof. Ma would just point to the sky. *Be good, and God will take care of the rest.*

At Frank's apartment, opened suitcases lay begging on the bed. Shaving kit, toilet articles, cigarettes, underwear and socks were scattered in typical disarray. Clothes draped over chairs and hanging from closet doors expanded the eyesore.

Frank picked up the phone on the first ring. "Yeah, Maggio. I'm getting it together. When's my flight? Sure, I'll make it. Got some personal stuff to take care of first."

The impact of the moment hit me. Frank had set aside his life, returning to the States solely to help solve my murder. Thanks to his efforts, the killer was identified, though now deceased himself. And if the instigator, Romano, didn't receive a lethal injection for his part, he would surely spend the rest of his life in jail.

Frank had also spent some quality time with Ma, easing her over the worst part and somehow transfusing some of his own Irish chutzpah into her soul. She came through much stronger than I would have predicted.

Now here he is, telling Maggio he's packed and ready to move on to his next assignment. Well, so am I.

Uh, hello, up there. I'm ready, I think.

No response. I feel as though I'm in a dentist's waiting room, not exactly looking forward to my appointment but anxious to get it over with. I wait. Still, there's no response. Patience. I have all the time in the world.

But just as I'm thinking this life is behind me, Frank's telephone interrupts my reverie. He punches the speaker button, and Martola's voice bounces into the room: "Before you take off, Frank, thought you'd like to know that it ain't over yet."

"What the hell are you talking about?"

Martola's breathing heavily. "Romano's escaped."

"WHAT?"

"Just got the call. They were transporting him and a couple

of other prisoners to Riker's. Van got sideswiped by a cab on the East River Drive. All I know is, Romano made off in the backseat of a dark sedan with tinted windows. It was a setup."

Hang on a second, Martola. Am I hearing right? I just called for the next bus and you're telling me the guy responsible for my current condition is on the loose?

Frank grabs for a cigarette. "Tell me this is an April Fool's joke."

"I know it sucks. We're sick about the whole thing. Can't believe they'd allow this guy to leave the holding cell. My partner swears someone on the job over there is . . . I hate to say it. I mean, how else could it have happened?"

Silence from our end. Frank must really be in shock.

Say something, hon. I'm getting nervous.

"Gotta be Luke Snyder," my guy finally blurts out.

"Sure, but get him to admit it! The thing is, would the big boss be looking to help out a friend or make sure his lips are sealed—like forever? Charlene and I are going over to talk with Snyder now. Of course, we don't expect to bump into his house guest."

"Shit. I don't know what to do now."

I know Frank's talking more to himself than to me or Martola, but the latter answers anyhow. "Don't change your plans." He adds, "There's nothing you can do now anyway. Give me the number of your contact here, and I'll get a message to you about what's going on."

I see Frank struggling with this. "No," he says, with absolute finality. "I'm hanging around awhile longer. You guys are going to need all the help you can get. Be right over."

He hangs up the phone, calls Maggio to tell him he's had a change of plans, and takes a long drag on his cigarette. Frank surveys the litter on his bed and shakes his head. Apparently he's made some momentous decision.

I was beginning to suspect that my own time on this level was nearing an end, but I still had unfinished business and a score to settle. Decisions, decisions . . . Okay, like it or not, I had to let go. So I observed Frank as he pulled on a pair of slacks, donned a clean shirt, ran a comb through his hair and slapped on some aftershave. This last was a dead giveaway. I sure hoped Charlene liked the scent.

Downstairs, my former honey slipped into the first available taxi. I heard him give the driver the address of the Mineola Precinct. Then I blew him a kiss just before the door closed and took off for my last errand.

It occurred to me that Romano had swung and missed for his third strike. Number one: slow-dancing with Fannie Shine (caught in the act). Number two: sent amateur crew to dispense with Frank (missed by a mile). Number three: left calling card at Harold Spurgeon's last hurrah (DNA doesn't lie). So, here's the big question: Did Romano really escape to freedom? Or did Snyder chuck him into the recycle bin? This was something I couldn't leave to chance. I pictured the sedan with tinted windows heading straight for the Meadowlands in New Jersey, notorious dumping ground for gangster has-beens. Well, he'd have to deal with me before going to his just reward.

Taking advantage of my newly developed radar system, I whooshed myself to Johnny Romano's last known whereabouts and began following the trail. The East River Drive traffic was, as expected, crawling along bumper to bumper. The police had set up barricades and were stopping suspicious vehicles. Time-wise, I knew the getaway car had long since passed this checkpoint, so I decided to go with my instinct. The wilds of New Jersey sounded like a happy solution for Luke Snyder's favorite son.

As was usual for this time of day, the Lincoln Tunnel traffic was practically at a standstill. Of course, I wasn't experiencing nearly as much frustration as those behind the wheels. I moved through the VIP lane (the one above the car roofs—no waiting), scanning all vehicles as I passed. A couple of dark sedans held out possibilities, but none contained any of the lead characters. Then, because I certainly deserved a break in all of this, I spied a dark green Mercedes with even darker tinted windows. Of course it was the car of my dreams, but not just because of the high polish and luxurious interior. It contained gangland's version of the Three Stooges. I didn't wait for it to slow down, but just simply oozed myself inside.

Romano was sandwiched between two very familiar, ugly faces. I easily recognized Luke Snyder's special envoys, otherwise known as the Orkin men, guaranteed to rid your house of every known pest from ants to rats. The latter, of course, was their speciality, and I stared at their recent catch in wonderment. Romano was still in his orange jumpsuit; only now he'd added a smile tinged with rancid oil. The sweat stains under his armpits reached down to his waist, and his hair had not seen a comb since he'd left civilian life. Unkempt and smelly, this was a far cry from the successful Greek god who had previously been able to invade any orifice of his choice. The overlord of Bronx's organized crime territory looked defeated. Well, if the shoe fits . . .

"Look, fellas . . . ah. . . ." He tried to sound normal but came off as the condemned man he probably was.

I guess this is where someone should ask you if you have any last words.

He was not up to responding.

"Hey, guys." (Romano tried to smile here, but his grimace came away looking like gas.) "Uh, Jingo, Sharkie," he pleaded.

The others, whose names sounded like some kind of seafood fest, sat like stones, but I couldn't resist. *What? The great Johnny Romano is begging?*

On the Jersey side, the car pulled off Four-ninety-five onto County Avenue and, according to the signs, was headed in the direction of the Hackensack River. Romano was *farshvitst.* Sweat rolled down his forehead, accumulated briefly onto his bushy brows, then dripped down his waxen cheeks. Not a pretty sight. When the car slowed near a deserted stretch of swampland adjacent to the river, I thought his eyeballs would pop out of orbit.

Does this look familiar, killer? Maybe you've done some business here before.

The goon nearest the door opened it and pulled on Romano's arm. The other shoved him toward his companion.

Both moves pointed the way. Romano stepped out, raised his hands, palms facing outward in a surrendering gesture, shrugged his shoulders and walked to where they pointed. He squeezed his eyes shut when, in unison, his escorts reached into their inside jacket pockets. He never saw the guns but surely heard the muted *pops* of their silencers; yet, no one was there to cry at the outcome.

I thought I was the only witness to Johnny Romano's execution, but I was wrong. Whispers filtered through the atmosphere, and as the two goons headed back toward their car, a low rumbling in a cloudless sky growled across the Hackensack River toward the swamp where Romano's body lay sprawled.

Strange, I hadn't noticed any signs of a weather change. But the noise escalated, and the two henchmen paused, now searching the heavens for an airplane off its course. Instinctively I knew this was no errant aircraft. Now claps of thunder exploded, and streaks of lightning appeared, not from above, but from below. Snyder's messengers looked at each other, shouted something to their driver and jumped into their car. The motor gunned, but the vehicle did not move. I could hear three loud voices arguing within, but my attention was diverted to the sudden darkness that rolled across the marshy area, engulfing Romano's body in an eerie hanging mist. Now the car's windows, previously too dark to see into, suddenly cleared. Three frightened faces stared out from within. I knew that whatever all of us were waiting for would soon be revealed. We didn't have long to wait.

Not human voices, but something akin to Halloween howls burst forth in threatening whispers. Shadows gathered around Romano's remains and ghoulish laughter resounded. While his body remained prone, an indistinct dark form gradually arose from the gangster's remains. As it took shape, the impression appeared to be that of a hunchback ensconced in a dark cloak. Quasimodo? It came to me that this was to be Romano's new afterlife identity. Oh, boy. Even I thought this a little extreme. But I didn't have time to linger on the problem. Darkness drowned out any remaining light, and additional shadows were gathering. The effect was otherworldly. I was sobered by the scene being played out but instinctively knew that I was not in any danger. However, the three trapped hoodlums wept behind the glass.

Now I heard Romano's voice, or what used to be his voice, pleading: "No, no, please don't . . . PLEASE!" His words ended in a shriek as the entities gathered round and dragged him off.

This was not a pretty sight to witness. I don't know which was worse: Romano's remains begging for mercy or the involuntary audience in the Mercedes howling to be set free. And as much as I might have wished for retribution, the reality of hell's messengers snatching up their victim was sobering.

Soon the darkness began to dissipate, and the former gangster's screams, now grotesquely distorted, became fainter. I heard the motor of a car and realized his former buddies were now free to go. It remains to be seen if any of them will take this lesson seriously. I stood there a few minutes, staring at Romano's earthly remains and willed myself back to more familiar territory.

Staring up at the window for the last time, I watched Ma and Manny toast each other. The last piece of the puzzle was in place. An inexplicable exhaustion overwhelmed me, and I felt vulnerable for the first time since that fateful day in Sands Point. Wow! Was this the Jewish version of an epiphany? It didn't matter. I felt light, happy, rewarded. My work here was done.